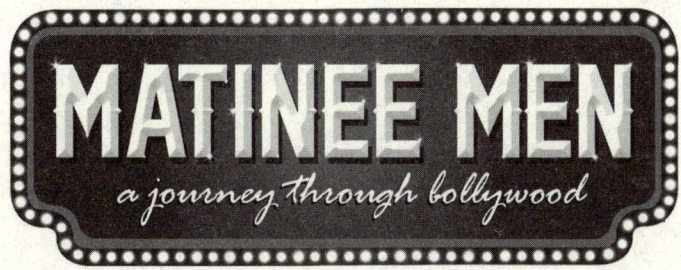

Roshmila Bhattacharya

RUPA

Published by
Rupa Publications India Pvt. Ltd 2020
7/16, Ansari Road, Daryaganj
New Delhi 110002

Sales centres:
Allahabad Bengaluru Chennai
Hyderabad Jaipur Kathmandu
Kolkata Mumbai

Copyright © Roshmila Bhattacharya 2020

All rights reserved.
No part of this publication may be reproduced, transmitted, or stored in a retrieval system, in any form or by any means, electronic, mechanical, photocopying, recording or otherwise, without the prior permission of the publisher.

The views and opinions expressed in this book are the author's own and the facts are as reported by her which have been verified to the extent possible, and the publishers are not in any way liable for the same.

ISBN: 978-93-90260-08-9

First impression 2020

10 9 8 7 6 5 4 3 2 1

The moral right of the author has been asserted.

Printed at Parksons Graphics Pvt. Ltd., Mumbai

This book is sold subject to the condition that it shall not, by way of trade or otherwise, be lent, resold, hired out, or otherwise circulated, without the publisher's prior consent, in any form of binding or cover other than that in which it is published.

*To my daughter Ranjika, the inheritor of my wonderworld,
may you always dream with your eyes wide open...*

CONTENTS

Introduction	vii
1. Ashok Kumar: Decoding Dadamoni	1
2. Dilip Kumar: The Last Mughal	20
3. Dev Anand: Evergreen at Eighty	37
4. Shammi Kapoor: The Original Rockstar	54
5. Dharmendra: Hero with a Heart	72
6. Amitabh Bachchan: Always the Shahenshah	89
7. Mithun Chakraborty: Not Just a Disco Dancer	107
8. Farooque Shaikh: The Extraordinary Actor	125
9. Aamir Khan: A Man for All Seasons	142
10. Shah Rukh Khan: Courting the Baadshah	160
11. Salman Khan: Peter Pan with a Swag	178
12. John Abraham: The Real Action Hero	194
13. Irrfan Khan: The Warrior	210

INTRODUCTION

Reaching for the Stars

As a child I wanted to fly, to where the stars twinkled. I imagined myself as an air hostess, soaring over the world, till one day, while sailing through the clouds, I discovered just how much work these 'aeroplane aunties' had to do. From serving meals and wheeling away leftovers to handing out blankets and repeatedly attending to call button requests, they were run off their feet. Not wanting to be sucked into this whirlpool of activity, I switched channels and instantly found myself a new hero in Captain Rakesh Sharma.

The first Indian to go into space, the captain spent 7 days, 21 hours and 40 minutes aboard the Salyut 7. When then Prime Minister Indira Gandhi asked him how India looked from up there, he quipped, '*Sare jahan se achcha Hindustan hamara*.' I repeated the words to myself and imagined myself in a spaceship, once again reaching for the stars. Then, I discovered that astronomy is a branch of applied physics and so requires a sound knowledge of mathematics which has always been my Achilles' Heel. With a thud, I came down to earth.

'Maybe I could be a typist,' I told myself, having pruned my wings. But I decided against this career option at the end of the first class because the idea of banging on a typewriter all day long was terrifyingly tedious.

My dad, a general manager with a nationalized bank, had a

better plan. Why didn't I follow in his footsteps? Banking was a safe and secure job, with perks guaranteed, he pointed out. I shuddered, seeing myself cooped up in a stuffy office, poring over figures. However, I didn't dare contradict him when he insisted that I appear for the banking exam, and got me loads of study material that I conveniently shoved into a dark corner and promptly forgot about. On the day of the exam, I breezed through GK, quit on maths halfway through and dashed off the precis writing with half an hour to spare, impatient to be gone.

'How did it go?' dad asked, as I hopped into the car, the first one to make a dash for freedom.

'Wonderful!' I replied, blithely.

He waited anxiously for the results and could not comprehend why I hadn't cleared the exams, little knowing that I had deliberately flunked them! Even today, I can't calculate capital interest.

Now, it was my mother's turn to intervene in my future calling. She pointed me towards a travel and tourism postgraduate diploma that a Mumbai polytechnic was offering. The daughter of her friend had just wrapped up the nine-month course and landed a job with Thomas Cook. 'You will get free holidays abroad,' she urged, hoping to reel me in with this bait since, till then, I had never visited a country outside of my own.

During the viva, when asked why I wanted to enrol for the course, I told the instructor with foolish bravado that I actually had my heart set on the mass media and social communications course that the polytechnic was also offering—this one was just a standby. Even as the words escaped my lips, I knew I had ruined my chances. I didn't care.

But mom did. 'What if you don't get through to the other course? What will you do then?' she raged.

'I can always be a typist,' I shot back.

She wasn't amused, reasoning that no one would hire a one-finger typist. More than a quarter of a century later, I still type with one finger.

Fortunately for the rebel in me, I did get into the mass communication course and ended up recording a radio play, scripting an audio-visual on noise pollution and clicking off rolls of film on our professor's trusted Nikon. But the real joy was a trip to the Film and Television Institute of India (FTII) where, over three days, we watched back-to-back classics, such as *Battleship Potemkin* (1925) and *Bicycle Thieves* (1948). I returned from Pune, cross-eyed and delirious.

Mom was beginning to imagine me as a hot-shot film director or a radio producer while dad figured advertising and public relations were more lucrative careers. I stumped them again by opting for journalism, a profession that paid peanuts. I trotted off for a six-week internship with *The Illustrated Weekly of India*, which, back then, was edited by Pritish Nandy. PN, as he is called, was the boss. People shivered when he walked past, his boots clicking on the floor with authority. When I wondered why he was wearing mismatched socks, I was told that it was fashionable. When I tried it, I was asked if I wanted to join the circus.

No, I wasn't eyeing the Big Top, but I did want to remain in the 100-year-old heritage building, which was *The Times of India* office. For that, I quickly realized, I had to unlearn all that I had learnt before. 'Good writing is not about using words that need a dictionary. Simple sentences which flow with a rhythm of their own and forge a connect with the reader is what you should aim for,' I was repeatedly told, every time I tried flaunting my English honours vocabulary.

I don't know when I connected with the words or rather when they connected with me, but one fine day, PN decided,

I could do some stories for the *Weekly*. Thereafter, artists were frequently pushed in my direction even though I didn't know the 'a' of art. Naively, I told them as much, and to their credit, they did not judge me. Rather, they sketched out their life stories for me with the same fluid strokes. I remember throwing random, untutored questions at Manjit Bawa, which the National Award-winning artist answered while sketching away on a piece of paper. On his way out, he left the doodle lying on my desk. Before I could take a closer look at the cat that he had gifted me, his gallery manager swooped down on it and pocketed the pencil sketch. I was too young to demand it back. Today, when I look at my walls, my heart breaks thinking that it could have been hanging there.

From art, I moved to television. A week or two into my internship, I was handed the 'Idiot Box' column. 'Get three or four news snippets on forthcoming television shows, on-air soaps and living room idols. It's once a fortnight, so it should be easy,' I was told. It wasn't, but I plodded along.

One day, while chasing a tip-off that a young actor who had recently debuted in a sports drama and stolen a piece of my heart, had signed a serial, I dialled him and in the course of the conversation, I inadvertently let slip my residence number. What followed was a stream of calls and invites to restaurants and movie theatres all over town till my dad threatened to go to the cops. That's when he backed off, telling me before we disconnected that I had dialled a wrong number the first time round, but he had played along, convincing me that he was the actor, in the hope that I would agree to meet him in person someday.

The column and the art pieces got me an extension in the *Times* after my internship ended. I was moved to the *Saturday Times* supplement, which Rauf Ahmed edited twice a month. He also helmed *Filmfare*, and I got to help with the production of the monthly film magazine. After three months of handling every page thrown at me, a flood of tears and a strong recommendation from the features editor Madhulika Verma, I was recruited as a trainee reporter with *Filmfare*.

My first interview was with Salim Khan, who after blockbusters such as *Zanjeer* (1973), *Deewar* (1975), *Sholay* (1975) and *Trishul* (1978), had recently split with his long-time scriptwriter-partner, Javed Akhtar. I was told to quiz him on the break-up. He came out strong, but for some reason, the interview was canned. I was disappointed, but not devastated because soon after, I was dispatched for a tête-à-tête with a promising new actress at a Versova bungalow where she was shooting for *Tridev* (1989).

Madhuri Dixit was beautiful, with a Madonna-like face, and answered my queries with rehearsed lines, stonewalling the unpleasant ones with icy hauteur, intimidating me from probing deeper. By the time we were done, I was friends with her mother, who fed me pieces of the apple she was cutting for her daughter, while Madhuri remained a stranger.

Soon after filing the interview, which ran into a dozen hand-written pages, I left for Kolkata. Meanwhile *Tezaab* (1988) released and Madhuri was an overnight star. I learnt to my great delight that my piece was going to be the lead story of the forthcoming issue. For fifteen days, I waited impatiently for the magazine to hit the stands. When it finally did, I riffled through the pages looking for my interview. It had been rewritten into a beautifully worded rhapsody, sprinkled with a few of my quotes and lots of dazzling pictures. It didn't matter that I had earned my first byline, the piece was no longer mine. This time I was truly devastated!

That day, I learnt that any kind of 'padding'—information

that was known previously—is a strict no-no unless it is a follow-up news story. Over the years, I have wielded the scissors too, dispassionately, watching hopeful faces turn baleful, betrayed and baffled as their Pulitzer-winning pieces were mercilessly cut short.

I also learnt the art of getting actors to shrug off their inhibitions and open up to me. The trick is to shove the dictaphone—now mobile phone—into an unobtrusive corner so its intrusive presence is quickly forgotten and the Q&A session grows into a casual conversation. That's how I discovered that Madhuri is a brilliant mimic and a lot of fun to be with, once the barrier came down.

That's also how I broke through Jeetendra ji's reserve, during a rare interaction at his office, and was told that disappointed by the lukewarm response to *Aasha* (1980), producer-director J. Om Prakash was contemplating changing the climax. The film ended with Reena Roy—in the title role of a famous singer Aasha—calling off her wedding at the *mandap* after learning that Jeetendra's wife Rameshwari is still alive and the child they have grown to love is his. Love turns to friendship again and Aasha returns to the stage to croon her signature song, '*Shisha ho ya dil ho, toot jaata hai*'. But before J. Om Prakash could heed the advice of well-meaning friends, the film, suddenly, inexplicably, picked up, and went on to become a blockbuster and spawn a Telugu (*Anuraga Devatha*, 1982) remake. It is anecdotes like these that sparked off a passion to learn the backstory of a film or a song and it turned into a weekly column in later years.

Of course, there were disappointments too. For close to six months I called up Rajesh Khanna, almost three to four times a week, with requests for an interview. After a point, Kaka ji came to recognize my voice, and I marvelled at all the excuses he managed to concoct. I persevered till one day he picked up the phone and informed me in a now-familiar voice that Rajesh Khanna was out of town. I told myself that day that some things were not meant to be and stopped calling. Today, I wish I had just landed at his place, unannounced, the way I did at Anil Kapoor's Juhu bungalow one afternoon. Maybe I would have got my interview then.

On learning that I didn't have an appointment, the security guard at Anil's told me I couldn't hang around. I walked out, sat on a boulder, conveniently placed just outside the gate, and told him that he couldn't stop me from waiting on a public road. After a while, the exasperated man reluctantly invited me in and offered me a chair on the porch. As soon as Anil's car drove up, I ran across, chased by the security, and as he stepped out, told him urgently that we needed to talk. Anil looked absolutely baffled, but the gentleman that he is, he invited me into his home, offered me tea, gave me my interview, and then, came all the way down to drop me, constantly repeating with a disbelieving shake of his head, 'I can't believe you are here.' I myself couldn't believe I could have been so audacious. Chalk it up to desperation.

Anil and I go back a long way to when I was a terrified South Bombay girl and he was a reigning superstar. After *Tezaab*, I was sent to meet him before he flew off on a long outdoor shoot, with explicit instructions that I return with a good interview. Having never ventured beyond Fort and Flora Fountain, I had no idea where RK Studio was. Sighing, my well-travelled colleagues pointed me in the direction of then VT station right across the road, telling me to hop off at Chembur.

It was my first ride on a local train and an autorickshaw because until then college and office had been just a bus ride or a cab ride away. Fortunately, RK Studio was too prominent a landmark for me to miss. But it was hours before Anil called me to his make-up room, courteously offering me sandwiches, samosas and even rasgullas from his dabba. Food was the last thing on my mind as I anxiously fired off a volley of questions, till he held up his hand to ask, 'Hey, what's the hurry?'

Naively, I told him that it was past 6 p.m. and I couldn't afford to miss the last train back to Mumbai. He looked perplexed for a moment, then burst out laughing, assuring me I wouldn't be stranded. 'We're still in the city, you know,' he told me gently, and years later, when my editor suggested I meet him at a way-out resort in Panvel, he told her he would rather I dropped by his Juhu residence instead. 'I don't want her to look at me with those big, frightened eyes and wonder how she was going to get back to Mumbai,' he guffawed.

I was like Alice when I stepped into wonderland, and my editor would frequently send me off to meet yesteryear legends. After stepping out of the spotlight, they had disappeared behind the imposing gates of their bungalows, become a nameplate in an impersonal apartment block or faded away into anonymity in a crowded chawl.

Yes, it was at a chawl in Dadar that I met Bhagwan Dada—the chartbusters from his musical comedy *Albela* (1951), *'Balma bada nadaan re'* and *'Sham dhale khidki taley'*, ringing in my ears. The actor-director recounted how he had quickly run out of finances after the first few weeks of filming and had to shoot all day for outside producers. With the money earned, he would return to *Albela* after 7 p.m. On his request, his leading lady Geeta Bali agreed to shoot from 7 p.m. to 10 p.m. 'Eventually, she would work till almost 6 a.m., and we wrapped up the film in eight months on a budget of just ₹5–6 lakh,' he reminisced, sighing over the fact that though the film ran to full houses at Taj theatre for eighteen weeks and celebrated a silver jubilee run at Imperial Cinema, he didn't make any money. 'My managers swindled me,' he rued. I met Bhagwan Dada just that one time, but the memory of that smiling, elderly man, content in his little one room, has stayed with me.

Soon, I was happily trooping off to meet Prem Nath ji, Dadamoni, Dilip Kumar sahib and so many others for nostalgia features, till one day, a reader came to the office wanting to meet me. She almost reeled when she discovered I was a fresh-faced, just-out-of-college recruit. 'I thought Roshmila would be at least eighty, considering she was writing with such authority on Madhubala, Shammi Kapoor and Guru Dutt,' she muttered, walking away visibly disappointed.

I did meet Dilip sahib and Shammi Kapoor ji, but it was through Madhubala ji's sisters and her mentor Kidar Sharma ji that I got to know the Venus of the Indian screen. Guru Dutt sahib was also gone by the time I became a film journalist, but that didn't make him any less loved. I traced his mother, Vasanthi Padukone ji, to an apartment in Matunga and barged in early one morning to 'discover' her son. She was surprised, but quickly warmed up to me and a couple of hours later, when I was leaving, pushed a sheaf of papers into my hands. I discovered later that they were an English translation of her life with her genius actor-filmmaker son, serialized in a Marathi paper. I understood just how precious they were only decades later. Her last words still resonate with me, 'With your kohl-lined eyes and big red bindi, you remind me of Geeta [her daughter-in-law singer Geeta Dutt]; I guess because you are a Bengali too. If I had another son, I would have got him married to you.'

Her words made me smile and were not to be taken seriously. But a few years down the way, I met Guru Dutt sahib's friend, writer-director Abrar Alvi, who regaled me with lots of anecdotes about *Pyaasa* (1957), *Kaagaz Ke Phool* (1959) and *Saheb Bibi Aur Ghulam* (1962). Abrar sahib liked the article and grew fond of me. One Sunday, I was woken up by his call, and after apologizing for disturbing me, he suddenly started talking about a filmmaker-friend who, though divorced, was a wonderful man. Even as I was wondering what this had to do with me, he informed me that the gentleman wanted to settle down again with a nice, homely girl and he had taken it upon himself to play matchmaker. 'I think you will be perfect for him,' he urged, and was terribly embarrassed when I told him I was already married. Wisely, I decided not to prod him on the identity of his friend, but I still wonder who it was!

While we are on the subject of matches, Lara Dutta once called me home for an interview and waited impatiently while I tiptoed around the subject of tennis ace Mahesh Bhupati. The couple was supposed to have been dating for a while, but they had smiled away all queries on the subject. When I finally brought it up, the actress held out her hand to show me the ring on her finger. Smiling at my expression, Lara admitted that Mahesh had designed it himself and had proposed marriage with it during a candlelight dinner in New York soon after the US Open. I couldn't wait to get back to the office with the news. But then, it was decided that we would break the 'exclusive' only on Sunday. The only problem was that Sunday was forty-eight hours away.

When I sounded out her publicist, she shared that Lara was scheduled to attend the Davis Cup matches in Chennai to watch Mahesh play. 'Sports journalists from across the country will be there. What if someone were to spot the ring and ask her about it?' she reasoned. 'Do something,' I begged, and the sport that she is, Lara promised to stay out of sight and away from the court to avoid any 'leaks'.

I have to admit that for the next two days I was on edge, wondering if she would be able to keep her word. Finally, Sunday dawned, and we could announce that Lara Dutta and Mahesh Bhupati were officially a match! The news grabbed headlines across the media and I had the satisfaction of sports journalists asking me how I had hit this ace when I was not even in Chennai. I notched it up to mutual trust.

Three decades later, I still feel like Alice. I've gone down many rabbit holes, crashed many a Mad Hatter's Tea Party, and occasionally heard a Queen of Hearts holler, 'Off with her head.' Happy to report that it's still attached to my body and filled with stories.

Every day in this fantasy world has been a story. And over the years, I have recounted several to family and friends and been told to chronicle some of them in a book, which is how the idea of *Matinee Men* came about. Thirteen of Bollywood's best, and stories that make them more 'human'. And I solemnly promise that what you read was no dream… It happened for real.

1

ASHOK KUMAR: DECODING DADAMONI

Rail gaadi, rail gaadi, chuk chuk,
chuk chuk, chuk chuk, chuk chuk

It was a Saturday afternoon, a little before three in the afternoon, when I pressed the buzzer of Bharti Jaffrey's Mumbai apartment. Ashok Kumar's eldest daughter opened the door and ushered me into her aesthetically done up living room, saying, 'Baba and Kishore [Kumar] kaka will be joining us as well.' Since both legends had long since passed away, I was momentarily taken aback till I noticed cushions with their faces embossed on them and burst out laughing. It's exactly the kind of joke the Ganguly brothers would have cracked.

On a stroll down memory lane, the first thing Bharti ji wanted to share about her father—whom I and several in the film fraternity fondly addressed as 'Dadamoni' meaning 'gem of an older brother' in English—was that he was a wonderful storyteller. When she was growing up, the family had lived in a penthouse in Kala Ghoda, which Mumbaikars still refer to as 'town'. Dadamoni had bought an entire building from a British gentleman and it came to be called Ashok Kumar House. He was at the peak of his career then, shooting every day, but whenever he was in the city, he would return home by 6.30 p.m. Once the children—son Aroop, and daughters Bharti, Rupa and Preeti—had finished their dinner, he would herd them up to the terrace. 'There, under the stars, with the muted sounds of traffic in the background, between 9 p.m. and 10 p.m., baba would tell us stories. He was a gifted raconteur and through the stories he narrated, many of which grew out of his own imagination, and the poems he recited, he educated us on everything, from tigers to complex 'grown-up' issues like apartheid in South Africa, which otherwise would have passed us by,' she reminisced.

Her Kishore kaka was a part of many of these *golpo* (storytelling) sessions. Since he was eighteen years younger than his Dadamoni and had been living with his elder brother since he was ten, he was more of a friend to the kids than their uncle. And on occasions, he would sit on Bharti ji's piano and play 'live' music to enhance the stories.

'Do you know that *Mahal* (1949) grew out of an eerie experience baba had during an overnight stay at Jeejeebhoy House?' Bharti ji informed me. I remembered Dadamoni telling me how one night while staying at the guest house in Khandala, he had been drawn outside by the sound of raised voices and had come upon a young lady arguing with her chauffeur near the gate where their car had stalled. Pointing out that the engine could have over-heated, Dadamoni invited the lady inside to wait while the chauffeur fixed the car. They were chatting amicably when the chauffeur returned to inform them that he hadn't been able to detect the problem. Unwilling to spend the night there, the lady ventured out again despite Dadamoni's request to stay back.

After they left, he retired for the night, only to be jolted awake by frantic cries for help. He ran out again to find the car still parked outside the gate. It looked dark and empty, but the voice calling for help was coming from inside the car. Peering through the window, Dadamoni spotted a man with his throat cut. He cried out one last time, then, died before his eyes.

Since he was alone and there was no one in the vicinity, Dadamoni prudently went back inside and spent a sleepless night waiting for the servant. As soon as the servant arrived early in the morning, Dadamoni ran out with him, saying there was a dead man in a car outside. But there was no one there... No car and no corpse.

Dadamoni learnt later from the local inspector that fourteen years ago, a young woman had slit a man's throat and leaving the car parked outside Jeejeebhoy House, had tried to flee the crime scene. She had died in an accident soon after.

So, was it their ghosts he met that night? No one can say for sure, but while Googling Jeejobhoy House, I came across a post about some boys who had spent three nights there. During a party one night, one of them had stepped out and seen the garden swing swaying, even though there was no one sitting on it and no breeze either. He called the others out, and even as they had watched, the swing continued to sway eerily, back and forth, till it came to a stop on its own as if an invisible someone had decided they'd had enough and strolled away into the darkness. Later, there were some inexplicable tapping sounds on the doors and windows that kept them awake all night, making them wonder if some nocturnal guests wanted to join the party. However, for the rest of their stay, the boys remained undisturbed.

The house, the swing and the mysterious lady all came together in *Mahal*, the chilling thriller produced by Dadamoni and Savak B. Vacha for Bombay Talkies Studio. He had started his career there and had bought the studio from its erstwhile owner and his former co-star Devika Rani after her husband and his mentor Himanshu Rai's premature demise. In *Mahal*, Dadamoni played the lead role of Hari Shankar, an aristocrat, who is drawn into a world of illusions and delusions by a ghostly apparition he is obsessed with. 'That was a film way ahead of its time, which baba sold to a distributor for just ₹4 lakh on the condition that he would buy it without wanting to see a trial show first as was the norm then. *Mahal* was a superhit and the distributor who was minting money, later came to my father asking why he had sold it so cheap,' Bharti ji chortled.

The film launched the careers of writer Kamal Amrohi as a director and Lata Mangeshkar as a playback singer with the haunting '*Aayega ayega, ayega aanewala, ayega*', which still echoes in our collective consciousness. A sixteen-year-old actress by the name of Madhubala also landed one of the most memorable roles of her career and went on to light up the screen as Bollywood's Venus. Kamal sahib's son, Tajdar Amrohi, shared that his father had insisted on Madhubala even though Suraiya, the numero uno star of the time, was the unanimous choice to play Asha—the gardener's beautiful daughter who masquerades as the ghostly Kamini.

Dadamoni himself admitted that he wasn't keen on being cast opposite a girl almost half his age and had only given in to Kamal sahib's persuasion, despite Madhubala ji having failed her first screen test because German cinematographer Josef Wirsching had deliberately used a different lighting on her, given that *Mahal* was not a conventional Hindi film romance. Kamal sahib took a second test, this time setting up the lights himself, and she got the nod of approval. The film was a surprise hit, and even today, Madhubala is Hindi cinema's most alluring bhoot.

Nine years later, the duo returned on screen with yet another murder mystery, *Howrah Bridge* (1958). The film was set in Kolkata and a world of smugglers and betrayals. A few years prior to this, Shakti Samanta, an aspiring actor who had previously played bit roles—usually that of an inspector giving chase—had found his way into the credits of Dadamoni's *Baadbaan* (1954) as a screenplay writer, translating director Phani Mazumdar's Bengali dialogue in Hindi. The following year, Shakti da debuted as a director himself with *Bahu* (1955) and soon after, in an ironic twist, signed Dadamoni to play the 'inspector' in a film by the same title. This was followed by *Sheroo* (1957), which released in the same year as *Inspector* (1957), a social drama starring Nalin Jaywant and Dadamoni. Revelling in its success, Shakti da was speeding down in his new car when he met with an accident. 'I broke three ribs and was in hospital for two weeks. It was during that time that *Howrah Bridge* was conceived,' Shakti da recounted one afternoon at his office in the now-defunct Natraj Studio.

The film is unforgettable for O.P. Nayyar's chartbuster, '*Aaiye meherbaan*', one of Asha Bhosle's evergreen club numbers, with Madhubala ji as the seductive crooner Edna. 'Since baba was very busy those days, we would tag along with him to outdoor shoots during vacations. We were in Kolkata when they were filming *Howrah Bridge*. Madhubala was one of the most beautiful women in the world,' Bharti ji reminisced.

The beauty, however, wilted before her time. During the shooting of *Ek Saal* (1957), she confided to Dadamoni that doctors had detected a hole in her heart and she was not expected to live long. 'Before I die, I want to be someone's wife,' she told him poignantly, her heart already broken by Dilip Kumar after he gave evidence against her in the *Naya Daur* (1957) court case.

Three years later, in 1960, she married Kishore Kumar after they lit up the screen in *Chalti Ka Naam Gaadi* (1958). 'When baba learnt about their wedding, he joked that Kishore kaka should now be called Mohabbat Khan,' an amused Bharti ji narrated.

I met Dadamoni for the first time as a just-out-of-college junior reporter. By then, he had shifted to a bungalow in a shady by-lane of Chembur's Union Park. His wife, Shobha, had passed away and his children had moved out. The living room I was ushered into was shrouded in a mausoleum-like silence, and as the minutes ticked by, I found it difficult to sit still. Jumping up, I restlessly prowled the room, stopping to inspect a Dresden china shepherdess in a showcase. She had the same porcelain fragility of an antique figurine in my mother's showcase. I was peering at her through the glass when a voice made me start, 'You like her?'

Dressed in a silk lungi and kurta, the man I had grown up idolizing, was observing me from across the room. I nodded, suddenly tongue-tied in his presence. Dadamoni gestured towards the shepherdess with his walking stick and repeated, 'You want to take her home with you?' I shook my head, telling him indignantly, 'You can't bequeath your treasures on perfect strangers. I was just admiring her.'

He laughed out loud, walking into the room and taking a chair, tickled to be reprimanded by a twenty-two-year-old girl. With a careless shrug he admitted that he had given away many such heirlooms to perfect strangers in the past. I rolled my eyes at such reckless disregard for priceless artefacts, and chuckling, he repeated his offer. I frowned at him darkly, and shaking my head again, took the chair opposite him and pointedly opened my notebook.

Observing my professional stance, he politely asked if I would like some tea. I shook my head again, and this time he frowned darkly, 'Why not?' I told him that I did not drink tea. His glance swept over me from head to toe, then nodding, he hollered for a glass of milk. When it arrived, he quipped, 'Little girls drink milk, so drink up like a good girl.' This time he would not take a 'no' for an answer. No one since has insisted I drink a glass of milk during an interview. But then, there has never been another Dadamoni.

He was decades older than me, but our birthdays were separated by only a day. His was on 13 October, mine the following day. When he learnt this, he laughed gleefully, telling me that I was his 'Didimoni'. I did not argue. Very early in our friendship, I had learnt that it was pointless to get factual with this Peter Pan. Before I got married and moved to Vashi, I had lived in Colaba and studied at Elphinstone College, which was in the vicinity of his Kala Ghoda home. Perhaps that's why my whereabouts had sparked his interest.

'Where did you say you lived?' he asked every time we met. 'Colaba,' I would repeat patiently. 'Not Colaba, Cobala,' he would correct me instantly. I had attempted to set him right on several occasions, but he would obdurately chime in a sing-song voice, 'Cobala...Cobala...Cobala...Cobala.' Eventually I had succumbed. 'Ok, Cobala,' and was rewarded with an approving smile. After that, every time the moustached darwan tried to stop me from entering his bungalow, I would tell him to inform Dadamoni that Roshmila from Cobala was there. Within minutes, the intimidating gates would swing open.

Years later, when I was interviewing actor Pran, we recalled director-producer Brij Sadanah's comedic romp *Victoria No. 203* (1972), in which Dadamoni and he had played a pair of lovable rogues. Pran sahib revealed that their punchlines that had prompted the audience to laughter did not come out of a dialogue sheet, but were improvised on the set. 'Whenever anyone tried to give him his lines, Dadamoni would wave them off saying he would only follow my cues. I would start a sentence and he would complete it and vice versa. We had an almost telepathic communication,' he shared.

They made a hit pair—two elderly gentlemen with hearts of gold and a love for Shobha ji's mutton curry. 'My mother was a wonderful cook. The pressure cooker would be placed on low heat every morning and the meat would be left to simmer in it. At 1 p.m., it would be taken off the gas stove and dispatched to the studio where everyone would be waiting to share my father's lunch. Once when I asked Pran uncle what he remembered most about baba, he told me that he would never forget my mother's lip-smacking mirchi gosht!' Bharti ji laughed.

Dadamoni and Shobha ji's match had been arranged by the elders in the family. He had been called home to Khandwa and pushed into a train. En route to Kolkata, he was told that he was getting married. He was introduced to his bride and within days they were married. Their love grew over a lifetime of living together. Persistent rumours of liaisons with his heroines, including gossip that he was all set to elope with the dimpled Nalini Jaywant, his neighbour in Chembur, could not shake her implicit trust in her husband. Shobha ji was a simple Bengali girl who was happy to live in Dadamoni's larger-than-life shadow, far removed from his world of glamour. Four days short of their golden wedding anniversary in 1987, she fell ill and passed away. 'My wife had been so excited about the party she had planned at Hotel Sea Rock. The guests had been invited and all the arrangements had been made. But she didn't live to attend it,' he mourned, shattered by the loss.

After the funeral, Dadamoni asked his youngest brother to sing a song for him. 'Kishore kaka chose the heart-wrenching "*Yeh jeevan hai, iss jeevan ka, yehi hai, yehi hai, yehi hai rang roop*" from the film *Piya Ka Ghar* [1972]. That was the last time I heard him sing that song. Six months later, Kishore kaka too passed away,' Bharti ji sighed.

The date is etched in my memory too. 13 October 1987: it was Dadamoni's seventy-sixth birthday. The brothers had spoken that morning and after wishing Dadamoni, Kishore da had coaxed him to stop by his Juhu bungalow, Gouri Kunj, on his way home from shooting. Though Dadamoni was still in mourning and wanted to ring in the day quietly, Kishore da was in the midst of organizing a surprise party for him when he succumbed to a sudden heart attack at around 4 p.m. Dadamoni never celebrated his birthday again.

∽

The eldest of Kunjilal Ganguly and Gouri Devi's four children, Kumudlal Kunjilal Ganguly was born on 13 October 1911 in Bhagalpur, Bihar. Everyone had expected him to follow in the footsteps of his grandfather, father and uncles, all of whom were lawyers. But much to the exasperation of the principal of Kolkata's Presidency College, Kumud was more interested in watching films than sitting in for lectures, which he dismissed as 'boring'.

Two films in particular by Debaki Bose—*Chandidas* (1932) on the life of a fifteenth-century Bengali Vashnavite poet and *Puran Bhagat* (1933), another devotional biopic—spawned the dream of becoming a film director in the young man. When he was in his second year of college, Kumud bought a third-class ticket for Bombay (present-day Mumbai) with the ₹35 his father had given him to pay for his law exams, and set off for the City of Dreams.

He chugged into Bombay on 28 January 1934. His brother-in-law Sashadhar Mukherji, an assistant sound engineer with Famous Cine Laboratories, had set up an appointment for him with actor-filmmaker Himanshu Rai. The founder of Bombay Talkies Studio was scouting for graduates from cultured families. Favourably impressed with Kumud, he persuaded him to shelve his plans of going to Universum Film-Aktien Gesellschaft, a German film production company, for a course in film direction, and suggested that he stay back in India instead and take acting classes at his studio to develop his sense of drama. He even coaxed the shy young man into facing the camera in the studio's in-progress murder mystery, *Jawani Ki Hawa* (1935). Dadamoni was a passenger in a night train in a blink-and-miss appearance without a single line of dialogue.

German director Franz Osten didn't care for Rai's protégé and after taking a look at his screen test, told Kumud bluntly that his jaw was 'too square' for him to make a career in front of the camera and he would 'never make it as an actor'. He hoped Kumud had the money to return to Kolkata. The twenty-two-year-old was not interested in acting, but he had no intentions of going back to law either. He wanted to be a director. After Osten's brusque dismissal, Rai assigned him to the camera department. He was later coached in editing by Savak Vacha and assigned several other production jobs. He may well have made a career behind the scenes had destiny not intervened.

The hero of *Jawani Ki Hawa*, the dashing Najmul Hussain, eloped with Rai's actress-wife Devika Rani during the shooting of their next film, *Jeevan Naiya* (1936). The off-screen drama brought shooting to a halt. Eventually, the runaway wife was cajoled by Sashadhar Mukerjee, who had since joined the studio to become Rai's trusted aide, to return home. Quite understandably, the boss was adamant that he would not take back Najmul Hussain and was scouting for a suitable replacement when he came across Kumud standing outside the lab, smoking.

Feeling someone's eyes on him, Kumud turned and came face to face with his boss. He paled, convinced that he would be pulled up for slacking, maybe even get the boot, as Rai stared intently at him. He was then instructed to walk slowly across the room. A jittery Kumud did what he was told. When he turned, Rai was smiling. 'You will play the hero in *Jeevan Naiya*,' he told his ashen-faced protégé. Much to Rai's amusement, Kumud who had been briefing other actors on their lines and scenes, wailed, 'Acting is not a befitting profession for someone with a science degree. Besides, it will jeopardize my match back home.'

Rai was firm. He told Kumud that he was contractually bound to the studio and had to do as instructed. As for his marriage prospects, his future in-laws had nothing to worry about because everyone who worked there came from respectable backgrounds. He pointed out that his leading lady, Devika Rani, was the grand-niece of Nobel Laureate Rabindranath Tagore. 'Now, no more arguments, we start shooting in four days,' he told his reluctant hero.

Four days later, the young star reported for work with half his hair shaved off hoping this would get him dropped from the film. His nonplussed producer simply ordered for a wig to cover up the hatchet job. Then, a nervous Kumud brought down his leading lady's elaborate bouffant during a romantic scene that required him to simply slip a gold chain around her neck. During a fight scene the amateur actor, who had been an ace boxer in college, swung at the villain. His punch left Massey with a fractured knee and shooting came to a grinding halt for four months. After this rocky start, everyone tried to convince Rai that Kumud was the wrong choice, but the filmmaker was obdurate. Kumud, just as he had feared, lost out on a prospective bride because the girl's parents didn't want to marry her off to an actor with an uncertain future.

Two days before the release of *Jeevan Naiya*, Kumud approached his mentor asking to be relieved from his contract, telling him that he had landed two jobs—one, of an income tax commissioner and the other, a police inspector, thanks to then chief minister of the Central Province and Berar, Ravi Shanker Shukla—and his father was waiting outside to take him home. Rai convinced Kunjilal Ganguly to leave his son with him and return home alone. Meanwhile, he offered Kumud another film, *Achhut Kannya* (1936), then, gifted him a suit and a premiere ticket to his debut film. 'Go, watch *Jeevan Naiya* with the audience,' he urged. Kumud, who had been rechristened Ashok Kumar for the screen, went to the theatre reluctantly. After the film was over, he was whisked off to meet some important guests sitting in the adjoining box. They were the Maharaja and Maharani of Gwalior, his first fans.

Jeevan Naiya was a hit, so was *Achhut Kannya*, which was released around the time Mahatma Gandhi launched his crusade against untouchability. The film revolved around a beautiful Harijan girl and a Brahmin boy separated by caste differences and societal pressures. It drew full houses and though Gandhiji could not be persuaded to watch the film, Congress president Jawaharlal Nehru saw it at a special screening, along with his daughter Indira and Sarojini Naidu. The latter nodded off soon after the film started and only woke up once when the song '*Khet ki muli, baag ki aam*' started to play. 'I was sitting beside her and she nudged me to ask who the actor was, who was singing so beautifully. Blushing, I admitted it was me, and after telling me that I was very good she went back to sleep,' he guffawed.

In the present, Bharti ji jogged my memory, asking, 'You

remember my father loved dogs?' and I was reminded how on my visits to Dadamoni's Chembur home I would be greeted by a volley of barks. They had around twenty dogs at various times, from Great Danes and Boxers to Alsatians and even a Shar Pei. 'Baba gave them the most fantastic names, from Stalin and Brutus to Chiang Kai-shek and Hitler,' she laughed.

Once Moushumi Chatterjee had dropped by at their place and asked Dadamoni the name of his new pet. 'Kukur,' he replied, shortly. 'That's hardly a name! It's the Bengali translation for dog. You need to give it a proper name,' she protested, only to be told that he couldn't be bothered with finding another dictator to name it after. 'So, Kukur it is,' he shrugged, leaving everyone chuckling.

While Dadamoni's humour never created any problems, his younger brother was infamous for his eccentric ways and whimsical demands. Filmmakers would come to Dadamoni complaining that Kishore da would insist on them dancing on a table before agreeing to come for a recording. Once, when a scene required him to drive, Kishore da who was still waiting for a part of his remuneration simply drove away, all the way to Panvel! 'After one complaint too many, baba called Kishore kaka home and confronted him. Kishore kaka stood before him, respectfully quiet, when my father suddenly burst out, "*Tu yeh sab kaise kar leta hai? Mujhse kyun nahin hota!*" [How do you do all this? How come I am not able to play such pranks sometimes!]' Bharti ji recounted, leaving me in splits.

∞

I have a vivid memory of Dadamoni on stage, accepting a lifetime achievement award. The trophy was shaped like a woman. Lovingly cradling it in his arms, he quipped with a straight face and a naughty twinkle in his eye, 'Today I will sleep well, I have a naked woman in my arms.' The audience responded with a roar of laughter.

On another occasion, I had stopped by his bungalow to drop off a copy of the magazine in which his interview had appeared. I had been in two minds about keeping my promise to him because there was a photo spread of voluptuous, scantily clad starlets from the South that made me blush in embarrassment. I watched him flip through the magazine, and as I had feared, he stopped at the pages featuring the sexy nymphs. Squirming awkwardly, I admitted that I had contemplated tearing out the pages. He looked at me with horror, 'You could tear out my interview but not these pages. These pictures are far better than mine!' I had no answer for the octogenarian Puck.

On the subject of pictures, Dadamoni was a gifted artist whose studio was his bathroom. Every morning, from seven to nine, he would lock himself up there. 'No one was allowed to disturb him during these two hours because that was when he painted,' informed Bharti ji. She revealed that one day, when she asked him if he would be the chief guest at her college event, her father refused, pointing out that there would invariably be requests to paint live and he would not be able to comply because he could only wield his brush when alone in the bathroom.

He made more than three hundred paintings, from self-portraits and ink sketches of his wife during various stages of their journey together to pastoral landscapes and his favourite subject, horses. 'When M.F. Husain saw baba's horses, he was amazed, and told him that these were not the strokes of an amateur artist,' Bharti ji recalled proudly, pointing out that Dadamoni had chosen the most difficult medium, watercolours. Also, without bothering with pencil drawing, he would always put brush to canvas directly. 'During the shoot of *Bhai-Bhai*

(1956), he got two days off, and with me tagging along, travelled from Chennai to Mahabalipuram to meet the self-taught artist G.D. Paulraj, he had read about. Baba stayed with him and learnt all that he could about the technique in the short time they had together,' she informed, admitting that because of his unquenched thirst for knowledge, Dadamoni was always looking to learn something new.

He also urged his children to explore, experiment and extend their boundaries, exposing them early to the classics of world cinema, such as Roland Colman's *A Tale of Two Cities* (1935), Vittorio De Sica's *Bicycle Thieves* (1948) and Akira Kurosawa's *Roshomon* (1950). These films had helped him hone his craft and adapt to a more 'naturalized' style of acting, which set him apart from his contemporaries whose over-the-top dramatics were more suited to the stage than cinema. 'Baba was not just a talented actor, singer and producer, he was also an astrologer, artist and a homeopath,' Bharti ji reminded, and I flashbacked to the nineties, when during one of my visits, I had noticed a box in his bedroom. Dadamoni opened it to reveal rows of neatly segregated glass phials with little white pills in them. He had admitted then that he was a qualified homeopath.

His interest in medicine had sparked off in 1951, when on their way to London for the shooting of *Naaz* (1954), Shobha ji had complained of breathing trouble. The moment they landed, Dadamoni had rushed her to a specialist and they had learnt that one of her lungs was blocked. On their return to India, she underwent a corrective surgery, but alarmed by her rapid weight loss, Dadamoni flew her to Bangalore to meet a practising homeopath. Under his treatment, she began to recover, and an impressed Dadamoni asked the miracle man to teach him all that he knew about this system of alternative medicine. 'He told me that I needed to learn anatomy and physiology first, which would take me at least a year. I studied these subjects for a fortnight before returning to him,' he recounted. The doctor, impressed by Dadamoni's intellect, imparted his knowledge, which the actor put to good use. 'I cured a girl with polio whose left leg had developed gangrene. A top surgeon her parents consulted had told them that the leg would have to be amputated. As a desperate, last-ditch measure, they came to me. I tried four medicines—I don't know which worked, but after six months she was completely cured and had only lost half a toe.'

When we met, he was still treating colleagues and strangers for everything, from cough and cold to aches, pains and even cancer. Rati Agnihotri confided that when they were shooting *Tawaif* (1985), Dadamoni had noticed that she was looking wan and drained. Eighteen-hour workdays without any breaks, had sapped her energy and left Rati vulnerable to infections. 'He prescribed some pills and they worked their magic on me,' she recalled.

Ironically, his pills couldn't cure his chronic asthma, which he had developed after drinking twenty-five glasses of ice-cold water for two days straight so he would sound suitably hoarse for the climax of *Rakhi* (1962). His voice remained unchanged, but all the ice water resulted in a serious chest infection, which subsequently led to the asthma.

Dadamoni was a prolific actor who had worked in almost 300 films, seamlessly making the transition from lead actor to character roles till asthma and a heart condition forced him to cut down on his work. I had watched his films for over six decades, from *Kismat* (1943) to *Khubsoorat* (1980). *Kismet* was one of the biggest grossers of Hindi cinema, enjoying an uninterrupted 192-week run at Kolkata's Roxy Cinema.

Dadamoni played Shekhar, an unrepentant, small-time crook who robs the poor and helps the rich. Bharti ji shared that his maternal grandfather, Raghu Thakur, eulogized in a poem by Rabindranath Tagore, had been something of a Robin Hood himself in the pre-Independence era. 'He would ride into weddings, rescue brides from dowry-hungry in-laws and get them married off to better men. Baba might have modelled Hindi cinema's first anti-heroes after his *dadu* [grandfather],' Bharti ji acknowledged.

While he got away with *Kismat*, despite a scathing review in *FilmIndia* that lashed out at him for glamorizing crime, the run of Gyan Mukherjee's *Sangram* (1950) was cut short in its sixteenth houseful week. In this film, Dadamoni played the wayward son of a cop who gambles and steals, abducts and even kills, not just a dancer but some police officers as well. 'The then chief minister of Maharashtra, Morarji Desai, sent the police commissioner to our place to tell baba that as a role model to youngsters, he couldn't do films like *Sangram*. My father argued that he was shot dead at the end by his own father, reiterating that crime does not pay in the long run. The commissioner wasn't appeased and insisted he should choose his roles with more care. After that, baba went on to do boring inspector roles,' Bharti ji rued.

Once in a while though, he accepted films such as B.R. Chopra's courtroom drama *Kanoon* (1960), in which he played Badri Prasad, a judge accused of murder. 'In the year of *Mughal-e-Azam*, *Kohinoor*, *Chaudhvin Ka Chand*, *Jis Desh Mein Ganga Behti Hai* and *Kala Bazar*, which boasted of unforgettable music scores, *Kanoon* was a film without a single song and with baba in a grey role. The distributors were appalled, till they saw a preview show. The role had struck a chord with my father because it was against capital punishment,' revealed Bharti ji.

One of my favourite films, however, is Hrishikesh Mukherjee's *Khubsoorat* (1980), in which Dadamoni played a fun-loving patriarch who allows his 'dictator' wife to turn their home into a military school, only rebelling against the rules through the song *'Sare niyam tod do, niyam pe chalna chod do'*. That for me epitomizes the Dadamoni I knew.

One of my fondest memories is sitting with him and his brother Anoop Kumar and listening to the duo re-live memories of Kishore da after his untimely end. There were no tears; instead, they celebrated their lives together with smiles, songs and delightful anecdotes. *'Babu samjho ishare horon pukare, pum pum pum',* they crooned, as they pretended to drive the 1928 Chrysler, the star attraction of *Chalti Ka Naam Gaadi* (1958), down an imaginary street in Dadamoni's bedroom, sending his nurse and me into a mirthful fit.

Unfortunately, as he grew older, the asthmatic attacks left him too ill to shoot or even entertain visitors. The Cobala password no longer worked. My calls were attended by his man Friday, Khursheed, who would tell me that Dadamoni was not in a condition to speak.

During one of our earlier meetings, he had confided that he had not seen two of his films—*Hospital* (1960), a progressive Bengali film with Suchitra Sen as an unapologetic, unwed mother, and Asit Sen's *Mamta* (1966), a Hindi remake of the black-and-white Bengali classic *Uttar Falguni*, again with Suchitra in a double role. Both were very close to his heart because they went against the formula. 'I am sure you could get a VCD,' I pointed out, and he sighed, saying he was too old to go hunting.

Soon after, when I was in Kolkata on vacation, I bought VCDs of the two films, and one Saturday afternoon, accompanied by my husband, dropped by his Chembur residence. When

I presented them to him, I could see a lifetime of memories flash in his eyes that had turned suspiciously moist.

After that, my visits grew increasingly infrequent, and eventually stopped. At the age of ninety, Dadamoni passed away, on 10 December 2001. His heart failed him. My heart broke.

Bharti ji recalled how frail her father had looked the last time she saw him. She had sat by his bed and remembering the poems he would recite to her and her siblings on the terrace of their Kala Ghoda home, had picked one, *The Slave's Dream*.

Beside the ungathered rice he lay,
His sickle in his hand;
His breast was bare, his matted hair
Was buried in the sand.
Again, in the mist and shadow of sleep,
He saw his native land...

As her words resonated in the room, bringing back a dark chapter of human bondage, her father's eyes had filled with tears. 'Looking up at me, he said with a tremulous smile, "*Tor mone ache?*" [You remember this poem?] I nodded and assured him that I remembered everything he had taught me. "*Amar shob mone achche.*"

'Ten days later, he was gone, leaving me with only a treasure throve of memories,' she had sighed, as the sun disappeared behind a cloud.

I had refused Dadamoni's gift of the porcelain shepherdess, but I accepted a small watercolour of a prancing stallion he had painted. I couldn't say no to Bharti ji even though this gift was far more priceless. The framed painting hangs in my bedroom, close to the bathroom—the space he was known to paint in—as a reminder of the man who brought Bollywood home to me.

2

DILIP KUMAR: THE LAST MUGHAL

Ude jab jab zulfen teri, kanwariyon ka dil machle

I met him for the first time as a twenty-something reporter. I had tagged along with my editor who sat chatting with his better half, Saira Banu, while I sat quietly in a corner, feeling distinctly out of place and out of depths at their Pali Hill bungalow. My eyes were fixed on the masala dosa on my plate—a perfect, golden-brown triangle. It wasn't that I was particularly hungry; it was just that I had never seen the South Indian dish served on exquisite china and with such old-world courtesy.

Suddenly a voice broke into my thoughts. Perhaps it was my unblinking gaze on the plate that made Dilip Kumar believe I was as fastidious about food as he was because he was offering to share his bowl of soup with me. 'It's bhindi,' he whispered. I took a quick peek, expecting a congealing mess and was surprised to find a clear broth with perfectly sliced bits of ladies' fingers floating in it. Though intrigued, I was too shy to accept his offer; instead, I was happy to hear the legendary actor meticulously explain how to make the perfect biryani.

We had come to the point at which the recipe called

for whole garam masalas to be tied in a sheer muslin cloth, simmered in a pot of water with the rice, while the mutton was marinating in a spice paste. Suddenly, Saira ji broke into our conversation, saying, 'Sahab, you are boring the child. Why would she be interested in learning how to make biryani?' He immediately retreated with an apologetic smile and to this day, I regret that we did not reach the end of the recipe. Perhaps then I would not have embarrassed myself trying to pass off a mess of a khichdi as home-cooked biryani to the family!

The next day, I was back at the bungalow, admiring the perfectly made sandwiches we were served while the boss interviewed Dilip sahib who flashbacked to his early days in Peshawar when they would be served pink milky tea with a type of tandoori bread called *bakarkhani* for breakfast. Then, natty in an inky blue suit, he faced the camera for a special photo shoot he had been coaxed into doing by the 'Home Ministry', as he laughingly referred to Saira ji. His array of expressions, playful improvisations and 'live' performance wowed me completely even though I remained in the background with the props.

A few days later, I saw him again, this time on stage with Lata Mangeshkar. I watched the two legends hand each other their respective Lifetime Achievement Award trophies, before he enveloped her in his arms in what was undoubtedly a Kodak moment. At the end of the evening, as I stood by the gate, watching the guests leave, some jubilant and some sulking, a familiar voice broke into my thoughts, '*Aji, hamare taraf bhi to ek nazar dijeye*' [Excuse me, spare a glance in my direction too]. I turned and came face-to-face with a smiling Dilip sahib with Saira ji beside him. That day I realized that little escaped his eagle eye, even if it was a young reporter trying hard to be unobtrusive.

Several years later, when he turned eighty-five, in response to my query about which birthday brought back the fondest memories, he recalled the night he had arrived in the world. Going by what his uncles and aunts told him later, a fire had broken out on the street in Qissa Khwani Bazaar, Peshawar, where their three-storeyed home was located, and caused much commotion. 'It took a while for the midwife to arrive and attend to my frail, delicate mother,' he shared, adding that nothing since had been quite as dramatic!

Mohammad Yusuf Khan was born to Ayesha Begum and Lala Ghulam Sarwar Ali, the fifth of thirteen children. His father was a fruit merchant with orchards in Peshawar and Deolali. In the 1930s, the family relocated to Bombay (present-day Mumbai) and moved into a fourth-floor apartment. However, when his mother started falling ill frequently, they moved out of the city to Deolali where the young Yusuf went to Barnes School in a horse-driven tonga, much like the one he is seen driving in *Naya Daur* (1957).

The dacoit drama *Gunga Jumna* (1961) that was filmed in Nasik and Igatpuri, also took him back to his Deolali days. He had grown up in a bungalow with a beautiful garden tended to by a gardener who lived on the premises with his wife. His mother would often send him to the outhouse with food for the couple or to tell the gardener to run some errands. Young Yusuf often heard him speaking with his wife, and sometimes his mother, in a dialect that he used in the film in later years.

Dilip sahib had never imagined a career in the movies. A keen sportsman, he had dreamt of playing Test cricket for the country and scoring a match-winning century someday. But since he needed a job, on his return from Pune where he ran a canteen in the Air Force cantonment, he approached a family friend, Dr Masani, for one. He was introduced to Bombay Talkies' boss lady, Devika Rani, who was favourably impressed by the young man and engaged him. Yusuf later confided in his director Amiya Chakrabarty that he didn't know the first thing about acting and was advised to hang around the sets. He learnt a lot simply from observing Ashok Kumar while the latter was filming *Kismet* (1943).

His debut film, *Jwar Bhata* (1944), at the age of twenty-two, gave Yusuf a new name. Talking to Mahendranath Kaul in an interview to BBC in 1970, he admitted that he changed his name for fear of a trashing from his conservative father who didn't care for the make-believe world of cinema. He recalled that when they were living in Peshawar, his father was not happy that their neighbour, Lala Basheshwernath Kapoor's son Prithivraj, a handsome, well-built lad, was wasting his time as an actor. So, when Yusuf's launch was being discussed, and three screen names were shortlisted—one of them his own— he, afraid of his father's wrath, begged the producers not to use Yusuf Khan. The other two names were Dilip Kumar and Basudev. He only learnt which of the two had been chosen when he saw the first advertisement announcing the film.

Dilip Kumar, the name stuck, but *Jwar Bhata* came unstuck, as did *Pratima* (1945) and *Noukadubi* (1947). But *Jugnu* (1947), which was released in the same year as India's Independence, was a hit. So was *Shaheed* (1948), which was set against the backdrop of the Quit India Movement. Dilip sahib played Ram, whose participation in the freedom struggle upsets his father and puts him in the path of a police officer who is his rival in love.

A nine-year-old schoolboy had gone with his uncle to watch *Shaheed*, the second film of his young life. Ghulu returned home in tears after watching the hero being hanged for treason. He had seen the same man die earlier in *Jugnu* and was absolutely distraught. That night, when his mother was putting him to sleep, the little boy asked her how a man could die twice. *Beeji* surmised that the impossible could happen only if he were a *farishta* (angel). At that moment, the youngster decided he wanted to be an angel too. A decade later, Ghulu aka Harikrishan Goswami ended up in the movies, playing the martyr Bhagat Singh in a film interestingly titled *Shaheed* at the end of which he too is marched to the gallows.

The actor was none other than Manoj Kumar who borrowed his screen name from Dilip sahib's character in *Shabnam* (1949), a film set against the backdrop of the Burma campaign of 1942. Dilip sahib played a refugee answering to the call of 'Manoj'. 'I watched *Shabnam* in a theatre in Delhi and told myself that when I became an actor, I would call myself Manoj too,' he recounted.

Three decades later, Manoj Kumar brought his 'hero' back from a five-year hibernation—Dilip sahib had disappeared from the silver screen after a double role in *Bairaag* (1976) had failed to impress—with his most ambitious home production *Kranti* (1981). His 'hero' in the film played Sanga, who spearheaded a revolution, and one of the songs in *Kranti*, '*Channa jor garam*', still continues to be played every year on Republic Day and Independence Day. 'I had written the song to lighten the grim mood of the film and ended up giving *chana* [Bengal gram] a patriotic touch and sowing the seeds of a revolution with the lines "*Mera chana hai apni marzi ka bhai marzi ka, yeh dushman khudgarzi ka, khudgarzi ka*", strange as it may seem,' Manoj Kumar sahib had recounted with a smile.

Another must-play patriotic song from *Karma* (1986) is '*Tu mera karma, tu mera dharma*' with Dilip sahib playing a retired cop-turned-jailer in the film, whose encounter with the terrorist Dr Dang changes the course of his life. Writer-director Subhash Ghai's original script had the line *'Har karam apna karenge, aye watan tere liye'.* Subhash ji took it to his music director duo, Laxmikant–Pyarelal, saying he wanted a song with the same line. 'Laxmi ji told me we could meet after three days and discuss the lyrics with Anand Bakshi sahib. I left his bungalow and ran into a producer friend below,' Subhash ji reminisced. They were chatting when the household help ran out saying that Laxmi ji was calling Subhash ji back to his music room. 'Mystified, I went back to find that he had set my words to tune!'

'Har karam apna karenge, aye watan tere liye' was the first song of *Karma* to be recorded. But before *Karma*, urged on by his producer Gulshan Rai, Subhash ji had taken the story of a grandfather and grandson duo to Dilip sahib. He was apprehensive about the thespian's reaction, but to his delight, Dilip sahib liked the plot and his role of an engine-driver-turned-smuggler. Approvingly, he told the Bangalore-based distributor who had fixed the meeting, 'The boy knows his job.' He, however, insisted on a bound script before the film went on the floors at a time when a script was usually written on the set while shooting was on. Subhash ji was quick to deliver and Dilip sahib came on board.

However, not everyone was happy when Subhash ji announced the film, *Vidhaata* (1982), with Dilip Kumar heading a blockbuster cast that included Sanjay Dutt and Padmini Kolhapure as the romantic leads, along with Shammi Kapoor, Sanjeev Kumar, Amrish Puri, Suresh Oberoi and Madan Puri in strong supporting roles. Subhash ji admitted later that over 300 filmmakers told him that he was making a mistake, signing the senior actor who would end up ghost directing the film.

So, during their second meeting, Subhash ji asked him straight, 'Who will direct *Vidhaata*, Subhash Ghai or Dilip Kumar?' He never forgot Dilip sahib's answer, 'It's your ship, you're the captain, I'm just the actor.'

The real casting coup for him however was getting Dilip Kumar and Raaj Kumar to play friends-turned-foes in *Saudagar* (1991). Subhash ji worked on the script for a year because he didn't want either of the veteran actors to feel cheated. Then, having ensured that both had equal footage and challenging roles, he approached Dilip sahib first, having worked with him earlier. He was ecstatic when Dilip sahib gave his nod to Veer Pratap Singh aka Veeru. As he was driving away, Dilip sahib asked, 'Who is playing my friend?' Subhash ji mumbled, 'Raaj Kumar,' and zoomed away before he could be asked any more questions, having been told by his writer that the duo hadn't worked together in thirty-six years.

No one could be sure if Jaani would take the bait, but like Dilip sahib, he too liked the role of Rajeshwar Singh, aka Raju. And just as Dilip sahib did, Raaj Kumar ji too asked who was to play his friend, Veeru. When told it was Dilip Kumar, he nodded approvingly and told Subhash ji that after him, if there was any actor of merit, it was Dilip Kumar. With the two legends coming on board, *Saudagar*, a story spanning three generations, was suddenly the biggest film of the year. It launched two new faces, Manisha Koirala and Vivek Mushran.

Subhash ji once confided that he had planned a fourth film with Dilip sahib, also featuring Amitabh Bachchan and Shah Rukh Khan. A war epic titled *Motherland*; the project however didn't materialize. *Saudagar* that released in 1991, is still remembered for the '*Imli ka boota*' chartbuster, featuring the seasoned duo. A night before it was to be filmed, Dilip sahib suddenly admitted to Subhash ji that he couldn't dance and was petrified of *naach-gaana* (song-and-dance) sequences. The filmmaker convinced him to give it a try. 'Once he was in front of the camera, there were no signs of nerves though. Dilip Kumar was always a consummate actor,' the filmmaker raved later.

Once, talking about Bimal Roy's *Devdas* (1955), Vyjayanthimala admitted that she had been told that Dilip Kumar was a temperamental and moody actor. But in reality he turned out to be very different. Flashbacking to one of her favourite scenes in the tragic romance where she, as the nautch girl Chandramukhi, is watching a drunken Devdas in 'full flow', Vyjayanthimala ji admitted that she was so mesmerized by his histrionics that she was afraid she would forget the one line she had been given, *'Aur mat piyo, Devdas.'* Interestingly, even though he played an alcoholic with such conviction in the film—bagging a Filmfare award for the performance—Amrit Shah, Bimal Roy's manager, once revealed that he had never seen Dilip sahib touch even a drop of liquor during the shoot.

Devdas turned him into a 'Tragedy King' at the age of twenty-six, and by his own admission, he was forced to consult drama coaches and psychiatrists in London to alleviate the depression that weighed heavily on him, long after the film was over. They advised him against signing any more films that took him into dark alleys, which was why he turned down Guru Dutt's *Pyaasa* (1957) about a poet trying to make a name for himself in an indifferent, cruel and materialistic world. The role was eventually played by the filmmaker himself while Dilip sahib moved to lighter roles as in *Azaad* (1955), *Kohinoor* (1960) and *Ram Aur Shyam* (1967).

Forty-six years later, Shah Rukh Khan also bagged the Filmfare Award for Best Actor for his portrayal of Devdas in Sanjay Leela Bhansali's adaptation of Sarat Chandra

Chattopadhyay's epic novel of the same name, and Saira ji confided that in one scene, he reminded her so much of 'sahab' that she was convinced that if they had a son, he would have looked exactly like Shah Rukh. The younger actor had grown up listening to his mother telling him that he resembled her idol, but it was only when Saira ji herself alluded to the striking resemblance between them, that Shah Rukh actually began to believe his mother's refrain.

※

Saira ji saw Dilip sahib for the first time when she was a twelve-year-old schoolgirl. She had accompanied her mother, actress Naseem Banu, to a film's premiere in London. It would have been *Aan* (1952), and by the end of the film, she had lost her heart to its dashing hero. After that, every night, she would pray to God to make her a famous actress like her mother—and Mrs Dilip Kumar.

The first dream was easier to realize, but the second took its time. Even the films they were offered together, be it *Palki*, *Leader* or *Habba Khatoon*, did not take off, or like *Leader* (1964), was made with another actress, Vyjayanthimala. Dilip sahib had himself turned down the suggestion that Saira ji be cast opposite him in *Ram Aur Shyam* (1967), saying 'she is too young to team up with me'. The role eventually went to Mumtaz with Waheeda Rehman playing the other leading lady in this twin drama.

For a decade, he treated Saira ji like a kid; his feelings only changing after she turned twenty-two. He had been invited along with several other industry big-wigs to her birthday party, which doubled up as a house-warming celebration. Dilip sahib flew in from Chennai where he was shooting and for the first time realized that the *chhoti bachchi* had grown up into a beautiful young woman. He told Saira ji as much when they shook hands that evening, and the next morning, he called for her. After that he was a regular visitor to their home and a few weeks later, proposed to a disbelieving Saira ji. She dismissed it as a joke, till he came down the next day, to officially ask her grandmother and mother for her hand in marriage. On 2 October 1966, gorgeous in a white sequined sari, she slipped a diamond ring on his finger. He reciprocated and in the presence of his siblings, Indian screen's most eligible bachelor committed himself to the beauty queen.

A quiet nikah was fixed for 2 November, but as soon as the news leaked out that they were engaged, it sparked off mass hysteria. Coincidentally, they were in Calcutta (present-day Kolkata) together for the shooting of their respective films at the time, and Saira ji recalled how enthusiastic fans had spilled into the tarmac of the airport and at the hotel, pounded on their doors. Exasperated, Dilip sahib decided to push back the date of the wedding, and Naseem Banu ji flew back to Bombay to scout for a maulvi who would perform the ceremony at short notice. On 11 October, Saira Banu, at the age of twenty-two, became Mrs Dilip Kumar and years later admitted that except for a 'year of distress' in 1981, when Dilip sahib is reported to have secretly married Asma, it has been a dream run. 'I love the man, I cannot live without him,' she asserted.

In 2004, when K. Asif's 1960 magnum opus *Mughal-e-Azam* returned to the theatres in full colour, with digitally restored sound, Dilip sahib walked into Mumbai's Eros theatre for the premiere with his begum by his side. It was an unforgettable moment for Saira ji because forty-four years ago, when the film had first been unveiled at Bombay's Maratha Mandir theatre, on 5 August 1960, she had been among the select invitees, which included Suraiya, Nutan, Dev Anand,

Prithviraj Kapoor and his sons, Raj and Shammi. Saira ji, a pretty teenager then, had come only to see her prince and had returned home disappointed because Dilip sahib hadn't turned up for the premiere that evening.

A few weeks before the second premiere, I pinned down Dilip sahib at his bungalow for a quick chat. He wasn't happy to be called away from a cricket match he was watching on TV. He had requested that the interview be pushed to another day, but with the deadline coming up, I had no choice but to impose. He was uncharacteristically short, grudgingly admitting that the idea of restoring and digitally colouring the film had come from him. After discussing it with the Indian Academy of Arts & Animation that specializes in restoring fine art, he had suggested the idea to the son of the late producer, Shahpoorji Pallonji. The original film was in black-and-white, the only splash of colour being Madhubala's rebellious taunt to Badshah-e-Hind Akbar in *'Pyar kiya to darna kya'*.

Today, it is hard to imagine anyone but Dilip sahib and Madhubala playing Salim and Anarkali. They embodied romance on screen, and down the years, the unanimous opinion is that the scene where the prince caresses the beautiful dancing girl with a feather on a moonlit night is one of the most sensuous moments in Hindi cinema. The film's director, K. Asif sahib, wanted Ustad Bade Ghulam Ali Khan sahib to sing *'Prem jogan banke'* in the background to enhance the moment. Composer Naushad sahib tried telling him that the maestro did not sing for films but that only made Asif sahib more obdurate.

With Naushad sahib, he turned up at Khan sahib's house and told him, *'Gaana to aap ko gaana hi padega*, just name your price.' Seething with rage over the young man's impertinence, Khan sahib quoted ₹25,000 for that one song as his remuneration, an unheard amount in those days. Without batting an eyelid, Asif sahib pulled out a wad of notes and paid him an advance of ₹10,000, assuring him that he would get the rest on the day of the recording.

On the day of the recording, Khan sahib reluctantly reported at Mehboob Studio and instantly threw a fit when he found that there was no *gadda*, *chaddar* or *takiyas* laid out for him. Within minutes, Asif sahib had turned the studio into a *baithak*. Mollified, Khan sahib sat down and launched into a rendition of the song in *Raag Sohini*, which Tansen sang between 3 a.m. and 6 a.m. to welcome the rising sun. Far from overwhelmed at having the legend sing for him, Asif sahib pointed out that the *gamak taan* was a tad too heavy and suggested something softer in keeping with the scene's romantic mood. The maestro flew into a rage and stomped out of the recording studio, saying that he would return only after he had seen the scene.

It was now left to Salim and Anarkali to woo Khan sahib back. Asif sahib quickly shot the scene set in the palace garden, rushed it through edit, cut a print and screened it for the singer. According to Naushad sahib, Khan sahib watched the scene in silence and at the end, nodded his grudging approval, '*Anarkali khubsoorat hai... Shehzaade bhi kafi khubsoorat hai.*' He then sang the song four times. Each time the reel had to be rewound and played for him so he could watch Salim and Anarkali in action. As he was leaving, he told Asif sahib to use what he wanted. 'But make sure it sounds good.'

When I had recounted the incident to Dilip sahib that afternoon, he admitted that Khan sahib had insisted on seeing the scene. 'But I don't think he was wooed just by the beautiful Anarkali. I think he was finally convinced by what he saw on screen, what we shot,' he reasoned.

Dilip sahib had been somewhat reluctant to accept the film

initially because he had never played a princely character like Salim before and nor had he done a role of such dimensions. But Asif sahib was convinced he would be able to do justice to it. Even Shahpoorji insisted on Dilip sahib playing Salim after the original prince, Sapru, had to be replaced following Chandramohan's sudden demise. Prithviraj Kapoor stepped in for Chandramohan to play Akbar while Madhubala replaced Nargis as Anarkali.

Mughal-e-Azam was in the making for fifteen long years, during which a lot of things changed off screen too, among them the Dilip Kumar and Madhubala break-up. The two actors had met on the sets of *Badal* (1951) when, from what Prem Nath ji told me, the beautiful heroine would woo both Dilip sahib and him with love notes on scented pink paper and red roses, which were delivered by her hairdresser. When the two actors who were friends exchanged notes, she was caught because she had sent the same notes to both! Prem Nath ji then decided to bow out of the picture, and during the shoot of *Aurat* (1953), met the love of his life, Bina Rai. By the time they returned from Mysore, they were engaged and married soon after.

Meanwhile, after the initial shock of losing Prem Nath ji, Madhubala ji grew closer to Dilip sahib. They were in love and contemplating a future together despite her father Ataullah Khan's opposition to the match, when the *Naya Daur* (1957) controversy blew up. Ataullah Khan refused to allow his daughter to go for an outdoors shoot to Bhopal and the film's producer-director, B.R. Chopra, moved court against his leading lady for breach of contract. He also forced his actor-friend and the film's hero Dilip Kumar to give evidence against his lady love. The betrayal broke Madhubala ji's heart and most of the scenes from *Mughal-e-Azam* were filmed in strained silence, with the couple not exchanging a single word between shots. To their credit however, they never let it appear that they were simply play-acting on screen. Three decades later, speaking about Madhubala ji, Dilip sahib had pointed out that though hers was not the most perfectly chiselled face, she was beautiful in totality, her greatest asset as an actress being her spontaneity.

Sashadhar Mukherjee's *Anarkali* (1953) with Bina Rai and Pradeep Kumar as Anarkali and Salim was a bigger grosser, but *Mughal-e-Azam* that opened seven years later with an ailing Madhubala, immortalized her. Nine years after its release, she bid adieu to the world.

Vyjayanthimala ji replaced Madhubala ji in *Naya Daur* and the film established the dancing star as an actress of note. After that the duo were roped in by Bimal Roy for the reincarnation drama *Madhumati* (1958). Dilip sahib was warned that the audience might be confused by the metaphysical layers inherent in the story, the only Hindi film Bengal's auteur Ritwik Ghatak had scripted. Yet, he accepted the film solely for the pleasure of working with Bimal da, as he was popularly known. Like him, his *Devdas* director too was a man who believed in perfection and hard work. The following year, high on the success of the film, Dilip sahib and Vyjayanthimala ji, reunited for *Paigham* (1959), which had the leading lady's own mother Vasundhara Devi playing the same role in reel life. By the time *Gunga Jumna* (1961) came along, the two were reported to be heading towards the altar. Then, Vyjayathimla ji signed *Sangam* (1964) with Dilip sahib's biggest rival, Raj Kapoor, and everyone concluded that this was the end for the duo. However, when accepting their best actor and best actress awards, for *Leader* and *Sangam* respectively, they were seen smiling happily together and a few weeks later, went on to sign *Ram Aur Shyam*, which had Dilip sahib in a double role.

Madhumati also brought another friend, Bimal Roy's editor, Hrishikesh Mukherjee, into Dilip sahib's life. Hrishi da was fascinated by a house adjacent to the studio and often wondered about its residents. One day, he came up with the idea of a film around the house—three stories of three different families who at some point had lived under its roof. They were stories of birth, marriage and death. No one was convinced—not even Hrishi da himself—that *Musafir* (1957) was a commercially viable project. But Dilip sahib coaxed him into directing the film, even waving away his remuneration. On his part, Hrishi da cajoled Dilip sahib to sing '*Laage nahin chhute Raama*' with Lata Mangeshkar. This little 'big' film opened in the same year as *Naya Daur*, but as expected *Musafir* did not work commercially. It, however, got the certificate of merit for Third Best Feature Film in Hindi at the National Film Awards and gave Hrishi da's career a new direction.

Another young film director who remembered Dilip sahib fondly was Yash Chopra, whose 1961 film *Dharmaputra*, based on a novel by Acharya Chatursen Shastri, revolved around a boy who grows up hating Muslims only to learn that his biological mother who had given him up to her Hindu neighbours during Partition, belonged to the 'other' community. After its release, the film, not surprisingly given its controversial subject, upset both communities and sparked off agitations across the country. To add to Yash Chopra ji's woes, even the collections were abysmally low. This was the young director's second movie after *Dhool Ka Phool* (1959). He was a disturbed and depressed man when he ran into Dilip sahib at a film function. The actor whisked him away in his car and drove him around the city till early morning. 'I don't remember what he said, but his words gave me a lot of solace,' Yash Chopra ji reiterated years later. He returned home to the news that *Dharmaputra* had been voted Best Feature Film in Hindi at the 9th National Film Awards.

Yash Chopra ji never forgot that gesture and cast Dilip sahib in *Shakti* (1982), followed by *Mashaal* (1984). The latter had been conceived with Dilip sahib in mind, along with Kamal Haasan in the role of a neighbourhood rowdy who turns into a responsible journalist under his guidance. When things didn't work out with Haasan, Yash Chopra ji took the role of Raja to Anil Kapoor who instantly came on board.

Rati Agnihotri who was cast opposite Anil Kapoor in the film—she had shared the screen with Dilip sahib earlier in *Mazdoor* (1983)—had grown up playing with Dilip sahib's nieces and nephews because she lived right next door. She recalled how the kids would sometimes stray into the garden. Dilip sahib would be there too sometimes, offering namaz, but not once did she remember him getting angry with them. After she married businessman, Anil Virwani, she would often bump into Dilip sahib at the Turf Club where over tea, he would read out excerpts from his life's journey in Urdu.

One of his nieces, Sayyyeshaa, was introduced by Ajay Devgn in his directorial *Shivaay* (2016). When I had asked her to pick a moment from one of Dilip sahib's films, she immediately zeroed in on his death scene in *Gunga Jumna*. Another unforgettable scene was the one in *Mashaal* when he is frantically trying to flag down a cab or a car to take his ailing wife to hospital. Waheeda Rehman's untimely death in the film changes the course of his character's life from a crusading editor into a criminal. Two versions of the scene were shot over four days and eight shifts at Ballard Pier. It's one of the film's highlights and Kamal Haasan, when he saw the film later, reportedly told Yash Chopra ji that had he known the role he had been offered would shape up so well, he would have grabbed it.

Dilip sahib himself baffled many when he had turned down David Lean's desert epic, *Lawrence of Arabia* (1962). The filmmaker, whose fourth wife Leela Welingkar was a beauty from Hyderabad, had approached Dilip sahib with the role of Sherif Ali. But content with his success back home, he turned it down. On the rebound it went to Omar Sherif who was initially supposed to play Lawrence's desert guide, Tafas. Sherif bagged an Oscar nomination for his performance of Sherif Ali, making him a big name in Hollywood. 'Any regrets?' I had once asked Dilip sahib, and without a second's thought he had replied, 'None. This is my home and this is my cinema.'

Dilip Kumar acted in sixty-two films. Fourteen remained incomplete or unreleased. He bagged the Filmfare award eight times, a Padma Bhushan, the Dadasaheb Phalke Award and the Nishan-e-Imtiaz in Pakistan, among many others. His last appearance was in Umesh Mehra's *Qila* (1998), which had him in a double role but failed to impress. *Aag Ka Dariya* never saw the light of day while *Afsar: The Impact* and his official directorial debut, *Kalinga*, were shelved.

On Dilip sahib's ninetieth birthday, I had called Manoj Kumar for a few words on the man who brought him into the movies. 'He may be ninety, but he still looks twenty-five,' he asserted, going on to point out that while many songs had been penned on a Hindi film heroine's tresses, only Dilip Kumar could have inspired Sahir Ludhianvi to come up with the lines, '*Ude jab jab zulfein teri, kavaariyon ka dil machle, kavaariyon ka dil machle jind meriye...*' Over six decades later, in this 'naya daur', Dilip Kumar wooing Vyjayanthimala still makes my heart trip.

3

DEV ANAND: EVERGREEN AT EIGHTY

Main zindagi ka saath nibhaata chala gaya,
har fikr ko dhuyein mein udata chala gaya

He was Raju, she was Rosie, and together they were making a movie that even though they didn't know it then, would immortalize them in celluloid history. They were shooting at the Maharaja's Palace in Udaipur when suddenly, a group of boisterous American tourists landed on the set and peremptorily ordered the young man, who was being addressed as 'guide', to show them the sights. He flashed his charmingly crooked grin and herded them into a motor boat, jumping in after them. The boat skimmed across Pichola Lake, leaving behind a bemused unit. He returned only after giving them a guided tour. And so convincing was he that none of the tourists guessed he was a popular Indian actor till one of them, a Texan oil tycoon, was formally introduced to him at dinner that evening. Dev Anand, he learnt, was a special guest of the maharaja and was there to film his Indo-American production, *Guide* (1965), which was being made in Hindi and English.

Today, I realize that what made Dev sahib special was that he wore his stardom casually, almost nonchalantly, as he breezed through life. His loose-limbed shuffle, as elder brother Chetan Anand often joked, made him look like a human Leaning Tower of Pisa. To me, the quintessential Dev Anand was *Hum Dono's* (1961) Captain Anand, puffing on a cigarette and warbling in Mohammed Rafi's voice, *'Main zindagi ka saath nibhata chala gaya, har fikr ko dhuyein mein udata chala gaya.'* He didn't need the high of nicotine—Sahir Ludhianvi's words reflected his own philosophy. 'I don't smoke but I do believe in shrugging off the cares of the world instead of letting them settle heavily on my shoulders. I don't like to carry baggage around, no one should,' he would point out. Untouched by success and unfazed by failure, life for Dev sahib was a joy ride. You were welcome to hop aboard, but he didn't enjoy strolls down memory lane. He didn't have a 'pause' or a 'rewind' button because for Dev Anand, life was always in the 'flash-forward' mode.

He also didn't care for Alexander Graham Bell's invention even though he was one of the few stars whose personal number was listed in the *Screen* telephone directory. If one called his office at Anand Studio, chances were he would pick up the phone himself. He answered every caller personally, but he didn't like conducting interviews over the phone. 'Why don't you hop across to Bandra, it would be better if we spoke in person?' he suggested when I tried to coax him into doing a 'phoner'. He eventually agreed, though reluctantly, with a lot of cajoling, after I explained that I was on a tight deadline. 'Next time I will drop by the studio,' I promised. However, once he agreed, one could chat with Dev sahib on anything, from kissing on screen to live-in relationships. Even at eighty plus, he zipped down life's fast lanes, chortling, 'I'm as young as my films.'

Dharamdev Pishorimal Anand's journey in showbiz began in 1943 when unable to go to London to pursue higher studies because money was short, the nineteen-year-old English literature graduate from Lahore's Government College boarded the Frontier Mail for Bombay with just ₹30 in his pocket. In the city, he bunked down with some friends from Gurdaspur, many of them clerks or mill workers, in a flat in Parel, starting out as a clerk at an accountancy firm for a salary of just ₹85. He then moved to the censor office at General Post Office (GPO). Here, letters written and received by Indian soldiers forced to fight with the British against their own, were minutely scrutinized. The letters, he admitted later, gave him an insight into human relationships, which came in handy when he was scripting his films. By this time, his salary had increased to over a hundred rupees, but he was quickly losing interest in the job. As Dev sahib often said, 'Reach for the stars, the moon is not your goal', and that's exactly what he did.

One day, he learnt from his friend Nasir Khan, Dilip Kumar's younger brother, that P.L. Santoshi had dropped one of the heroes from his first film, *Hum Ek Hain* (1946), and was looking for a replacement. He sent across his photographs and was invited to meet the debutant director and the film's producer, Baburao Pai, in Pune. He impressed them with an impromptu performance from his play *Zubeida*. He was hired on the spot by Prabhat Studio, on a three-year contract, for a monthly salary of ₹450.

A parable about communal amity and national unity, *Hum Ek Hain* (1946) was released a year before Independence. Its theatrical run was cut short when Hindu–Muslim riots broke out. The film is remembered today because it cemented a bond between Guru Dutt—Santoshi's young assistant and the film's choreographer—and its leading man. Thanks to a mix-up by their dhobi, Guru Dutt sahib turned up on the set wearing Dev sahib's shirt because he didn't have a spare one and immediately caught Dev sahib's eye. Soon they were eating samosas at Lucky Restaurant and sharing their dreams.

The buddies made a pact: If Dev sahib turned producer, he would sign Guru Dutt sahib as the director. And should the latter land an opportunity to make a film first, he would sign his actor-friend as the hero. Fortune favoured Dev sahib first. After Prabhat Studio shut down and his contract was deemed null and void, he came to Bombay and bagged *Mohan* (1947) with Baburao Pai, an independent producer at the time. One day, as he was running after a train at Churchgate station, he was spotted by Shaheed Latif, who, sitting in a stationary train watched the young man race by. Nudged by his begum, author Ismat Chugtai, Shaheed Latif sahib called out to him. When Dev sahib went across to them, he asked him to drop by Bombay Talkies Studio the next day and meet the boss, Ashok Kumar.

Dev sahib was delighted. He idolized Ashok Kumar whose *Achhut Kannya* (1936) had pointed him in the direction of cinema. When the senior actor and studio boss asked him how much remuneration he was expecting, Dev sahib quipped that his fee would be people saying that Ashok Kumar had given the industry a star. His self-assurance, rare for a newcomer, landed him Shaheed Latif's debut directorial *Ziddi* (1948), which was based on his wife's short story and had been conceived with Ashok Kumar in mind. Dev sahib's starting salary as an actor was ₹7,000 a month, but it quickly doubled after *Ziddi* was a hit.

The following year, with his elder brother Chetan Anand, Dev sahib launched Navketan Films, named after his brother's son Ketan. Their first production, *Afsar* (1950), directed by Chetan sahib, was based on a German play *The Inspector*

General. It featured Dev sahib and the woman of his dreams, Suraiya, in the lead. It bombed. After that, true to his word, he signed his friend Guru Dutt to direct *Baazi* (1951). Guru Dutt sahib's mother, Vasanthi Padukone ji, confided to me years later, that throughout the making of the film, there were many arguments between her son and Chetan sahib who had wanted Balraj Sahni to write and direct their next production. However, Dev sahib was resolute and always sided with her son, despite him being a first-time director.

On the day of the mahurat, cupid struck when Guru Dutt sahib heard Geeta Roy singing, *'Tadbeer se bigdi hui taqdeer banale, apne pe bharosa hai to yeh dav laga le.'* She was a top singer, he, only a struggling director, but love is blind. Her car would often be parked outside his Matunga residence with Geeta ji in the kitchen helping his mother and sister, Lalita, with the chores, and sometimes singing a Rabindra Sangeet for them. But she had another suitor too, a Bengali man her family was keen she marry, and whom Guru Dutt sahib knew about. One day, he took her to Haji Malang dargah and asked her to choose between them. They tied the knot three years later, on 26 May 1953.

Baazi paid off for both friends. *Jaal* (1952) followed, which Guru Dutt sahib wrote and directed, with the same pair—Geeta Bali and Dev Anand. Zipping down in his Impala, en route to Bombay after the shoot, his chauffeur and Geeta Bali ji's sister at the back, Dev sahib, urged on by his exuberant co-star, pressed down on the accelerator. 'The previous night, he had been tricked into tasting a glass or two of Feni after pack-up by K.N. Singh, the film's baddie, and Dev sahib was nursing a hangover when he took the wheel. For a fraction of a second his eyes closed while he was on the road and the car smashed into a tree. The steering wheel pierced his chest and he broke a few ribs while Geeta ji was hit in the head,' recounted Mohan Churiwala, a close associate of the actor. They were rushed to Pune's Sassoon Hospital where Dev sahib was attended to by a wonderful doctor, Dr Shreeram Lagoo, whom he later cast in *Des Pardes* (1978) and *Lootmaar* (1980).

Meanwhile, Guru Dutt sahib himself turned producer, in partnership with Geeta Bali ji's sister Haridarshan Kaur, with *Baaz* (1953), an action adventure set in a ship. He chose to play the lead himself but the film sank faster than the Titanic. It took two more films, *Aar Paar* (1954) and *Mr. & Mrs. '55* (1955), both with him as the hero, before Guru Dutt sahib sent his assistant Raj Khosla, across to Dev sahib with the script of *C.I.D.* (1956). It was directed by Raj Khosla ji and introduced Waheeda Rehman in a vamp's role. And finally, the pact, made years ago, was sealed with a hit.

Dev sahib went on to become a huge commercial star while Chetan sahib remained an artistic filmmaker. This sparked off creative differences between the two brothers over Chetan sahib's choice of subjects for their banner and his treatment of them. During the screening of *Aandhiyan* (1952) at the prestigious Karlov Vary Film Festival where it was one of the five official entries, differences cropped up over Chetan sahib editing out the courtroom scenes at the end, which his brother believed was among his best emotional performances. They cropped up again after *Humsafar* (1953) bombed and put Navketan in the red. *Taxi Driver* (1954), directed by Chetan sahib with Dev sahib in the lead, co-written by their younger brother Vijay Anand and the director's first wife Uma, bailed out the company then. However, things got so bad between them during *Funtooshi* (1956) that Vijay Anand aka Goldie sahib was called to direct a song for it. The film was a hit, but soon after, Chetan sahib relinquished his 50 per cent shares in Navketan and launched his own banner Maha Shakti Films, with *Anjali* (1957).

Meanwhile, Goldie sahib finally had his moment in the sun when he was able to sell another script to Dev sahib on the condition that he would direct it. The demand was too ludicrous to merit consideration when he first made it, but two months later, with Raj Khosla failing to deliver the script of *Khali Botal* as promised, Dev sahib reached out to his younger brother. This time Goldie sahib hopped into a Chevrolet, with Dev sahib and Kalpana Kartik ji, and en route to Mahabaleshwar, narrated his story of a young man who unexpectedly inherits some money and property, and on his way to claiming it, gives a ride to a runaway bride and ends up being thrown into prison for abducting an heiress. As soon as they reached Hotel Fredrick, Dev sahib called his manager in Bombay and informed him that their next yet-untitled production could wait; they were launching a new film with Goldie as the director. *Nau Do Gyarah* (1957) shot in forty days, in a truck from Delhi to Bombay, was a runaway hit—and Vijay Anand the successful director was born. Raj Khosla sahib's *Khali Botal* was eventually made as *Kala Pani* (1958) and bagged Dev sahib and Nalini Jaywant Filmfare Award for Best Actor and Best Supporting Actress, respectively.

In their struggling years, Guru Dutt sahib and Dev sahib would often gaze out at a quaint bungalow in suburban Bandra from Chetan sahib's apartment. After he became a star, Dev sahib purchased it and renamed it Anand. There, in his study, he scoured newspapers and books for true-life stories, scouted out new talent and made movies with indefatigable energy. It didn't matter that after Padmini Kolhapure, Tabu, Jackie Shroff and Tina Munim, none of the new faces he launched made an impression. He continued to play the benign godfather, telling me that introducing a newcomer gave him more satisfaction than a million bucks. Indeed, there was no stopping Dev Anand.

Zaheeda, whom he introduced in *Prem Pujari* (1970), remembers her mentor as India's Gregory Peck—dashing, debonair, always speaking at such a breakneck speed that you had to stop him mid-sentence and ask, 'Excuse me, *aap kya keh rahe the?* What were you saying?' He was friends with her actress-aunt, Nargis, and uncle, Sunil Dutt, and one day, her father was surprised by a call from Navketan informing them that Dev sahib had heard they served a hearty Sunday breakfast and wished to join them. 'My father immediately extended an invitation. Eventually, Dev sahib didn't turn up, and without thinking too much about the unexpected call, we all sat down and finished off the keema-toast, fruits and juice,' the actress recounted.

From their later conversations, Zaheeda ji believes Dev sahib may have had her in mind to play Rosie, the young wife of a years-older archaeologist, who is lured away by a charlatan in *Guide*. 'He shared the story based on R.K. Narayan's novel with me, discussed the role and asked me if I could dance. He even introduced me to Pearl S. Buck at a party at Hotel Sun-n-Sand,' she informed me.

Dev sahib had met Pearl, the Pulitzer-winning author of *The Good Earth*, with American director Tad Danielski, at the Berlin Film Festival, and the trio had agreed to collaborate on an Indo-American co-production based on a book by an Indian author during a party at Hotel Sun-n-Sand. They eventually agreed on *Guide*. Danielski had his heart set on Leela Naidu, but she was not a classical dancer—a must for the role. Danseuse-actresses like Padmini and Vyjayanthimala didn't impress him. He eventually gave the nod to Waheeda Rehman who was playing the dutiful Sita in films at the time, but was ready to gamble with the 'adulteress' Rosie. She however refused to work with Raj Khosla with whom she had an altercation during *Solva Saal* (1958). He was directing the Hindi *Guide* at the time, and unwilling to lose his heroine, Dev sahib turned to his elder brother. The idea was to film the two versions simultaneously to cut down on costs, but it was soon apparent that Chetan sahib and Danielski were not on the same page. As a result, Dev sahib decided to wrap up the English film first and then start the Hindi one.

Danielski's English *Guide* was made in ten weeks, but just as the Hindi *Guide* was about to roll, Chetan sahib got permission to shoot his war epic, *Haqeeqat* (1964), in Ladakh. The film had a huge cast, was being made with the cooperation of the government, including then Prime Minister Jawaharlal Nehru and the army, and there was no time to be lost since the location would be snow-bound and unreachable after a month. This time it was Goldie sahib who bailed out *Guide*.

'But I didn't want to keep anything of the Americans in my film. I had gone through the screenplay; in the first shot, Marco and Rosie disembark at the station, and in the next shot you see her in bed with Raju. Who would accept such a hero even if he became a saint later? The cuckolded husband would have walked away with all the sympathy,' Goldie sahib had pointed out to me years later. He took off to Khandala for eighteen days and rewrote the original script before flying out to Udaipur and wrapping the Hindi *Guide* in eighty shifts.

Meanwhile the English version premiered in New York City in February 1965. The reviews and the box office collections were disappointing. The only silver lining was that David O. Selznick, the producer of *Gone with the Wind* (1939) and *Rebecca* (1940), signed Dev sahib for a Hollywood film which was to be shot in Kashmir. Sadly, Selznick passed away suddenly after four months and the film was shelved.

Back home, there were no takers for the Hindi *Guide*. After a few distributors thumbed it down as being 'too risky', the Anands refused to show it. Yash Johar, Dev sahib's production controller, however, quietly screened one song, *'Piya tose naina laga re'*, for a Delhi distributor, and got his nod.

This film too opened slowly, but then, packed full houses at Bombay's Maratha Mandir for ten weeks. It celebrated a silver jubilee in Ahmedabad as Gujarat, grappling with a real drought, prayed to Raju 'Guide' to bring rain. The legendary Howard Hawkes who had made over fifty films for MGM Studio, watched it and wanted to sign Goldie sahib to direct a film for him, but suggested he get himself an Oscar first. *Guide* was India's official entry to the 1966 Academy Awards in the Best Foreign Language Film category and on Hawkes' suggestion, the Anands submitted a thirty-minute shorter cut, minus many of the songs and with English subtitles. It cleared the first round but lost out to a Norwegian film in the second. 'If Goldie and I had stayed back in Los Angeles and lobbied, we may have well brought the Oscar home,' Dev sahib mused later, but they barely had money to settle their hotel bills and so had no choice but to return to Bombay.

Desperate to move on, the Anand brothers then partnered on a thriller, *Jewel Thief* (1967), which grew out of a story by K.A. Narayan revolving around mistaken identity and a man whose very existence is suspect. Dev sahib persuaded his ailing mentor, Ashok Kumar, to play the 'intellectual villain', promising him that he would not be inconvenienced by shootings delays and even his afternoon siesta would be worked into the schedule. 'His casting as the villain was the big talking point, though Goldie sahib gave away the plot in the poster's tagline: "Ashok Kumar in and as Jewel Thief". But very few caught on,' Churiwala pointed out.

Over the years, there have been speculations of a *Guide* sequel titled *Bhookh*, but while admitting that Goldie sahib and he had toyed with the idea, Dev sahib had added that it was not as a follow-up to *Guide*. In fact, when a contemporary remake of *Guide*, to be directed by the late Rituparno Ghosh, with Akshay Kumar and Vidya Balan in the lead, was proposed, Dev sahib had vehemently opposed it, saying, 'I won't let it happen', even as he prepared to take the original to the Cannes Film Festival to be screened in the 'Classics' section. He argued that he had never remade a film in his career. Yes, despite a string of forgettable flops in his later years, Dev sahib was never short of original ideas. *Prem Pujari* (1970), *Hare Rama Hare Krishna* (1971), *Tere Mere Sapne* (1971)—so many of his films were way ahead of their time.

With *Prem Pujari*, he finally partnered with Zaheeda. Nargis was filming *Raat Aur Din* (1967) at Mehboob Studio, and one day, during a break in shooting, she decided to drop in on Dev sahib who was picturizing a song for *Teen Devian* (1965) on another floor. Zaheeda ji tagged along with her aunt, and after meeting her again, he offered her the role of a spy in *Prem Pujari*. 'I was getting lots of offers at the time. One of them came from Guru Dutt, but since he had a reputation of screen-testing actresses and rejecting them, I didn't want to risk the "jinx" tag and turned him down. Navketan was a big banner, the role had many shades to it and Dev sahib was a superstar. So, I accepted *Prem Pujari*,' Zaheeda ji recounted. She also said that when she had gone for a music sitting to composer S.D. Burman's house, he had welcomed her with snacks and rasgullas. 'When Dev sahib groused that Dada never offered him more than a cup of a tea, he pointed out that I was the granddaughter of Jaddan Bai.' Jaddan Bai was a successful actress-filmmaker, one of India's best thumri singers and among the first female composers of Hindi cinema.

Prem Pujari written by Dev sahib, revolved around his character, the peace-loving Lieutenant Ramdev Bakshi, who is sent by his war hero father to the Indo-Chinese border where he refuses to pick up the gun and so is court-martialled. Soon after, he is abducted by the Chinese and coaxed by a beautiful spy to work for them. He redeems himself by joining the Indo-Pakistani War of 1965 and gunning down many enemy soldiers. The film sparked off much curiosity, as did its debutante, with the who's who of the industry flocking to the newly revamped Shalimar Theatre on Grant Road, for its premiere. 'But after the show, all the guests melted away. Only Kishore Kumar stayed back with the team for the after-party at the Taj Mahal Hotel, complimenting Dev sahib and me with a "well done",' Zaheeda ji reminisced.

The scenario was not new to Dev sahib. In later years, his career graph was dotted by a string of debacles. His protégé admitted watching his last film, *Chargesheet* (2011), a crime drama partly inspired by late actress Divya Bharti's mysterious death, with her filmmaker son Nilesh Sahay, in an almost empty theatre. It took Zaheeda ji back to the release of *Prem Pujari*, which, because it had touched upon the Indo-China and Indo-Pakistan conflicts in the 1960s, and had Dev sahib playing an anti-hero, had sparked off violent protests across the country. In Bengal, it was forcibly removed by the ruling Communist Party of India (Marxist) because a sequence alluded to the cultural revolution in China and even in Bombay, theatres were vandalized. 'The film suffered, Dev sahib suffered,' Zaheeda ji sighed.

He compensated her for the disappointment by casting her in a typical heroine's role in *Gambler* (1971), then offering her the role eventually played by Zeenat Aman in *Hare Rama Hare Krishna* (1971). 'I told him that after seeing me as his leading lady in *Gambler*, the audience would never accept me as his sister. He wasn't happy with my decision,' Zaheeda ji recounted.

Tere Mere Sapne, a film on medical ethics and malpractices, was Goldie sahib's favourite film, both as an actor and a director. 'It was inspired by A.J. Cronin's 1937 novel *The Citadel*, as also the disillusionment of a surgeon-cousin of the Anands. Dr Avinash Chadda, who, after a failing battle with non-existent infrastructure and government apathy in the villages where he wanted to practice, migrated to the UK,' informed Mohan Churiwala. What made it personal was Goldie sahib's decade-long suffering because of a kidney stone. In a rare interview, he revealed how two doctors had fought over his surgery and their commission. He was eventually operated upon by a new surgeon for whom it was a 'big break' to attend to Dev Anand's brother.

The film was also a love triangle, with Dev sahib's character, Dr Anand, drawn to one of his patients, a glamorous actress, which distances him from his wife to the extent that he doesn't even realize she is pregnant. 'He had wanted me to play the actress, but once again, Vijay Anand believed Hema Malini was better suited,' Zaheeda ji informed me.

∞

Dev sahib's own personal life had sparked off plenty of rumours of romances with his heroines. He has himself admitted to nightly rendezvous with Suraiya ji with whom he worked in seven films, on the terrace of her Marine Drive apartment. He even sent her an engagement ring which she accepted, but then, was forced to throw it into the sea following her grandmother's threats of suicide. That they belonged to different communities and Dev sahib was still just a struggling actor while Suraiya was the reigning box office queen, went against the madly-in-love couple. She stayed unmarried; he married Kalpana Kartik, his *Taxi Driver* co-star, during the shooting of the film, in the make-up room at Mohan Studio. Their secret was revealed when the cinematographer noticed a sparkling ring on Kalpana's finger that hadn't been there before, and worried about continuity, he pointed it out.

Dev sahib had bought one of the cottages at Iris Park and settled down in Juhu to raise a family there. Two years after *Taxi Driver*, their son Suneil was born on 30 June 1956. His wife, an army girl from Shimla, retired from the screen after *Nau Do Gyarah* (1957) and reverted to her original name Mona. She was happy to remain out of the spotlight and raise their children, Suneil and daughter Devina. They stayed married till his death.

To him, family mattered. Goldie sahib revealed how after Chetan sahib's demise on 6 July 1997—which he believes could have been precipitated by a hurried transfusion—a subdued Dev sahib confronted by the transience of our existence, had come to him. Chetan sahib had directed *Jaaneman* (1976), a contemporary remake of *Taxi Driver*, in Navketan's silver jubilee year. 'Twenty-five years have flown past, it's time to make another film together,' Dev sahib told his younger brother. *Jaana Na Dil Se Door* was to be a tribute to their *bhaiji* Chetan sahib who had kept the family together after their mother passed away and their father had become a freedom fighter. Goldie sahib was game, provided his brother forgot that he was Dev Anand, the star, and surrendered to him completely.

The emotional family drama revolved around a man—Dev sahib playing his age—whose life is turned upside down when his daughter, whom he hasn't seen in twenty years and who is the mirror image of her mother, suddenly reappears. The film starring Indrani Banerjee in a double role, featured the Anand brothers, along with Kamini Kaushal and Moushumi Chatterjee. Goldie sahib passed away on 23 February 2004 at the age of 70; Dev sahib continued to make films, alone.

During our last interview, Dev sahib revealed that he was planning to take forward *Hare Rama Hare Krishna*. This film about hippie culture and the perils of drug abuse had launched Zeenat Aman and remains unforgettable. 'Maybe I'll return to Nepal to shoot it,' he mused, saying the script for the sequel was ready. There were three other films on his mind, one which he wanted to shoot in India, the second demanded a trip to the United States and the third to Croatia. He didn't reveal more but admitted that he also wanted to write a follow-up to his bestselling memoir, *Romancing with Life*. I didn't for a minute doubt that he could do all this and more, even though he would be turning eighty-nine in a few weeks. Unlike other occasions, this time I had dropped by at his makeshift office in Khar because Anand was under renovation. He sat behind a desk piled high with papers and spoke enthusiastically about his 1960 black-and-white film *Hum Dono*, which was returning to the theatres as the colourized and digitized *Hum Dono Rangeen* (2011), fifty years after it was first unveiled. He was just as excited about his new film *Chargesheet* that was also releasing the same year.

A younger colleague—an ardent Dev Anand fan—had begged to accompany me for the interview. I told her to swing by a little later, after I had taken his permission. She popped up with a delighted smile and an instamatic camera. Once I was done with my questions, she asked him for a picture for her album. He graciously posed with her while I clicked them. As I was handing the camera back, he beckoned me over, and throwing an arm around my shoulder, asked her to take a photograph of the two of us together. I must have looked somewhat bemused because no star before, or since, has asked for a picture with me. I have never wanted one either. This one I wanted because the man in the frame was so special. I kept asking for it—my colleague never did mail it to me.

A few months after that meeting, on 3 December 2011, I woke up to the news that Dev sahib had passed away in his sleep in a hotel in London. For some reason I flashbacked to his television rendezvous with Simi Garewal. When she had asked him if he feared anything, he had shaken his head, 'No, no fears, not even death… You close your eyes, and you are in a different world.' Perhaps that's how death had come to him. Quietly, gently leading him away while he slept.

I switched on the TV and was drowned in a deluge of tears as his leading ladies wept unabashedly. I was just as distraught, but strangely, my eyes were dry. I wondered why I didn't feel his absence, which I knew was forever. Vyjayanthimala ji, when I connected with her at her Chennai residence, wasn't crying either as she remembered how relieved she had been to discover that her *Amar Deep* (1958) hero was taller than her by a few inches. She went on to confide that by the time *Jewel Thief* came along nine years later, he had found a nickname for her—Papa. That day, when the world was saying Dev Anand was gone forever, Vyjayanthimala ji was telling me that she could still imagine him walking into the room that very instant and telling her in his usual staccato style, 'Where have you been, Papa? It's time to make another movie together.' And I could see them singing '*Dil pukare aa re aa re*' rather than

'*Rulake gaya sapna mera*'. Even as our shared laughter carried across the wire, I could imagine him smiling approvingly from somewhere near. Dev sahib, like Rajesh Khanna in *Amar Prem*, had always hated tears.

4

SHAMMI KAPOOR: THE ORIGINAL ROCKSTAR

Aasmaan se aaya farishta, pyaar ka sabak sikhlane

'Once upon a time,' he reminisced, with a faraway look in those hypnotic, blue-grey eyes, 'I would ring in my birthdays in Kashmir on a shikara at night on the Dal Lake.' The picturesque valley sparked off memories of many enjoyable film shoots, and typically for Shammi Kapoor, these memories had a musical ring.

Mohammed Rafi's evergreen chartbusters, *'Chahe koi mujhe junglee kahe'* for *Junglee* (1961) and *'Yeh chand sa roshan chhera, yeh jheel si neeli aankhen'* for *Kashmir Ki Kali* (1964), were filmed there in the swinging sixties. Nasir Hussain's *Tumsa Nahin Dekha* (1957) that put him on the road to stardom, was also shot there in the month of October, and the melody of its title track, *'Yun to hamne lakh haseen dekha, tumsa nahin dekha',* set his feet tapping decades later when confined to an electric wheelchair, he could no longer walk, let alone dance.

There were no signs of regret for the man he had been and one he had become as Shammi ji discussed plans for his seventy-seventh birthday. The wild all-night parties had given way to quiet dinners at home and the guest list had dwindled down to a handful of doctors he met during dialysis thrice a week and who, over time, had become his friends. In 2003, while trying to save his lungs, he had lost his kidneys to heavy antibiotics and that is when dialysis had become a part of his life. In fact, when I had called, he informed me that he was at that very moment at Mumbai's Hinduja Hospital undergoing dialysis. Apologizing for catching him at a bad time, I quickly tried to hang up, but he had stopped me with a laugh, pointing out that we could speak while the solutes and toxins were being cleansed from his blood. 'I have nothing else to do anyway for the next three hours,' he rumbled across the wire.

Chatting with someone who was undergoing treatment was a first for me, but because Shammi ji was so matter-of-fact about it, I quickly forgot about the dialysis. Hospitals have always depressed me since I had spent much time in and out of them as a child, having suffered from acute tonsillitis. Recalling my resentment as I watched other kids go to school or out to play while I was cooped up inside, it made me wonder if his health problems upset him as well. Didn't he miss the revelry? Didn't he miss acting, which had been a part of his life for decades? There was a long, reflective pause, followed by a sigh, 'More than acting, I miss running around at will, like I used to once. I would have very much liked to travel with my wife to different parts of the world now, but these thrice-weekly dialysis sessions cannot be missed. More than a cure, this is the treatment.'

I sighed with him, knowing how it felt to be tied down. Then, he said something I will never forget. 'But only three days in the week are for the hospital, the remaining four days are mine to live, right?' I learnt later that four of his toes had been amputated due to diabetic gangrene, but he would still take off in his new Mercedes, with his chauffeur sitting in the backseat and his wife Neila Devi beside him, driving 180 kilometres to Pune.

Till almost his last days, Shammi ji's joie de vivre sparkled in those blue-grey eyes. A week before he passed away—two months short of his eightieth birthday—he had rolled his wheelchair into his daughter Kanchan's golden jubilee celebration, and for the short time that he was there, he had been the life of the birthday party.

After his demise, Shabana Azmi revealed that plans had been underway to take Shammi ji back to his beloved Kashmir where so many of his reel-life romances had bloomed. In 2011, Jyotsna Suri, wife of hotelier Lalit Suri and chairperson and managing director of Bharat Hotel Limited, had met him at his South Mumbai apartment. She had invited him to Srinagar for the centenary celebrations of The Lalit. Back when it was the Oberoi Palace, Shammi ji had a favourite suite at the five-star hotel where he always put up, and Mrs Suri wanted him to return to it in its hundredth year. When he reluctantly turned down her invitation, telling her that he was tied down to Mumbai because of the dialysis sessions, she promised him that they would make arrangements to ensure that his treatment continued uninterrupted in Srinagar. An excited Shammi ji was looking forward to the visit with his real-life leading lady Neila Devi by his side, when on 14 August, death came knocking on his door and whisked him away.

In early September, his children Aditya Raj Kapoor and Kanchan Desai—with a handful of industry friends such as Biswajeet, Asha Parekh, Shabana Azmi, Amitabh Bachchan, Vinod Khanna, Tina Ambani, Vinod Chopra and Poonam Dhillon—flew down to Srinagar with his ashes. After the last rites, everyone got into a shikara and rowed around Dal Lake, singing and dancing to his chartbuster numbers, including

'*Yeh chand sa roshan chehra.*' Indeed, that was the way Shammi ji would have wanted to exit the world.

One of O.P. Nayyar's biggest hits, the song '*Yeh chand sa roshan chehra*' was one in which he serenaded Sharmila Tagore in Shakti Samanta's *Kashmir Ki Kali*. The composer had been strongly recommended to Shakti da by Pacchi, Om Prakash's brother and the producer of his *Howrah Bridge* (1958). With his heroine Madhubala also rooting for him, Shakti da entrusted the film's score to Nayyar sahib and to this day, Geeta Dutt's '*Mera naam Chin Chin Choo*', picturized on Helen, and '*Aye meherbaan*', on a sensuous Madhubala, remains unforgettable. Thereafter, the duo collaborated on *Jaali Note* (1960), another noir thriller and Madhubala-starrer, whose '*Chand zard zard hai*' and '*Gustakh nazar*' were equally popular.

In 1963, high on the success of *China Town* (1962), the three Musketeers—Shammi, Shaky (Shakti Samanta) and Jacky (Jaikishan of the Shankar–Jaikishan composer duo)—were gearing up for *Kashmir Ki Kali*, when Shakti da ran into Nayyar sahib. 'He was going through a professional low and requested my father to come to his music room in Mahalaxmi and listen to some of the tunes he had in stock in the hope that he would pick up a few. My father found it difficult to refuse him, and for old time's sake, dropped by one evening,' Shakti da's son Ashim told me. The gratified music director played almost a hundred tunes for him and Shakti da shortlisted a dozen.

Shakti da returned to the studio a second time, this time dragging a reluctant Shammi ji along. The latter was afraid Jaikishan would hear about the visit and it would upset him. He only agreed after Shakti da assured him that they would go ahead with Nayyar, only if he liked the songs. If not, they would return to their original choice of Shankar–Jaikishan.

This time, Nayyar sahib played fifty-two tunes and Shammi

ji picked out a dozen. Eight were used for *Kashmir Ki Kali*, including '*Yeh chand sa roshan chehra*' and '*Deewana hua badal*'. Four found their way into *Sawan Ki Ghata* (1966), which Shakti da produced and directed two years later, with Sharmila Tagore, Mumtaz and Manoj Kumar.

Shakti da flew to the Valley to shoot '*Yeh chand sa roshan chehra*' with a crew of a hundred and forty. It rained for three weeks before the sun peeked through. While the rest of the team sat in the hotel, chatting and playing cards, Sharmila ji used the time to rehearse her Bollywood style *jhatkas* and *matkas*. Shammi ji never joined her and Shakti da knowing that his friend never worked with a choreographer, didn't insist. 'When the skies finally cleared up, they shot for twelve hours at a stretch for four days and wrapped up the song,' Ashim concluded.

During the recording, Shammi ji had badgered Nayyar sahib, the music director, to give him different variations of the line '*Tareef karoon kya uski jisne tumhe banaya*'. No one could figure out why he had been so insistent till they started shooting. Then, Shammi ji spontaneously came up with different ways of enacting the line. His moves got more and more frenzied towards the end of the song, when clapping his hands to the catchy beat, he swayed in the shikara, before stumbling over its edge—the unexpected splash taking everyone by surprise. That was the magic of Shammi Kapoor!

Shammi ji also discovered R.D. Burman, this time thanks to Vijay Anand's persistence. Goldie sahib, as Anand was fondly known within the film fraternity, had been roped in by Nasir Hussain to direct a film for his banner. It was initially meant to star his brother Dev Anand in the lead. However, the producer and the hero had a fallout at R.K. Nayyar and Sadhana's engagement ceremony and Dev sahib exited the project. Having worked with him in *Tumsa Nahin Dekha* (1957) and *Dil Deke Dekho* (1950), Nasir sahib offered the film to Shammi ji. His 'yes' triggered off a mad scramble to find an appropriate script for him.

Teesri Manzil (1966), Goldie sahib informed me one afternoon at the White House during his tenure as Censor Board chairperson, was born from a one-scene idea that Nasir sahib narrated. Two girls are on their way to Mussourie, where Rupa (sister of one of the two girls), has fallen from the third floor of a hotel and died. While everyone believes she committed suicide, the sister, Sunita, is convinced she was murdered, and that a drummer, Rocky, is behind her untimely demise. When asked how she would recognize this Rocky, Sunita says she has heard that he always wears dark glasses. Hearing this, a young man on a motor bike, who has stopped to fill petrol at the pump and has been listening to them, surreptitiously takes off his glares and tucks them into his pocket before they can register his presence.

I won't give away the identity of the murderer and spoil the suspense, but I can reveal how R.D. Burman scored over O.P. Nayyar and Shankar–Jaikishan. To start with, Shammi ji was far from impressed with Goldie sahib's choice of the music director, even if Pancham, as R.D. Burman was fondly called, was veteran composer S.D. Burman's son. Goldie sahib had known him since he was a child and knew that he could play every musical instrument—from the harmonium, tabla and sitar to the mouth organ, drums, trumpet and banjo—and would constantly assure his worried dad that the boy would make his mark in the industry. In fact, Goldie sahib had planned on signing Pancham da for *Jewel Thief* (1967). When *Teesri Manzil* came along, he decided that the musical thriller would be the right break for the maverick genius.

Anu Malik added that he had heard from his father, music director Sardar Malik, that after hearing some of Pancham da's tunes, Jaikishan whom Shammi ji had convinced to slash his fees by half for the film, urged his actor-friend to give the youngster a hearing, pleading, '*Sun to le ek baar*.' Shammi ji mulishly shook his head, 'If you are not composing, I'm not listening.' When he finally agreed, it was evident to both Nasir sahib and Goldie sahib that he was simply going through the motions, having already mentally dismissed Pancham da when he drove in for the music sitting.

It was around seven in the evening and Pancham da who had prepped for this sitting for days, started with a folk song. Shammi ji who was lolling disinterestedly on the settee, sat up after hearing the first few notes. He listened to a dozen songs, then, told his producer and director that from now on this boy would compose music for all his films.

Teesri Manzil's revolutionary album was a generous mix of rock 'n' roll and jazz, Blues and Latino—all with a twist. It offered a bouquet of classics by Mohommed Rafi, from the soul-stirring ballad '*Tumne mujhe dekha*' to the pahadi '*Deewana mujhsa nahin*'. It also boasted of four Rafi and Asha Bhosle duets, from the seductive '*O haseena zulfonwali*' to the sweetly playful '*O mere sona re*', from the spirited '*Dekhiye sahibon, woh koi aur tha*' to the almost orgasmic '*Aaja aaja mein hoon pyaar tera*'. It was the perfect showcase for Pancham da's brilliance, a fusion of the East and the West. Like Shammi ji who changed the face of the Hindi film hero with his leather jackets, cocky swagger and unabashed sensuality, Pancham da with his inventive orchestration gave Hindi film music a new zing.

'Shammi uncle was like Salman is today. He had a terrific ear for music and as soon as he heard "*O haseena zulfonwali*" and "*Aaja aaja mein hoon pyaar tera*", a unique blend of Indian melody and Western orchestration, he was won over. My daddy used to say Pancham da turned the page for Indian music, giving it a completely new sound. He brought along jazz and lounge, which were unheard of at the time,' Anu Malik pointed out. Nasir sahib and Pancham da went on to collaborate on a number of films, including *Baharon Ke Sapne* (1967), *Pyar Ka Mausam* (1969), *Caravan* (1971), *Yaadon Ki Baaraat* (1973), *Hum Kisise Kum Naheen* (1977), *Zamaane Ko Dikhana Hai* (1981) and *Manzil Manzil* (1984).

Teesri Kasam reinforced Shammi Kapoor's image as the 'desi Elvis Presley'. It was an adage he didn't care for, arguing that they didn't have access to videos—pirated or otherwise—back then, so he couldn't have copied the King of Rock 'n' Roll. 'Maybe he copied me,' he quipped, adding with a laugh, 'Aamir calls Elvis the "videshi Shammi Kapoor". I like that better!'

∞

Born Shamsher Raj Kapoor to Prithviraj and Ramsarni Kapoor, he joined his father's theatrical company, Prithvi Theatre, in 1948 as a junior artiste on a monthly salary of ₹50. He stayed on for four years, his remuneration going up to ₹300. Despite belonging to Bollywood's first family with his father being a legendary actor and elder brother, Raj Kapoor, a star and filmmaker, Shammi ji neither entered the film industry with glowing testimonials nor was he launched by the RK banner. It was only when he was fifty that Raj Kapoor cast him in *Prem Rog* (1982) as Bade Raja Thakur, modelled after their Papaji, Prithviraj Kapoor.

Shammi ji made his acting debut with Kardar Film Company, when the producer spotted him on stage in a play by Prithvi Theatre and cast him in *Jeewan Jyoti* (1953). It was a disaster, and for the next four years, till he was twenty-five, all his films failed. He had a string of nineteen flops despite working with some of the top actresses of the time—Madhubala (*Rail Ka Dibba*, 1953), Nutan (*Laila Majnu*, 1953), Suraiya (*Shama Parwana*, 1954), Nalini Jaywant (*Hum Sab Chor Hain*, 1956) and Meena Kumari (*Mem Sahib*, 1956). The only silver lining was that he found the love of his life while shooting for *Miss Coca Cola* (1955).

The romantic thriller revolves around a night club dancer, Ganga, whose stage name is Miss Coca Cola. Her father is implicated for a murder he didn't commit. While helping the damsel in distress prove her father's innocence, twenty-three-year-old Shammi ji fell head-over-heels in love with his leading lady, the vivacious Geeta Bali, who was a year older than him. The film was directed by Kidar Sharma who gave Geeta ji her first hit, *Suhaag Raat* (1948), opposite Raj Kapoor.

After *Miss Coca Cola*, Sharma ji signed Shammi ji for his next film *Rangeen Raaten* (1956) with Geeta ji's protégé, Mala Sinha, and Chand Usmani as the female leads. 'Geeta accepted the bit role of a mad village boy called Gullu so she could be near Shammi during the shoot,' Sharma ji informed. They left for Ranikhet for the shoot on 2 April 1955. Four months later, on 24 August, they were married.

'It was a beautiful age for romance. I missed her so much when she was away, that I started crying,' Shammi ji reminisced, adding that they would drive side by side, gazing at each other. Somewhere along the way they would get into one car and continue, imagining that they were journeying through life together. It took Geeta ji four months to accept his proposal.

Geeta ji wasn't, however, his first love, and Shammi ji was known to fall in and out of love since he was a little boy. He had once bitten the leg of a young rival who had crawled under the couch to retrieve a ball and impress his first love at her birthday party.

A year before he gave away his heart to Geeta ji, he had met Nadia Gamal, an Egyptian belly dancer, during a four-day visit to Sri Lanka for a charity cricket match. He saw her performing at a cabaret one evening, and before he left, he asked the seventeen-year-old dancer to be his wife. There's even a picture of the two of them along with his grandparents at a silver jubilee function of one of Raj Kapoor ji's films at Liberty cinema when she had stopped in Bombay en route to Cairo. She told him they would have to wait five years to be married; he was ready. He was even prepared to migrate to Egypt to be with her. But once Nadia returned home, they lost touch.

Meanwhile, Shammi ji met Geeta ji and started proposing to her every hour! Before her, he had been like a car without brakes. She was fun to be with, but she also steadied him and gave his life purpose. Within days of meeting her, he knew she was the one for him. She was just as crazy about him, but turned him down every time he proposed, pointing out that at twenty-four, she was a year older. She had worked with his Papaji, Prithviraj Kapoor, in *Anand Math* (1952) and his brother Raj in *Suhaag Raat*. She wasn't sure if his family would accept an actress as a daughter-in-law of the Kapoor family. Then, there was her own family; her father was blind and her mother, brother and sister partially deaf. She couldn't just walk away from her responsibilities, she reasoned. However, Shammi ji refused to take 'no' for an answer.

Then on 23 August after four months of refusal, Geeta ji suddenly surprised him by saying 'yes' when they were shooting together at Juhu Hotel. There was, however, a condition: 'It has to be now.' Perhaps she had hoped that it would put him off. But Shammi ji simply jumped into a car with her and drove to actor-comedian Johnny Walker's house for advice (since he had got married just a week back). Johnny bhai pointed out that they couldn't have a nikah like him since Shammi ji was a Hindu and Geeta ji was a Sikh. 'Go to a mandir,' he suggested.

Temple? Which temple? Hari Walia, the producer of their film *Coffee House* (1957) that they were still shooting for, escorted them to Banganga near Malabar Hill where there are around ninety temples. By then it was past 10 p.m., pitch dark and raining. All the temples had closed for the night. The priest they roused, told them that the Gods were asleep and that they should go home and sleep too. 'Return at 4 a.m. tomorrow,' he told the couple.

Shammi ji didn't dare let his lady love return to her own home in case she changed her mind. Instead, he escorted her to his Matunga residence and spent the rest of the night counting the hours till they could return to Banganga. They were back at the crack of dawn. This time the temple doors were wide open and the Gods were waiting. The priest recited the mantras while they took the pheras—he in a kurta-pyjama and she in a now crumpled salwar-kameez. They hadn't thought to shop for new clothes and weren't even carrying the customary sindoor. After they had exchanged garlands, the bride fished out a lipstick from her bag and offered it to the groom asking him to fill her maang with it.

The deed done, he took his bride home to his grandparents who lived in a house opposite theirs. He told his 'Bade Papa'—grandfather—that he had brought home his daughter-in-law and asked for his blessings. His grandparents conveyed the news to his parents who were away in Bhopal, touring with their theatre troupe.

Shammi ji himself called up his elder brother. His sister-in-law Krishna Raj Kapoor performed the traditional ritual of pouring oil on the bride's feet and welcomed her into the family that evening. The day after their marriage, he gave Geeta ji six files with details of the girls he had once dated. She made a bonfire of his past as they prepared for their future together.

Geeta Bali was a top star at the time and her producers were aghast when news of her marriage was leaked. Though she assured them that she would not give up her career, she had been working since she was twelve, having made her debut in choreographer Pandit Gyan Shankar's documentary on chorus girls, *The Cobbler*. By this time at twenty-four, the magic of stardom had begun to pall. She had done more than seventy films in a little over a decade and now was ready to play house.

She completed *Coffee House* and *Mohar* (1959) before bowing out of the arc lights, despite the fact that her twenty-three-year-old husband was still struggling for that elusive hit and they were broke. 'It was good to return home to her every evening after pack-up and discuss my work with her,' Shammi ji had smiled at the memory.

A year after they tied the knot, on 1 July 1956, they were blessed with a son whom they named Aditya Raj. The following year, Shammi ji got his first hit, *Tumsa Nahin Dekha*. The musical romance was conceived as a launch for Ameeta, the protégé of Tolaram Jalan, the owner of Filmistan studio. The hero's role had initially been offered to Dev Anand and then Sunil Dutt. They didn't have the dates, so it came to Shammi ji on the rebound, with a meagre fee of ₹25,000, much against the wishes of its debutant director Nasir Hussain. In fact, the original lyricist, Sahir Ludhianvi, who had written the title track, dropped out after Dev sahib's exit. Majrooh Sultanpuri sahib, who replaced Sahir sahib, came up with some wonderful songs along with Nayyar sahib, such as '*Chhupnewale samne* aa', 'Jawaniyan yeh mast mast' and 'Sar pe topi lal hath mein resham ka rumaal'.

In a do-or-die gamble, Shammi ji who till then had been seen only as a bad copy of brother Raj, shaved off his pencil-thin moustache, swept back his hair and grooved to these chartbusters. An Indian James Dean was born who stood up against the triumvirate of Dilip Kumar, Raj Kapoor and Dev Anand. A rebel without a 'pause', he was Hindi cinema's first rock star.

Two years later, came another Nasir Hussain film *Dil Deke Dekho*, which launched Asha Parekh. During the shooting, Geeta ji would help the debutante, whom she fondly called 'Tea Cosy', with her make-up. On the day of the film's release, Geeta ji accompanied her husband, his heroine, their director, lyricist Majrooh sahib and his wife, to the film's premiere. They were all wearing brave smiles and flashed the victorious thumbs up sign as they trooped through the foyer of Naaz cinema. The response was positive and jubilant. Mrs and Mr Kapoor, with Nasir sahib and Majrooh sahib, returned to their Chembur home and spent the night celebrating on the terrace, in a tent they had rigged up.

After that there was no looking back. *Junglee* (1961), *Professor* (1961), *China Town* (1962), *Kashmir Ki Kali* (1964), *Janwar* (1965), *Teesri Manzil* (1966), *An Evening in Paris* (1967), *Tumse Achha Kaun Hai* (1969)—there was no stopping Shammi Kapoor. With each film, he got bigger and better.

Meanwhile Geeta ji delivered a daughter on 8 August 1961. She wanted to name the baby Kajal. He was stuck on Kanchan after his *Professor* song '*Aai Kanchan*'. He won. She scribbled Kajal all over the walls of their bedroom in protest.

Their married life was full of laughter and banter, a few rows and a lot of love. Boredom started to creep in when

Aditya was sent away to boarding school. Geeta ji returned to the screen with *Jab Se Tumhe Dekha Hai* (1963). She had seen Satyajit Ray's *Pather Panchali* (1955) at Bombay's Naaz cinema with Shammi ji. The film made them both cry and while he continued to sing and dance, Geeta ji decided to adapt Rajinder Singh Bedi's novel, *Ek Chaddar Maili Si*, on screen. She was playing the lead, a widow who is married off to her younger brother-in-law after her husband's sudden death as per custom in then Punjab. She was also producing the film, which was titled *Rano*. Towards the fag end of 1964, she rushed off to Moga, a small village in Punjab, with her co-star Dharmendra and her two kids, for the shoot. It was the dead of winter. On 9 January 1965, she hosted a party for the unit to ring in the new year. The next day, she fell ill.

Shammi ji was shooting for *Teesri Manzil* when he learnt that his wife had contracted measles. He cancelled his shoot and brought her home. She was burning with fever. Turned out, it was smallpox, and within eight days, it had ravaged her face and attacked her eyes. He didn't leave her bedside, praying that the fever would subside and she would come out of coma. She did, on 21 January. She opened her eyes and looked straight at him. He looked back and assured her that he would take her to Switzerland where doctors would fix the pox marks and make her beautiful again. He had no idea if she heard him. Five minutes later, she was gone.

Ten years after their marriage, he returned to Banganga, at five in the evening, carrying his wife's body. After performing the last rites, Shammi ji returned home, alone and inconsolable. Nasir sahib waited for him to come out of his stupor, so they could resume shooting for *Teesri Manzil*. Weeks went by, he remained unreachable. Then, one day, his director stormed into his house and dragged him to the location, telling him they were going to complete the song '*Tumne mujhe dekha*', that very day in two long shots, with the camera going around him in circles on a trolley. 'I can't do it, I'm a broken man!' Shammi ji protested. 'His hands were shaking, his voice was wavering, he looked like a man on the verge of a breakdown,' Goldie sahib reminisced years later.

He assured his hero that they would call it a day if it got too much for him, then, gently pushed him in front of the camera. Shammi ji braced himself—and gave a perfect take. Everyone was ecstatic. Then, the unthinkable happened. Goldie sahib wanted a retake. Shammi ji quietly went back and gave another perfect shot. This one satisfied even his perfectionist director.

He continued to shoot for the rest of the day. In the days that followed, grateful to Goldie sahib for having brought him back from the dead, he recommended him to all his producers, but surprisingly, they never worked together again. Goldie sahib attributed it to the difference in their lifestyles. While his hero liked to hit a bar after pack-up, enjoyed poker and the races, the introverted director enjoyed long, solitary walks. It was understandable that their paths wouldn't cross again.

But even for Shammi ji the wild bachelor's life quickly lost its charm. The devil-may-care Casanova yearned to return home to a wife again and proposed to his *Brahmachari* (1968) heroine Mumtaz. She was only eighteen and was getting a lot of offers. She turned him down with a polite 'no'.

The woman, who eventually came into his life and stayed by his side till his last day, was Neila Devi. She belonged to the royal family of Bhavnagar, and Shammi ji knew her father and brother well. They had met when he was nineteen and she was nine. A chubby little kid in pigtails, she had watched him perform on stage from the wings with other kids. Four miserable years after Geeta ji's death, his sister-in-law Krishna ji called him to Sun-n-Sand Hotel one afternoon for lunch and showed him Neila ji's photograph. She surprised him by saying that the family believed she was the right woman for him and his children.

On 26 January 1969, after returning to his lonely apartment, Shammi ji called Neila ji. It was around 11 p.m. and he asked her to take her parents' permission to speak with him. Then, over the next two to three hours, he told her all about himself and his life. He ended the conversation, which was more of a confession, by telling her that he wanted to marry her. If she was ready, she should come with her parents and family to his residence that day for lunch and stay on for a lifetime. She accepted his crazy proposal.

The next morning, he called to invite his own family to his wedding. This time, the pheras were taken in his own home. Neila Devi kept all the promises she had made to him, bringing up his children as her own and standing by Shammi ji through good times and bad. When I met him years later, at his South Bombay residence to talk about Geeta ji for a nostalgia piece I was doing, it was Neila ji who wheeled in the tea trolley. She was a picture of dignified grace as he showed me all the pictures he had restored and put up on the website he had designed, one in which he had virtually traced his family tree.

The Internet was still in its nascent stage then, but Shammi ji had always been ahead of his time. He had logged on to the Web once during a trip to the United States and was instantly hooked. Back home, he was one of the founder members of the Internet Users Club and campaigned to make schools, colleges and individuals from different streams understand the advantages of the Internet.

At an age when other boys were busy sowing their wild

oats, Shammi ji had enjoyed playing house with his wife and kids. At the time when other retired men were drinking, reading or playing cards, he bought himself an Apple Macintosh and taught himself computers. With the mouse in his hands, it was easy to give up smoking, even though he had once smoked a hundred cigarettes a day.

Back in 1961, while filming Subodh Mukherjee's *Junglee* in Kashmir, they couldn't get skies or sledges. Unfazed, Shammi ji had simply rolled down the slope, from fifty feet up, without any safety measure, not even gloves, and ended up with frost bites. Three years later, while shooting for a song for *Rajkumar* (1964), he had broken his knees. Other accidents followed, and by the time he was in his sixties, there was no more sliding down the slopes to the jungle cry of 'Yahoo!' There was no more cavorting wildly in shikaras; no more gate-crashing parties or jumping out of windows so he wouldn't have to confront his host. Cut off from the world, Shammi ji used the Internet to bring the world to him.

Sitting in his den, surrounded by computers, a modem, printer and fax machine, he was the master of his universe. He didn't have to go to the theatre to watch a film. There were DVDs and then the LED screens. 'I don't watch too many Hindi films now, it's mostly foreign films,' he admitted. In 1974, he adapted *Irma la Douce*, a French play he saw in London years ago, for his directorial debut, *Manoranjan*. It didn't work—nor did *Bundal Baaz* (1976) that had him playing a genie. With his directorial urge satiated, life took a 360-degree turn. Shammi ji quietly settled down to a life of domesticity and found spiritual solace in his guruji. With his expanding girth, flowing saffron robes, prayer beads and red tilak, he was almost unrecognizable from the rock star of the 1960s.

In later years, Subhash Ghai was one of the few filmmakers to get his nod for *Vidhaata* (1982) and *Hero* (1983). Shammi ji also played Salman Khan's grandfather in Majrooh sahib's son Andaleb's directorial debut *Janam Samjha Karo* (1999). In his last film, Imtiaz Ali's *Rockstar* (2011), he played a classical musician, Ustad Jameel Khan, mentoring grandnephew Ranbir Kapoor who was already being touted as the next Shammi Kapoor. Comparisons had always made him frown. 'Ranbir is a good dancer, but he's not my reflection. He's an original, like Shammi Kapoor was,' he asserted when I brought this up. When I watched Ranbir groove to *'Budtameez dil'* in *Yeh Jawani Hai Deewani* (2013) I had to admit that Shammi ji had been right. Ranbir was good, very good in fact, but he was not Shammi Kapoor. There can never be another Shammi Kapoor.

5

DHARMENDRA: HERO WITH A HEART

Main jat yamla pagla deewana

Growing up, I spent five blissful years in Shillong, a small town tucked away in the hills of Meghalaya. Sunday was shopping day and once we had loaded up on essentials for the week, my parents, with me tagging along, would duck into one of the three theatres in the town centre to catch the latest film. It was in a dark auditorium during a screening of Hrishikesh Mukherjee's *Guddi* (1971)—my parents had been dragged for the night show by some friends—that I was introduced to the 1970s matinee idol Dharmendra, playing himself in a slice-of-life drama.

A year later, I saw him again, this time in Prakash Mehra's dacoit drama *Samadhi* (1972), in the double role of father and son. To my surprise, as the son he was romancing Jaya Bhaduri, the schoolgirl for whom he had engineered a match in *Guddi*. Then came *Kahani Kismat Ki* (1973) in which he climbed up a crane to croon '*Rafta rafta dekho aankh meri ladi hai*' to a blushing Rekha in the same year that he serenaded Hema Malini from the skies to the tunes of '*Tera peecha na chhodunga soneye*' in *Jugnu* (1973). By then I had grown to understand that reel-life romances were as fickle as the weather in our rain-drenched hill station. Still, when it was time to vote for my favourite screen couple—my friends were divided between Amitabh Bachchan and Rekha and Rajesh Khanna and Sharmila Tagore—I gave the thumbs up to *Sholay*'s (1975) Veeru and Basanti who ended up together even in real life.

Decades later, when I was interviewing Hema ji at her Juhu bungalow, she abruptly broke off in mid-sentence and, jumping to her feet, announced that we would have to complete it another day. 'Dharam ji is here,' she offered by way of explanation. Turning, I watched the man who had won my heart many years ago, step out of his car and walk up the stairs towards his 'Dream Girl'. Neither of them spared me a glance as I slipped out.

It would be a few more years before I was properly introduced to Dharam ji. It was at a bungalow in suburban Mumbai where he was shooting for Sriram Raghavan's neo-noir thriller *Johnny Gaddaar* (2007). The quiet hum of an industrious unit at work and the late afternoon sun, which had tinged the sylvan surroundings with a golden glow, contributed to a feeling of mellow well-being. But it quickly dissipated as I stepped into his vanity van. Dharam ji was over seventy by then, but togged out in a pair of trendy jeans and matching denim jacket. The moustache he had glued on added to his machismo. He still looked every inch the hero I had grown up idolizing, except that in person he seemed even more larger-than-life and possibly a trifle intimidating.

Watching his fingers flex and fist as he spoke, I wondered where I would land if the trademark *'dhai kilo ka haath'* flipped me over for an impertinent query. When I abruptly voiced my thoughts, he answered with a guffaw, reassuring me that while the 'He Man' image had sparked many fights on screen, it was not a true reflection of the man. 'The world sees me as "He Man", but I prefer the tag "Darling D" because that's who I am,' he asserted earnestly.

Dharam ji then went on to recall a scene in *Kartavya* (1979). Since he was playing a forest officer, he was required to wrestle with wild animals and was lowered into a pit with instructions to fight off a couple of snarling panthers. 'I tried to ward them off, jabbing ineffectually with the pitchfork in my hand. But before I knew it, one of the wild cats had snatched it out of my hand and chewed it up, then, turned to contemplate me hungrily,' he recounted.

With his superhero image imprinted on my mind, I imagined him leaping on the panthers and taming them single-handedly. But to my surprise, Dharam ji admitted that he had simply hollered for the cage to be lowered. 'It arrived just in the nick of time to whisk me away from the jaws of death even as the panthers leapt against it. I still remember the day—8 December—the day I came into the world. Thank God I lived to see another birthday,' he concluded with a wry smile.

My smile in response to this anecdote was rather forced because the memory of him subduing lions and tigers, panthers and elephants in films such as *Maa* (1976) and *Kartavya* was still too deeply etched in my mind for me to regard him as just another man! In *Loha* (1987), which was released a decade after *Kartavya*, he had hit a man on the head and the man had sunk halfway into the sand. When I reminded him of this, an embarrassed Dharam ji admitted that when Veeru Devgan had sketched out what he wanted, he had dismissed it as 'absurd'. But the action director was convinced that though a trifle exaggerated, his hero would be able to carry it off convincingly. Reluctantly, Dharam ji had obliged. To his dismay, Veeru ji had then insisted that his red-faced hero flex his biceps triumphantly after delivering the mighty blow. Squirming awkwardly, Dharam ji complied. Much to his surprise (and Veeru ji's satisfaction), when the scene played out on screen, it was greeted with resounding claps and ear-splitting whistles by the audience. 'I saw the reactions for myself when I accompanied Veeru to a neighbourhood cinema hall,' Dharam ji marvelled, still dazed by the appreciation.

In his first diamond jubilee hit, *Phool Aur Patthar* (1966), he had rushed into a blazing fire, scooped up Baby Farida into his muscular arms and dashed out unscathed. 'That's not true; we were both hurt, but those days one simply ran into a fire when the director called "Action!" without caring for safety measures. The scene was effective on screen, but it could have cost us our lives. Don't believe everything you see, hear or read,' he cautioned, and I was instantly reminded of the lessons he had preached in *Guddi*, which had presented a true-life picture of our film industry and its heroes.

Only a brave man with a really big heart would have allowed a director as astute as Hrishi da to unmask him on screen. Dharam ji confided that through the making of the film, he had worried that people might not see him as a 'hero' after its release. 'But to my surprise, *Guddi* made me an even bigger hero!' he exclaimed, with the wide-eyed wonder of a child. By the time I left him, the sun had gone down and the six-foot-tall Jat, while still an imposing figure, no longer seemed intimidating.

∞

Dharminder Singh Deol had grown up in the village of Sahnewal in Punjab's Ludhiana district, playing hockey and kabaddi in the fields and swimming in the ponds. His friends at the Government Senior Secondary School in Lalton Kalan often discussed the films they had watched. Young Dharam had no idea what they were talking about because his strict schoolmaster father, Kewal Kishan Singh Deol, kept him away from the 'talking pictures'. Lightning struck when he was in standard eighth and watched his first film. Ramesh Saigal's *Shaheed* (1948) was set against the backdrop of the freedom struggle and revolved around two star-crossed lovers, played by Dilip Kumar and Kamini Kaushal. He returned home in tears after Dilip Kumar's character, Ram, died a martyr.

When Dharam ji was sent to Phagwara for higher studies, he would queue up for the latest Hindi film every Friday. Slowly inching his way towards the ticket counter, he would fervently hope that they didn't run out of tickets or that the second bell signalling the start of the film would not go off before his turn came. He was fascinated by this wonder world and convinced that the heroes he watched on screen every week, from Dilip Kumar and Motilal to Raj Kapoor and Dev Anand, along with their shehzaadis, Suraiya, Kamini Kaushal, Madhubala and Nargis, would never grow old, but remain forever beautiful. He dreamt of seeing these celestial beings in person, talking to them and God willing, becoming a part of their world.

In 2017, Dharam ji had shared a throwback picture of himself and admitted that while cycling to work in those early years, he would imagine that it was his face on the film posters he passed every morning. '*Raton ko jaagta, anhonee khwaab dekhta, subah uthkar aaine se puchhta, "Main Dilip Kumar ban sakta hun kya?"*' His cousin, filmmaker Guddu Dhanoa, recounted how his elder brother would make all his younger siblings climb up a ladder and welcome him with a chorus of 'Dharam aaya, Dharam is here'. Perhaps this was his way of imagining himself as a movie star being serenaded by his fans.

While working as an assistant driller for an American tube well sinking company, he clung on to this dream and one day, told his confidante, his mother Satwant Kaur, that he was thinking of running away to Bombay (present-day Mumbai). 'Alarmed, she told me to never voice such thoughts aloud, apprehensively pointing out that if my father heard me, he would turn both of us out. She suggested instead that I fill out job applications and send them off to these film-wallahs, assuring me that *arzi dene se koi bhi naukri mil jaati hai* [with the right job application you can bag any job]. I had laughed at her words, thinking how bholi...how innocent...my mother was,' Dharam ji reminisced.

He returned to his job, stoically boring holes for tube wells, but a few days later, came across a copy of *Filmfare* magazine announcing the United Producers' Talent Hunt contest. It invited participants from across India and promised that the winner would land roles in films made by Bimal Roy and Guru Dutt. Remembering his mother's advice, Dharam ji immediately sat down and meticulously filled out his name, address and other details, sending off the application with some recently clicked photographs. 'I didn't have much hope of being selected, but to my surprise, I was shortlisted for the auditions and sent money for a first-class train ticket to Mumbai,' he narrated.

He arrived in the 'City of Dreams' and after several rounds of auditions and an interview, he was declared the winner of the contest. The elation was short-lived because the promised films did not materialize. He made frequent trips to Bimal Roy's office, but the filmmaker didn't have anything to offer. Disheartened, he returned home after three months, only to rush back to Bombay after receiving a telegram from Bimal Roy Productions informing him that he had been cast in *Bandini* (1963).

Dharam ji played a young prison doctor in the film. His character, Devendra, falls in love with a woman serving a life sentence and even after learning how Nutan's Kalyani had come to murder the wife of her first love, Bikash Ghosh, wants to marry her. After convincing his mother to accept the convict as her daughter-in-law, Deven sets out for home with his bride-to-be. En route, they run into an ailing Bikash, played by Ashok Kumar, and Kalyani opts to sail away with him. Bimal Roy's wife, Manobina, confided to me decades later, over tea and cake, that she had tried to convince her husband to change the film's ending inspired by Jarasandha's Bengali novel *Tamasi*. She didn't think Kalyani owed loyalty to a man whose life she had saved by tarnishing her own reputation, only for him to leave her without a word and marry another woman. She thought the girl deserved a second chance at happiness, and along with several others, wanted Kalyani to settle down with the handsome Deven.

Momentarily swayed by the argument, her husband had brought up the suggested change with his screenplay writer Nabendu Ghosh. The latter was aghast, pointing out that Kalyani's whole life had revolved around her ill-fated love. After learning that Bikash had not consciously betrayed her, she would definitely go with him, even if he were old and ill. That was the only way to justify her crime of passion and the film's title. 'Three days after this discussion, Bimal da's assistant, Debu Sengupta, told me that he wished to see me. He was on his way to the editing room, and as we were walking through the garden, Bimal da looked up at the sky and said, "Nabendu, you were right, we will keep the end. And that was it,"' the veteran scriptwriter shared with me. Dharam ji was disappointed to be left alone at the end but agreed with his director and scriptwriter that the end justified the title—

Bandini, a prisoner of love. The film remains one of his best performances and won him plenty of accolades.

However, even though *Bandini* was the first film he signed in 1958, it was released five years later. For two years, Dharam ji made daily rounds of studios and producers' offices, returning to the garage where he lived, empty-handed, sometimes with no money even for a meal. During this period, he befriended two struggling actors, Shashi Kapoor and Manoj Kumar, who, like him, were looking for that elusive break in films. There were times when the trio would land up at a studio together when they heard that a filmmaker was scouting for an actor, hoping that at least one of them would walk away happy. Soon, they were referred to as the 'Three Musketeers' by the studio regulars and security.

Back then, films were hard to come by and Dharam ji who was already married and a father, was beginning to despair. Uncertain about his future in the movies and unwilling to shirk his responsibilities, he often wondered if he should return to Punjab and find a steady job. One day, when Manoj Kumar was at their regular haunt, Shanbhag Restaurant in Dadar, opposite Ranjeet Studio, he was handed a note. It was from Dharam ji and read, 'Manu, *ab mujhse nahin hoga*, I can't continue like this. I am going back home.' As soon as he read this, Manoj sahib rushed to the Matunga Railway Quarters to find his friend all packed, ready to leave for the station and board the Frontier Mail. 'I raged and cried, beat myself up and begged him to stay back for another two months. I even promised to bear his expenses in the interim,' Manoj sahib flashbacked. He was eventually able to convince his friend to stay back.

On the third day, Dharam ji bagged Filmistan's *Picnic* (1966). But soon after, he contracted jaundice, and by the time he recovered, he looked too gaunt to play an army officer. The film went to Manoj sahib on the rebound and Dharam ji made his debut in Arjun Hingorani's *Dil Bhi Tere Hum Bhi Tere* (1960). The filmmaker who was like a brother for over half a century, had been chasing him since they met in a bus when Dharam ji first came to Bombay for the Filmfare contest. After landing the role in *Bandini*, Dharam ji didn't pay much heed to Arjun sahib's prophesies that he would make him a star one day. Eventually, however, he gave the nod to the dental surgeon-turned-director's *Dil Bhi Tera Hum Bhi Tere*, that also featured Balraj Sahni. Just before its release, Dharam ji bought his first car, a second-hand Fiat, for ₹18,000. 'I drove straight to the studio to seek Bimal da's blessings. I even took him for a quick spin. Bimal da was so happy and sitting beside me in my car, assured me that lots of good things were in store for me. He was confident I would make it,' Dharam ji had smiled at the memory.

His first film didn't make much of an impression though, with Dharam ji going unrecognized at the premiere and Balraj sahib hogging all the limelight. However, *Shola Aur Shabnam* (1961), which followed, was a huge hit. The film had a memorable score by Khayyam. *'Jeet hi lenge baazi hum tum, khel adhura chhute na'* mirrored his own determination.

Interestingly, Manoj Kumar had been the first choice for this Ramesh Saigal-directed love triangle. Dharam ji himself lost another film to his friend, the Dilip Kumar-starrer *Aadmi* (1968). He didn't mind it at the time, but later regretted missing out on the chance of sharing the frame with his matinee idol, whom he visited every year on his birthday till Dilip sahib, in the grips of Alzheimer, stopped recognizing anyone.

Meanwhile, after seeing him in *Shola Aur Shabnam*, Ramanand Sagar offered Dharam ji the role of a spy in his *Aankhen* (1968). It was the *'dhai kilo ka haath'* that ultimately landed him the film because both the filmmaker and his son, Prem, thought that this hand had been made to hold a gun. However, before the crime thriller could take off, *Phool Aur Patthar* (1966) opened and went on to become the biggest hit of the year. It owed some of its popularity to the fact that a Hindi film hero had gone bare-chested on screen. Even though it was a gallant gesture, to cover up his lady love played by Meena Kumari, the action made Dharam ji a 'He Man', whose rippling biceps made heartbeats accelerate. Delighted by his new-found fan following, distributors insisted Ramanand Sagar rope in a bigger heroine opposite him and Mala Sinha stepped into the picture. Dharam ji's fee also increased, and he took off for his first shoot abroad, filming in Tokyo, Tehran and Beirut.

Aankhen was a blockbuster too. By this time, Dharam ji with his classic good looks, bashful smile and Greek God-like physique had become every woman's dream lover. A decade later, he appeared in Manmohan Desai's action-adventure *Dharam Veer* (1977), dressed somewhat incongruously in Scottish kilt-like skirts, riding horse-driven chariots and fighting an army bare-chested. A far-fetched fantasy, but after watching the film that earned him the adage of 'Garam Dharam', his *Anpadh* (1962) director and one of his mentors, Mohan Kumar, told Dharam ji that God and his parents needed to be complimented for giving the world such a fine specimen of physical beauty. The hyperbole notwithstanding, the observation was bang on. In a poll conducted in the 1970s—Dharam ji was forty-plus by then—he was voted one of the ten most handsome men in the world.

∞

Filmmaker Ketan Anand recalled meeting Dharam ji for the first time in Kashmir where he was filming his father Chetan

Anand's war drama, *Haqeeqat* (1964). Ketan was accompanied by a friend, an English boy named Christopher Hardwick, and when they arrived in Sonmarg, Chetan sahib was chatting with a handsome army officer. Spotting the boys, he walked up to them and Ketan asked his father about the soldier he had been speaking with. 'Dad told me that he was his hero, Dharmendra, who was playing Captain Bahadur Singh, and I told him that I wished all officers looked as beautiful in a uniform,' Ketan smiled.

The officer, however, went missing in action one day during the shoot in the Valley. 'We found him sleeping peacefully in a real jawan's tent in the camp in Bartal after one drink too many,' the film's art director M.S. Sathyu guffawed. Incredibly, Dharam ji's love for the bottle did not mar his good looks. He eventually quit alcohol and still makes heads turn without Botox shots or cosmetic surgery as he drives around his farm in Lonavala. The farm has become a second home to him today, where organic farming keeps him occupied. His lifelong love affair with the camera, however, continues uninterrupted.

'*Naam aur shauhrat ek nasha hai, chadta hai toh utar bhi jata hai, par mohabbat woh jazbaa hai jo dil mein ghar bana leta hai*,' he once explained, borrowing phrases from Bachchus's well-thumbed dictionary, to help me understand why his first love keeps bringing him back to the studios, if not as an actor, then, as a producer. 'It's the only way I know to stay in the hearts of the people,' he often tells me, the words simple and straight from the heart.

Dharam ji has worked in over 300 films, delivered six blockbusters and several super hits in a career spanning six decades. He has been a largely bankable name, a saleable star, except for one period, from the late 1990s to 2003, when he featured in a string of quickly forgotten disasters, which sparked off memes like *'kutte, kaminey main tera khoon pe jaoonga!'* When I asked him why he had chosen to do them, he explained that they helped bankroll his farm. 'Forget them,' he urged. I have. Today, I remember him as one of our best all-rounders, who stood up to the star power of Rajendra 'Jubilee' Kumar and Shammi 'Yahoo!' Kapoor in the 1960s and matched Dilip Kumar's histrionics with finely nuanced performances in *Devar* (1966), *Anupama* (1966) and *Satyakam* (1969). *Satyakam* was a film after his own heart. As Satyaprakash Acharya—the idealistic engineer who marries a rape survivor, gives his name to her illegitimate son, loves her all his life, yet never touches her—Dharam ji admitted he didn't need to 'act' in this Hrishikesh Mukherjee film. 'Satya was so much like me,' he acknowledged.

Between 1969 and 1974, when Rajesh Khanna was 'The Phenomenon' with fifteen straight hits, Dharam ji quietly notched up as many strikes. *Mera Gaon Mera Desh* was the second biggest grosser of 1971, *Seeta Aur Geeta* was the highest earner of 1972, while 1973 brought along four big hits—*Yaadon Ki Baaraat, Jugnu, Loafer* and *Kahani Kismet Ki*.

Guddu Dhanoa remembers the fan frenzy his Veerji brought home whenever he visited. Crowds of strangers, from school students to starry-eyed army jawans, would barge in for photographs and autographs. Often, the jawans would even block off the entrance to their lane with their trucks so he couldn't get away!

From the mid-1970s through the 1980s when Amitabh Bachchan reigned as the 'Angry Young Man' of Bollywood, Guddu revealed that the price per territory of Ramesh Sippy's Curry Western *Sholay* (1975) fell from ₹25 lakh to ₹12 lakh when there was talk of his Veerji dropping out of the project due to date hassles; this was despite other big stars such as

Sanjeev Kumar, Amitabh Bachchan, Jaya Bachchan and Hema Malini being on board. A decade later, in one defining year, Dharam ji notched up a record seven hits. *Loha, Hukumat, Aag Hi Aag, Insaniyat Ke Dushman, Watan Ke Rakhwale, Jaan Hatheli Pe, Mard Ki Zabaan* and *Dadagiri*—all released in 1987 and reinforced his image of a natural-born 'He Man'. 'And, yet, even when he was flexing his muscles, there was a vulnerability about him that tugged at the heart strings and made you want to protect him,' Rajkumar Santoshi pointed out.

On Dharam ji's eighty-third birthday, I had sent Raj ji a message wondering if he wanted to speak about the producer of his directorial debut, *Ghayal* (1990). He was busy with a shoot and didn't respond. Meanwhile, Dharam ji himself called for some other reason the morning I was to file my story. No sooner had he disconnected when the phone rang again. It was Raj ji, insisting he wanted to have his say. He went on to eulogize Dharam ji's versatility, the way he made romance seem real on screen, his two left feet that had spawned a new kind of *naach-gaana* and his impeccable comic timing seen in films like *Chupke Chupke* (1975), *Dillagi* (1978) and of course, the scene in *Sholay*, where bottle in hand, he totters on top of a water tank, telling the *gaonwalon* that he is going to do what Majnu had done for Laila, Ranjha for Heer and Romeo for Juliet—'soocide'. He then goes to warn them saying 'when I dead, police coming...police coming, *budhiya* [Basanti's mausi (aunt)] going jail...in jail *budhiya chakki peessing, and peessing and peessing, and peessing*' 'I improvised and added a "ji" to "mausi" to pile on the maska,' he confided later, thrilled that Shah Rukh Khan insists they should make this scene the national anthem of the Hindi film industry because of its everlasting popularity.

Thirty-six years later, Sameer Karnik wanted to replicate the scene in *Yamla Pagla Deewana* (2011) with Dharam ji's younger son. On the day of the shoot, Bobby Deol looked down at the sea of faces staring up at him, among them his brother, Sunny, and almost suffered a heart attack. To his credit, Bobby, who started his career playing the young Dharam in *Dharam Veer*, pulled it off, and seven years later, replayed the scene in *Yamla Pagla Deewana Phir Se* (2018). 'Who better than his sons to do what papa has done before,' Bobby pointed out with a laugh. Dharam ji and his two *puttars* (sons) are undoubtedly Bollywood's most under-rated actors and it's because, as he reasons, they are men who think with their hearts. *'Hamare dimag bhi hamare dil mein hai.* We could never learn the art of manipulation and self-promotion. Since I am not a shopkeeper, I could never sell or market myself,' he often sighs.

The box office however has never been a deterrent to his popularity. I remember sacrificing one Sunday for a Father's Day interview with him and his sons at his Juhu bungalow. Sunny never turned up; Bobby held fort till his father arrived. Then, he was ordered out and Dharam ji held court, quickly weaving his magic over the assembled journalists and photographers. No one complained about it turning into a one-man show, not even his sons. That's the kind of love and respect 'Darling D', as he likes to be referred to, inspires without even demanding it.

That Sunday, he spoke about his boys, and he spoke about his daughters too because Vijeyta and Ajeta, Esha and Aahna, are as precious to him as Sunny and Bobby. Esha once recounted how during the shooting of *Tell Me O Kkhuda* (2011), directed and co-produced by mom Hema Malini who also acted in the film, stepping out of his vanity van, Dharam ji who played a mafia don, Anthony Castello, had spotted a girl hanging upside down from a crane on a ship anchored in the middle of the sea. When he learnt that the daredevil was his daughter, he roared his head off. It didn't matter that he had done a similar stunt in *Samraat* (1982) or that Esha was a strong swimmer and in no danger of drowning. It was only when she was standing next to him, safe and sound, that the tirade stopped.

In the 1980s, Dharam ji launched his banner, Vijeyta Arts, named after his eldest daughter. His first production was *Betaab* (1983), to launch his elder son, Sunny. The film was a superhit, but the banner today is best remembered for *Ghayal* (1990), which bagged two National Awards (a Special Jury Prize for Sunny and the Best Popular Film Providing Wholesome Entertainment) and seven Filmfare Awards, including Best Film. The 'Black Lady' was accepted by Sunny, who was also adjudged Best Actor, on behalf of his father, who had stayed home despite getting a new suit stitched because he couldn't stomach the disappointment of returning home empty-handed. Sunny had been sent to the Filmfare Award function with instructions that if he got the slightest hint that the film was likely to win, he should call. His son did call, past 9 p.m., but by then a disheartened Dharam ji had taken a sleeping pill and gone to bed. 'In my sleep, I could hear firecrackers bursting, and asked myself groggily whose success were they celebrating?' he rued, when the realization dawned upon him the next morning that he had missed his moment in the spotlight.

∞

I guess one of the reasons I have always felt close to Dharam ji is because he is not just an actor, but a storyteller too. Once when we were discussing *Sholay*, he sketched out an idea he had visualized for its sequel. After Jai's death, a heartbroken Veeru, leaves Ramgarh with Basanti. They get married, settle down someplace else and have two sons who grow up to be Abhishek Bachchan and Bobby (who is brought up by Radha—Jaya

Bachchan returning to reprise her role). Something happens (he didn't say what) to take them back to Ramgarh where the boys unite to avenge Jai's death. *Sholay 2* didn't happen, but down the decades we have seen two generation of Deols follow in their father's footsteps. He had once confided that when he first came to Bombay, he would look with awe and admiration at 'Papaji' Prithviraj Kapoor and his three sons—Raj, Shammi and Shashi—who were growing up together, as actors and filmmakers. Today, he must feel the same pride when he sees Sunny in Parliament, Bobby staging a valiant comeback after a self-imposed hibernation and grandson Karan taking the baton forward. During the making of *Pal Pal Dil Ke Paas* (2019), he had dropped by unannounced at the Budd Track in Delhi, seen his grandson sitting behind the wheel of a racing car and flashbacked to *Betaab*, when on a surprise visit to Kashmir Valley, he had come across his Sunny playing football on camera. It had reminded him of Raj Kapoor's *Mera Naam Joker* (1970), which he was a part of, and the iconic song, '*Jeena yahan maran yahan, iske siva jana kahan*'. Karan's brother, Rajvir, is waiting to make his acting debut and Bobby's sons, Aryamann and Dharam, may also follow their cousins into showbiz.

The title of Karan's first film was borrowed from Dharam ji's evergreen number from *Blackmail* (1973). Rewinding to this Kishore Kumar track and watching Dharam ji woo Rakhee with his letters, I am reminded that he is a *shayar* himself, just like his mother. After she moved to Bombay to be with her son, Satwant Kaur ji would sit up late every night, playing a solitary card game, Sequence, as she waited for her Dharam to return home from shooting. He always stopped by her room on his way up to his own, and the two would chat for a few minutes. Sometimes, she would read out snatches of poetry. 'I still have some of her writings,' he admitted, emotionally. And in 2001, having studied Urdu as a child, he picked up his pen to give words to the emotions churning within him. 'I never thought I would become a poet, but I guess it's in my genes,' he mused.

One evening, while I was penning his interview, he called me, and despite the deadline, lured me away from my desk for a good half hour, with the most exquisite Urdu poetry. He rhapsodized about the *anokhi kashish* and *anjana ehsaas* of childhood infatuation. He sighed over Partition, which in 1947 divided not just a country but also homes and hearts. He philosophized about the transience of fame and spoke eloquently about how words could be used to bond hearts.

Over the years, I have become used to these sudden phone calls after long stretches of silences. Sometimes they are in response to a message I had sent days ago, sometimes to spontaneously share something and sometimes simply because it is a special day. They are my connection with a man I feel I have known all my life who always ends the conversation with his heartfelt blessings. To borrow a few of his lines:

Shayari meri, baat yeh dil ki teri meri,
Jis dil ne suni, uss dil ne kaha,
Tab usne suni, chupke se keh di,
Dil hi har dil ko chhu gayi,
Dil ne dil se jab bhi dil se keh di...

6

AMITABH BACHCHAN: ALWAYS THE SHAHENSHAH

Arre deewanon, mujhe pehchanon,
kahan se aaya, main hoon kaun

Amitabh Bachchan was my dad's favourite actor and so an integral part of my childhood. When VCDs turned televisions into home theatres, I would bring a Big B movie home from the video library every few days so dad would not crib about our date nights with the stars. I laughed through his professor act in *Chupke Chupke* (1975), crooned '*My name is Antony Gonsalves*', sighed through the tedium of *Jaadugar* (1989) and teared up with Babumoshai when he lost his Anand to lymphosarcoma of the intestines.

Then, I grew up to become a cub reporter with a prestigious film magazine. And one day, to my utter disbelief, was sent to speak to Mr Bachchan about a controversy over then Sheriff Nana Chudasama's 1989 'I love Mumbai' campaign that he was endorsing. He was shooting at Bombay's Mehboob Studio, and after I had sent in my card, was invited in and though I was an obvious greenhorn, he answered all my questions gravely in that now-familiar baritone. It was only when I was getting ready to leave that he politely requested a copy of the article to be shown to him before it went into print. This was not encouraged, but my editor who knew him well, realized that his intention was only to ensure that the interview did not whip up any more controversy so gave me the go-ahead.

Those were the pre-emails, pre-WhatsApps, pre-cell phone, even pre-computer days. Copies were hand-written on double-lined sheets and typed out on old-school typewriters. A few days after our interaction, I was in Juhu to meet another actor and decided to drop off the pages I had laboriously typed at Mr Bachchan's bungalow, Prateeksha.

As always, there was a crowd of fans hanging outside hoping for a glimpse of their demi-God. I muscled my way through them and reached the gate. With all the authority my five-foot-two-inch frame could muster, I told the burly security guard that I was there to meet Mr Bachchan. '*Inn sabko bhi Bachchan sahib se milna hai* [They also want to meet Bachchan sahib],' he smirked, pointing to the onlookers. With affronted dignity, I pointed out that I was not one of his fans but was there for work. The guard laughed out loud, 'In that case, you should speak to his secretary on phone and set up an appointment.'

By now the crowd had stepped closer to listen to our exchange. I was jostled by one of the bystanders and inadvertently took a few steps forward. Immediately, the guard grabbed my arm roughly and shoved me back, assuming that I was trying to push my way in. I saw red. Whirling on him, I snapped that I had no desire to enter the sanctum sanctorum. Scribbling my name, along with my office and residence phone numbers on the top sheet, I flung the pages at him, telling him the article would go to press in a day or two. 'If your boss complains that he was not kept in the loop, I will know whom to point fingers at,' I shouted, flagged down a passing autorickshaw and zoomed off, leaving behind a crowd of wide-eyed star-gazers and a bemused security.

I did not hear from Mr Bachchan all day and returned home wondering if I had acted impetuously. I was staring unseeingly at the television when the telephone rang. My sister took the call and after the first 'Hello', did not utter another word. After a few minutes of silence, she held out the receiver to me with rounded eyes, stuttering, 'It's him... Amitabh Bachchan... He wants to speak to you.'

Why would Amitabh Bachchan call me? If he had something to say or rather complain, he would dial the editor, I muttered, and picked up the proffered receiver. The voice I had grown up hearing enquired politely, 'Is this Roshmila Mukherjee?' [Mukherjee was my maiden surname]. I confirmed my identity and he introduced himself, saying, 'This is Amitabh Bachchan. I called to say that the interview is fine and you can go ahead and publish it.' My eyes were as wide as my sister's when I put the phone down and looking at dad, I whispered, 'It was him.'

Years later, filmmaker Suneel Darshan admitted he had also been taken by surprise when one day, as he was driving home, his cell phone rang and a familiar voice boomed across the wire, 'Amitabh Bachchan *bol raha hoon* [This is Amitabh Bachchan].' He quickly pulled his car to the side of the road and focused his attention on the legendary actor who baffled him further by expressing his desire to be a part of *Ek Rishtaa: The Bond of Love* (2001), which Suneel was producing and directing, based on a story he himself had written. 'Only a man who is tall, not just in height but in stature too, could have made that call,' the filmmaker asserts.

Suneel wrapped up the film in just four months, despite a star-studded cast of Akshay Kumar, Juhi Chawla, Karisma Kapoor and Rakhee, and a special thanks to a cooperative Mr Bachchan who was simultaneously filming *Kabhi Khushi Kabhie Gham...* (2001) at the time. 'He would shoot for Karan

[Johar] from 9 a.m. to 6 p.m., then, report for *Ek Rishtaa*, working from 7 p.m. to 2 a.m. every day. Only once did he turn up late, arriving an hour and a half late for a 9 a.m. shoot with Akshay at Hiranandani Gardens. No one was unduly perturbed by the delay, but as soon as he drove up, Mr Bachchan called me and apologized, informing me that his parents [Harivansh Rai Bachchan and Teji Bachchan] were very old and terribly unwell. He had been up all night with the doctor tending to them. My respect for him increased even more after hearing this,' Suneel shares.

The man himself has always been courteous with me, coming all the way down to drop me after an interview despite my protests. He is also one of those rare actors who is always punctual. Only once was I kept waiting when director Sujoy Ghosh sailed into his office in a rumpled kurta-pyjama and whisked him away for an out-of-turn meeting. He also is one of the few B-townies who always responds to a text. I remember back in 2015, when it was announced that Shashi Kapoor had been awarded the prestigious Dadasaheb Phalke Award, I reached out to his frequent collaborator for a quote. Mr Bachchan was busy with meetings all day and had no time to answer the questions I had sent. But the next morning, I woke up to find them in my mailbox. After a long day, he had returned home well past midnight and sat up to pen his memories of the actor with whom he had worked in eleven films. I learnt that during *Deewar* (1975), the two would shoot all night at Ballard Pier, then, along with director Yash Chopra, would breakfast on *baida pav*—the quintessential Mumbai street snack made with buns and eggs—before returning home to catch up on lost sleep. I have always looked forward to his mails, even if sometimes they went way beyond the expected word count. But, when it is about Big B, you can trust your readers to be interested in everything he has to say!

However, it is not easy, winning his trust. Always technology savvy, Mr Bachchan was one of the first actors to go on social media and publicly reprimand a journalist on his daily Twitter blog, if he was misquoted, misinterpreted or misrepresented.

If he answered you on email, he would post the interview in its entirety on his social media accounts—at times even before it was published. Sometimes it was to point to a discrepancy, sometimes because he wanted what had been edited out to also be there in the public domain. In later years, he even had his own videographer tape every interview he gave, so he had a copy for reference. The first time I was videotaped, I was disconcerted to have a light shining directly into my eyes and a cameraman recording my every word and gesture. Over time, I learnt to take it in my stride and have to thank Mr Bachchan for helping me warm up to being on camera.

In fact, he is the only actor whose picture I have up on the wall of my home. I had gone to meet him just before the release of *Paa* (2009), and, as usual, the interview was documented. One afternoon, soon after the interaction, a fellow journalist congratulated me for making it to his blog. My first reaction was, 'What did I do wrong?' Running back to my desk in the office, I frantically Googled and sighed with relief when I discovered that I was only part of a photo gallery of journalists he had met during the film's promotions. I sent the link across to my husband, quipping, 'See, I am a star now.' He had the photograph enlarged and framed, and hung it up in our bedroom where the electrician spotted it one day during repairs. 'Is that really you with Bachchan sahib?' he asked, staring at the picture with a dazed expression. When I nodded awkwardly, much to my husband's delight, he gave a discount without us even asking.

In *Paa*, Mr Bachchan played Abhishek's son, Auro, a

happy-go-lucky twelve-year-old trapped in a fast-wilting sixty-year-old's body. Only writer-director R. Balki would have thought to reverse their real-life roles. When he sounded out the junior Bachchan, Abhishek protested, saying, 'It's an awesome task man, I can't do it.' Balki convinced him to give it a shot while they were shooting a commercial. He later pointed out that both went back to being 'Paa'—which is how Abhishek addresses his father in real life—and son as soon as he shouted, 'Cut.' However, the comedy-drama gave Mr Bachchan the opportunity to do all those things he had enjoyed as a child, from reading and playing pranks with the kids on the sets to spontaneously dancing in the rain with Vidya Balan who played his mother.

The film fetched him his third National Award after *Agneepath* (1990) and *Black* (2005). He won a fourth for *Piku* in 2015, followed by the Dadasaheb Phalke Award in 2019. Balki recalled he had been trying out shoes in a shop on the outskirts of London, when his 'Auro' called to give the good news. Later, he watched as Mr Bachchan accepted the coveted award from the president. Later, they went to his daughter Shweta Bachchan Nanda's house for dinner.

Though Shweta and Abhishek were sent away to a boarding school in Switzerland, the kids always shared a great bonding with their Paa. I got an inkling of it, when unable to connect with Abhishek who was shooting near the North Pole for *Players* (2012), I re-routed a questionnaire for him through Mr Bachchan who was vacationing abroad. Despite everyone's best efforts, Abhishek remained unreachable, so his Paa did the next best thing: He answered some of the questions himself!

I finally got my interview with Abhishek when I flew to Auckland to cover the shoot of the official Hindi remake of the Hollywood heist thriller *The Italian Job* (2003). One of the biggest attractions of *Players* (2012) were the Mini Coopers that zipped across the screen. AB Jr had been adamant about getting original Minis, and it was a sight to watch the six-foot-plus actor fold his length into the tiny two-seaters, then, brave bumps on the head and knock his knees to whiz around in the tiny cars. At five-feet-two, the only Bachchan I am at eye level with is his mother, Jaya.

It was on the sets of Hrishikesh Mukherjee's *Guddi* (1971) that the parents met. Mr Bachchan was the first choice for Navin who Guddi's family believes is the perfect match for her even as the giddy-headed schoolgirl romanticizes about her favourite matinee idol, Dharmendra. The film made Jaya ji 'Guddi' for life, but the man she was to spend the rest of her life with was replaced with Bengali actor Samit Bhanja after five or six days when Mr Bachchan's secretary told Hrishi da that he had no dates to spare after *Anand* (1971). So, Hrishi da imported a real *Babumoshai*, Samit Bhanja, for the role.

During one of our many conversations, Hrishi da had admitted that he had initially wanted to cast Mehmood in the role of Dr Bhaskar Bannerjee and Raj Kapoor as his Punjabi friend, Anand. But when he had balked at the thought of his Raju dying on screen, Rajesh Khanna landed the role. Mr Bachchan walked into the picture when he accompanied his mentor Khwaja Ahmad Abbas, in whose film *Saat Hindustani* (1969) he was working at the time, to Hrishi da's Bandra residence. The filmmaker was unwell and lying in bed. Abbas sahib sat by his side while the tall, young man with piercing eyes and a brooding expression, stood by, silent and unsmiling. Looking up at him, Hrishi da knew instinctively that he was Anand's Babumoshai.

Suneel, whose father Darshan Sabharwal distributed *Saat Hindustani*, recalled that even standing shoulder-to-shoulder with six heroes, one could see that Mr Bachchan who played

Anwar Ali, a Muslim poet from Bihar, was destined for glory. But he had to struggle through thirteen duds before *Zanjeer* (1973) broke the jinx. The revenge drama had first been announced with Dharmendra and Mumtaz after Dharam ji brought the Salim-Javed script to Prakash Mehra. But a family commitment came up just when the film was to roll and unwilling to wait, the director took the role of Vijay to Dev Anand who thumbed it down because he didn't know Prakash ji well. Raaj Kumar whom he approached next, wanted Bombay to be recreated in a studio in Chennai where he was shooting another film with Mumtaz. Meanwhile, Pran sahib was signed on to play Sher Khan and it was his son, Amit, who recommended his friend and namesake for the cop's role. 'After watching Mehmood's *Bombay to Goa* (1972), I was convinced that an actor who could take on Shatrughan Sinha, would be able to match Pran sahib's fiery Pathan too,' Prakash ji recounted, adding that soon after, Mumtaz too dropped out but Jaya ji bailed them out to play the *chappan churiwali* heroine, Mala.

Suneel, whose father distributed *Zanjeer*, met Mr Bachchan for the first time as a thirteen-year-old boy at family friend Farida Jalal's party. It was just before the film's release and Mr Bachchan looked really anxious. 'Having seen the film, I was confident, like my dad, that *Zanjeer* would do well. Mr Bachchan's aggression and energy set the screen on fire,' he marvels.

The 1970s was a decade of simmering anger after Indira Gandhi imposed Emergency. Flashbacking to the era, Salim Khan, who, with Javed Akhtar scripted many Bachchan blockbusters, from *Zanjeer* (1973), *Deewar* (1975) and *Sholay* (1975) to *Trishul* (1978), *Don* (1978) and *Shakti* (1982), told me that in Bombay's local trains, he could see this impotent anger reflected in the faces of his fellow commuters. On screen, it exploded through Amitabh Bachchan and found an answering response in his audience. That was why the writer duo could take some audacious calls, such as having Vijay violently hurl Madan Mohan's naked body from the window in *Deewar* or ignite a stick of dynamite with the tip of his beedi in *Trishul* and stroll away. They went a step further and wrote both *Deewar* and *Shakti* without any songs believing they were superfluous to the plots. But the distributors rebelled and eventually the directors, Yash Chopra and Ramesh Sippy, had to oblige them. R.D. Burman's '*Keh doon tumhe ya chhup rahoon*' in *Deewar* and '*Jaane kaise kab kahan*' in *Shakti* were chartbusters, but both films are remembered for their fiery histrionics rather than their musical scores.

Amitabh Bachchan was a hero unlike any the audience had seen before. He didn't give up on life for love; rather, he fought for it and would even kill for it. Sometimes he ended up dead, but death didn't diminish his anger, rather it immortalized him on celluloid. For two decades, he ruled the box office, unchallenged and unconquered. Ramesh Sippy's *Sholay* (1975), which arrived in the Emergency year on Independence Day, was initially dismissed by the critics as 'all smoke, no fire', but it went on to set a record with a five-year uninterrupted run at Mumbai's Minerva cinema. During the shoot, Jai and Gabbar bonded off camera and went on to sign Shakti Samanta's *The Great Gambler* (1979).

Those days, actors shuttled between different projects. Amjad Khan sahib was hoping to wrap up his work on another film quickly, so he could hop on the evening flight to Goa and join *The Great Gambler* unit, but his co-star Sunil Dutt was delayed by his own home production, *Nehla Pe Dehla* (1976). Not wanting to upset Shakti da's plans, Amjad sahib decided to drive overnight.

En route, he met with an accident on the Goa–Bombay highway, which left him with a dozen broken ribs, a broken leg and other injuries. His two-year-old son shattered his collar bone and his seven-month pregnant wife, Shaila, was hurt too.

Looking at his crumpled body, not many gave him a chance, but Mr Bachchan who rushed to the hospital and signed the necessary documents needed for an emergency operation, spent long nights by Amjad sahib's bedside, repeatedly telling his buddy he couldn't die. Amjad sahib eventually pulled through, but the next time, it was his friend who landed in hospital when a stunt during the shooting of *Coolie* (1983) went wrong.

The headline-grabbing incident happened on 26 July 1982. It was first-day-first-shot for first-time villain Puneet Issar. Mr Bachchan was to dodge Puneet's punch, fall on a table and roll to the floor. He mistimed his jump and banged into the table instead. Its sharp edge caught him in the middle and left him with a ruptured intestine and massive internal bleeding. He was rushed to Bombay where he underwent an emergency splenectomy at Breach Candy Hospital. He survived that surgery, and the many others that followed, but every day was tense.

The whole country prayed for him, but no one prayed harder than a guilt-stricken Puneet. Reading newspaper reports of Mr Bachchan's deteriorating condition, he had rushed to Breach Candy Hospital with his wife where his 'hero' assured him that he was not to blame. Mr Bachchan recounted how while shooting for a Prakash Mehra film, the glass he had flung at Vinod Khanna had caught the actor on the chin and resulted in a deep cut, which needed four stitches. 'I can only repeat Vinod's words to me. Relax, it was an accident,' he told Puneet who was flooded with hate mail after the incident, even death threats, and dropped from several projects.

Six months after the accident, on 7 January 1983,

Mr Bachchan returned to Bombay's Chandivali Studio to pick up from where he had left off. This time the shot went off without a hitch. *Coolie* was released on 14 November 1983. It was a blockbuster. The punch that had taken down Big B was frozen at the point of impact with the words 'This is the shot in which AMITABH BACHCHAN was seriously injured' superimposed in English, Hindi and Urdu.

In the original script, Kader Khan's antagonist, Zafar Khan, was supposed to kill Iqbal. But director Manmohan Desai rewrote the climax and like in real life, on screen too, Mr Bachchan's Coolie No. 786 ended up cheating death.

While his accident is a part of Bollywood film lore, not many know that he had another close shave during a shoot at Natraj Studio in Bombay. 'We were filming the flood scene and both of us were waist deep in water when someone shouted out a warning about a live wire. Before I knew it, Amit ji had picked me up in his arms and jumped on to the train berth, saving his life and mine,' Rati Agnihotri revealed, three decades later.

Eighteen years after the accident, during a regular medical test, Mr Bachchan learnt that he had cirrhosis of liver. It's an ailment commonly associated with excessive alcohol consumption, but in his case, he had been given sixty bottles of blood during his treatment and one of the two hundred donors had been carrying the Australian antigen hepatitis B that damaged seventy-five per cent of his liver. He has been spearheading the hepatitis B campaign since, along with those for polio vaccination and diabetes.

When I met him in 2015 soon after the release of *Piku*, the legendary actor, who was then a sprightly seventy-two-year-old, arrived straight from the gym dressed in tracks. In the course of our interview, he casually listed all his ailments, adding that he had set himself up as a medical specimen to prove that tuberculosis is not a 'poor man's disease' and incurable.

Ironically, in Shoojit Sircar's film he played another 'Bhaskor' Banerjee (his character in *Anand*), who could have very well stepped out of one of Hrishi da's films, only here he was not a doctor but a constipated hypochondriac whose day revolved around his motions. The film ended with him passing away peacefully in his sleep. The film took him back to Kolkata, a city he feels close to and not just because he is its *'jamaibabu'* (son-in-law) after marrying Jaya ji. He had lived in Kolkata for around eight years in the 1960s. I have heard from him about the four-anna *puchkas* in Victoria Maidan and a visit to Manik da's (Satyajit Ray) messy study, which mirrored his own. Mr Bachchan too has been close to several Bengali directors, from Hrishikesh Mukherjee to Shoojit Sircar and Sujoy Ghosh. Sujoy, who has worked with him in *Aladin* (2009), *Te3n* (2016) and *Badla* (2019), even convinced him to render the popular Rabindra Sangeet *'Ekla cholo re'* for his film *Kahaani* (2012), whose release coincided with the Nobel Laureate's 150th birth anniversary celebrations. Though he had done playback singing for many films, Mr Bachchan was wary because it was in a language he was not very conversant in. After reluctantly agreeing, he insisted on recording the song for a second time despite Sujoy's assurance that it was fine. 'If it doesn't match up, my head will be chopped off, not just by the Bengalis but in my own house,' he pointed out with a straight face, referring to his petite wife.

That's Amitabh Bachchan for you. Everyone who has worked with him swears by his sincerity, dedication and commitment. Shoojit recalls how the day before he was to shoot the climax of his courtroom drama *Pink* (2016), he was jolted awake by a phone call at two in the morning. It was Mr Bachchan, who is usually up half the night writing his blog, answering mails or simply prepping for the next day's shoot, wanting the director to hear the 'No means no' speech that he had been practising for hours. He had prepared two different pitches and Shoojit quickly told him which he wanted, and they said 'goodnight'. The next day, the scene was canned in one take.

Singer-composer Bappi Lahiri while talking about his duet with Kishore Kumar, *'Jahan char yaar mil jaye'*, the *Sharaabi* (1984) chartbuster, recalled how Mr Bachchan had conscientiously turned up at his bungalow twice to rehearse his rap portions. 'On the day of the recording, the call time was 9.30 a.m. I arrived at ten to find Amit ji already there and rehearsing with the musicians,' Bappi da raved, adding that because of all the prep he had done, they were finished in two hours. 'He is one of the most dedicated actors I know, and one of the most cultured. I have been to Holi parties at his bungalow, when his parents were alive, and there was so much *sanskaar* and *sanskriti* even in the midst of revelry.'

Interestingly, Manmohan Desai was contemplating making *Sharaabi*, an adaptation of the American comedy *Arthur* (1981), around an alcoholic millionaire, with Randhir Kapoor. But Prakash Mehra announced the film first with Amitabh Bachchan. It was their sixth straight hit, and Mr Bachchan's drunken Vicky became a textbook act for actors down the years.

The simmering rivalry between the two filmmakers came to the fore eight years later. For twenty-three years, Amitabh Bachchan was the 'Shahenshah' of the box office. Then, in 1988, ironically, a film with the same title, sounded the first warning bell. Despite a great opening, the vigilante film quickly lost steam. In the same year, Manmohan Desai's *Gangaa Jamunaa Saraswati*, despite being the fourth-highest grosser with a hundred-day run at Kolkata's Metro cinema, was still certified a flop. In 1989, the Ketan Desai-directed *Toofan* opened on

11 August 1989, and in producer, Man ji's own words, 'The Toofan mail was racing ahead at full speed only to hurtle into a head-on collision with an incoming goods train with the result that both derailed.' The goods train he was referring to was Prakash Mehra's *Jaadugar*, which came just two weeks after *Toofan*, on 25 August, and was the only Bachchan starrer not to get an opening. It sounded the death knell for him.

Hrishi da had predicted the downfall, pointing out that in the seven films they did together, he had been careful not to stereotype his 'Babumoshai'—turning *Anand*'s introverted doctor into the playboy Vicky in *Namak Haraam* (1973), then the brooding recluse of *Mili* (1975) into Dr Sukumar Sinha, a professor of English who has to masquerade as botany professor Dr Parimal Tripathi, in *Chupke Chupke* (1975). However, other filmmakers repeatedly cashed in on Mr Bachchan's 'angry young man' figure, making him a prisoner of his image. 'He could have broken away, but he didn't, and ended up creating a Frankenstein,' the veteran director had sighed while discussing one of his favourite actors.

Perhaps Mr Bachchan himself realized this and tried to experiment with *Main Azaad Hoon* (1989) and *Agneepath* (1990). Director Mukul Anand told me that at their first meeting itself, Mr Bachchan had asked him if they could do something different. Mukul, inspired by the Hollywood classic *Scarface* (1983), modelled his Vijay Dinanath Chauhan on Manya Surve, the first underworld gangster to be shot dead in a police encounter in Mumbai, pushing up his age from twenty-five to thirty-seven. It was a National Award-winning performance with Mr Bachchan even trying to copy the gangster's husky voice. But the experiment fell flat with panicked theatre owners believing there was something wrong with the soundtrack and viewers thinking a 'double' had dubbed for their hero. Eventually he had to re-dub his lines and the film was re-released in his familiar baritone. *Agneepath* grossed ₹80 lakh per territory, which is more than what a 'superhit' with another actor would earn, but it was still dismissed as a flop and broke its producer Yash Johar's heart.

Yash Johar's son, Karan, was present on the set in Mandwa and had watched Mr Bachchan as Vijay Dinanath Chauhan run through the flames in the film's climax, eliminating his nemesis Kancha and pulling his mother, Rohini Hattangadi, along as he recited his father's verses, '*Yeh mahan drushya hai, chal raha manushya hai, asru, swet, rakht se lathpath, lathpath, lathpath, Agneepath! Agneepath! Agneepath!*' before going to sleep forever with his head cradled in his mother's arms. Karan remade the film twenty-two years later, with Hrithik Roshan as Vijay and Sanjay Dutt as Kancha Cheena. This time, it worked. Mr Bachchan continues to recite his father's verse with which the film ended, sometimes in the same husky voice, and admits it now brings him a lot of compliments.

Mukul went on to do *Hum* (1991) with Mr Bachchan—the film has been immortalized by the song '*Jumma chumma de de*', which was originally conceived for *Agneepath*. I was told by the director that Mr Bachchan had heard the original Mory Kanté version '*Yeke Yeke*' and suggested it to composers Laxmikant–Pyarelal. It didn't fit in there and was subsequently offered to Ramesh Sippy for *Ram Ki Sita Shyam Ki Gita* but since the film didn't materialize, it eventually went to Anand Bakshi who came up with the words '*Jumma chumma de de*'. While the word 'Jumma' got it banned on All India Radio following protests from certain Muslims, the ban only served to increase cassette sales. It was shot in the derelict Mukesh Mills, and choreographer Chinni Prakash has admitted that their hero grooved his way through fifteen rehearsals and twenty retakes to making musical history. The film was a hit and he went on to do a third film, *Khuda Gawah* (1992), with Mukul.

After *Khuda Gawah*, Mr Bachchan did not sign a film for five long years even though he received many offers during the time. He was back after the hiatus with Mehul Kumar's *Mrityudaata* (1997), which also crashed despite all the hype. It was Aditya Chopra's *Mohabbatein* (2000) that gave him a new lease of life, followed by others such as *Ek Rishtaa: The Bond of Love* (2001), *Kabhi Khushi Kabhie Gham...* (2001) and *Baghban* (2003)—all mainstream movies with him in the role of the traditional patriarch. During this phase he also brought Marlon Brando's *Godfather* into Hindi cinema with Ram Gopal Varma's *Sarkar* (2005, 2008, 2017) trilogy. After Hrishi da, Mr Bachchan admitted that he has done the maximum films with RGV as Ram Gopal Varma is popularly known. 'The reason that draws me to him is the fact that he has continuously offered me films; several others did not or offered those that did not interest me,' he reasoned. 'His approach to films changes according to the subject. He is keen to challenge himself and the artiste he works with.'

The director himself admitted that in all these years only once did they have a difference of opinion. This was during a scene from the original *Sarkar* in which his character, Subhash Nagre, throws his elder son, Vishnu, out of his house. While Ramu wanted him to execute the scene in a cold-blooded and emotionless manner, Mr Bachchan believed that it should be done with some anger. Eventually, they did it his way. But that night, after returning home, Mr Bachchan called the director and admitted that having thought it through, he agreed that they should have shot it the way RGV wanted and reshot the following day. It is things like this that makes Mr Bachchan stand tall amidst the competition.

A year after *Sarkar* came *Aks* (2001), a truly path-breaking film for Indian audiences with Mr Bachchan playing a cop, Manu Varma. Debutant director Rakyesh Omprakash Mehra's brief to him was simple, 'Let's for a moment think that you are not Amitabh Bachchan and reinvent him.' And at fifty-nine, Mr Bachchan took a leap of faith. *Aks* wasn't a hit, but it proved that he could still fly through air, fearlessly, three hundred feet into a waterfall and take us into a world so dark it left me shivering long after I had come out of the air-conditioned theatre.

After that, there was no slowing him down. A Best Actor National Award for *Black* in which he played an elderly teacher who leads a deaf-blind girl towards light while fighting Alzheimer's himself; a sexy item number, '*Kajra re*', with son Abhishek and yet-to-be daughter-in-law Aishwarya in *Bunty Aur Babli* (2005); his first English-language film *The Last Lear* (2007); a true-life Malayalam film with southern superstar Mohanlal, *Kandahar* (2010); a Hollywood debut with Baz Luhrmann's *The Great Gatsby* (2013); a spirited centenarian dad to a seventy-year-old morose son in *102 Not Out* (2018), a wily lawyer in the cerebral revenge drama *Badla* (2019) and a slimy, scheming fox engaged in a game of upmanship in the slice-of-life comedy *Gulabo Sitabo* (2020). He's relishing what he calls his 'third innings' with directors who allow him the creative freedom to push the envelope. Sitting up there, Hrishi da must be smiling to see his Amit finally live up to his potential.

But what makes him truly unique is that despite being voted the 'star of the millennium' at the turn of the century, he is still a familiar face in our living rooms thanks to *Kaun Banega Crorepati* (KBC). The first season of the game show, with him as the host, was flagged off on 3 July 2000. It returned in 2005 as *Kaun Banega Crorepati Dwitya* (KBC 2) and after one season with Shah Rukh Khan, the baton was handed back to Mr Bachchan who, in the eleven seasons so far, has touched many lives in fifty minutes.

When it started, my daughter was just over a year old, and every evening at nine, as soon as the familiar music came on, Ranjika would clap her little hands over her face and coyly peep at Mr Bachchan from between her splayed fingers. For the next hour, till the '*bhoopu*' (bugle) went off, she would sit in the rocking chair, giggling, mumbling gibberish and leaving me confounded with her interest in a quiz show that was miles beyond her orbit.

Mr Bachchan became grandfather for the third time on 16 November 2011, when Aradhya Bachchan was born to Abhishek and Aishwarya. Baby Bachchan was the most discussed baby even before she came into the world. In the months leading up to her birth, I had come to dread the almost-daily calls from office enquiring if she had 'arrived'. Once I called up Aishwarya's publicist at around 11 p.m. She sounded just as weary as me and told me even before I had articulated the question that Aishwarya was still at home and the baby hadn't popped out yet. We both sighed with relief and went back to helping our respective kids with their homework. Aradhya was considerate, choosing to show up a few minutes before 10 a.m. Almost immediately she acquired an imposter Twitter handle #BabyBachchan, which started with a shout-out to papa, was bemused that she was already a celebrity and gushed over how pretty her mother was. I sketched out the ordeal of being a 'B' in my weekly column and got a sweet message from her grandfather that the piece would be in her baby book waiting for her to read when she grew up. I don't know if it has, but my photograph with Aradhya's grandfather is still up on my bedroom wall.

7

MITHUN CHAKRABORTY: NOT JUST A DISCO DANCER

I am a Disco Dancer, zindagi mera gaana,
mein kissi ka deewana

I saw him for the first time across the suite of a suburban five-star hotel in Bombay. He was surrounded by dozens of gentlemen, all of them clamouring for two minutes of his time. Mithun Chakraborty who was holding court at the far end of the room didn't even notice me. I wanted more than just two minutes of his precious time, but at five-feet-two, was almost obliterated by the crowd around him. Wondering how to get his attention, I nudged a place for myself next to the door and patiently waited to catch him on his way out.

A quarter of an hour later, an assistant director hurried into the room and headed towards him. I smiled knowing that the AD had come to tell him that the shot was ready. My heart beats accelerated as I watched Dada fight his way towards the door. Suddenly, he was there in front of me, but before I could say anything, he was gone, the crowd once again between us. Panic-stricken, I called out to him. 'Dada... Dada... Mithun da...' He didn't hear me, and I slumped in my corner, defeated.

I knew my editor would be upset that I had failed to make contact. Dada had moved to Ooty by then and his visits to

Mumbai were few and far between. We had no idea when he would be back. I was cursing my lack in inches and my luck when suddenly, I felt someone's eyes on me. Looking up, I saw that Dada had stopped and was looking straight at me, expectantly. He had heard me!

Those around him had fallen silent, and in the sudden hush, I blurted out that I was a journalist and wanted an interview. I could see him sizing me up—a just-out-of-college reporter couldn't have cut an impressive figure. I heard a few sniggers, quickly stifled, but to my relief, I didn't see even the flicker of a condescending smile on Dada's face. Instead, he asked me gravely, 'Why do you want to interview me?' I pointed out that he was one of Bollywood's top stars. 'So? There are bigger stars than me.' he retorted. I nodded, 'Yeah, but they haven't won two National Awards [Best Actor for *Mrigayaa* (1976) and *Tahader Katha* (1992)].' He didn't react. And I continued, almost tripping over my words in my anxiety to make a favourable impression, 'You are the pride of every Bengali and I'm one of them.' A smile suddenly lit up his face, 'Ok little girl, you will get your interview.' My hopes soared and my heart sang. But, too soon! 'Today looks difficult with the shoot and my other commitments, maybe next time I am in Mumbai,' he told me gently. My disappointment was evident, and even as the AD was pulling him away, he paused to gesture towards his make-up man, saying, 'Be in touch with him, you will get your interview, I promise. You called me Dada [elder brother] just now, how can I disappoint my *Bon* [younger sister].' Before I could say any more, he was gone.

I did take down his make-up man's number before I left the newly opened suburban hotel, and a couple of mornings every week, for the next three months, I would call him up religiously to ask when Dada was expected to return to Mumbai.

I had almost resigned myself to the fact that we were never going to meet again, when, one day, he informed me that Dada was flying down the next day. 'Come over to Mehboob Studio tomorrow and try your luck. It's a 9 a.m. to 6 p.m. shift, but he won't be there before noon,' his make-up man told me over the wire even as I did a happy jig.

The next morning dawned grey and depressing. It was pouring cats and dogs, but nothing could keep me away from the Bandra studio. I arrived, dripping wet, an hour before noon, just so I wouldn't miss him. Dada drove up around noon. I handed my visiting card to his man Friday after he had settled in. A few anxious minutes passed before the door of his vanity van swung open and I was ushered inside.

He was looking out at the grey sheet of rain from behind the chintz curtains framing the windows. 'Bad day,' he observed, acknowledging me with a nod. I wondered if he remembered me from our last meeting. He did. 'Didn't you say that you wanted to interview me because of the two National Awards? I was beginning to think no one was interested,' the brilliant smile flashed again. I beamed back, 'Of course I am interested; it is a prestigious honour and you were felicitated twice.' He acknowledged this with a nod, 'Yeah, I proved *Mrigayaa* was not a fluke,' and went on to share that when he learnt he had been voted Best Actor again by the National Award jury for Buddhadeb Dasgupta's 1992 drama, he had cried, and then, whisked off his parents to Vaishno Devi. 'I walked all the way up to the temple without any breaks as I had promised. Jai Mata Di!'

I had cried too, watching *Tahader Katha*, my heart going out to Shibnath. Once a fearless freedom fighter in pre-Independence India, his body is broken and mind unhinged after eleven years of tortured incarceration for the murder of a

British officer. But a bigger shock awaits him when he steps out of his prison asylum to travel back home with a former comrade, Bipin Gupta, now a conniving businessman wanting to cash in on Shibnath's reputation to further his political ambitions. But the broken man is stronger than anyone believes and resolutely refuses to sell his 'patriotism' to better his life and that of his family. Instead, he retreats into his own fractured mind. 'The East Bengal dialect he spoke was a little difficult to master but it wasn't completely unfamiliar as my ancestors were from Bangladesh and Shantipur,' Dada told me that afternoon, as we waited for Rekha to get her make-up done.

Born on 16 June 1950 in Barisal, then East Pakistan and now in Bangladesh, Gouranga, like many impressionable Bengali boys in the late 1960s, got sucked into the Naxal movement in West Bengal. He was agitating for a perfect society when his brother's death in a freak accident made him question his ideals. He returned to the family fold, but a police crackdown on Naxals forced him to go into hiding again. After a few narrow shaves, he fled Kolkata and found a safe haven in Pune's Film and Television Institute of India (FTII). He graduated with a gold medal and went on to win the National Award for Mrinal Sen's Bengali film *Mrigayaa*, in which he played Ghinua, a tribal hunter from Odisha who does not understand why he is being led to his death for the same act for which a British officer is rewarded.

Dada arrived in Bombay to make a career in Bollywood, carrying the tag of an 'art cinema' actor. After that, the only time he associated himself with the ghosts of his political past was when he featured in Khwaja Ahmad Abbas's *The Naxalites* (1980). He had accepted the film for the pleasure of working with the legendary writer who had scripted films such as Chetan Anand's *Neecha Nagar* (1946), which won the Palme d'Or at the first Cannes Film Festival, as also Raj Kapoor's *Awaara* (1951), *Shree 420* (1955), *Jagte Raho* (1956), *Mera Naam Joker* (1970), *Bobby* (1973) and *Henna* (1991).

Dada's initial years in the 'City of Dreams' were a nightmare. Despite the National Award, he was rebuffed, told that an adivasi in a dhoti would never be accepted as a suited-booted Hindi film hero. Yet, he didn't give up and continued to make the rounds of producers' offices. With the money he earned from stage shows under the pseudonym of Rana Rez, he was able to rent a room in a slum. When he bagged his first Filmfare Award for Best Supporting Actor for Mukul Anand's *Agneepath* (1990), Dada admitted that the coconut-seller, Krishna Iyer M.A., had been modelled on a south Indian gentleman with whom he had shared the *kholi* in Koliwada. 'The man slept on the lone cot in the room while I would stretch out on the floor. But whenever he was late coming home, I would claim his bed. One day, he spotted me lying on it and thundered, *"Hum lungi uthayega to pata chalega",* Dada recounted. Anand Bakshi incorporated the line in the song '*I am Krishna Iyer M.A.*' with Dada answering Neelam's dare, '*Can you sing? Can you dance? Can you disco?*' with '*Hum ye lungi uthati, tumko disco dikhati, josh me aati to phir sabki chhuti hum kar jaati, bari bari hum tum, sabki dholak bajati.*' These quirky lines in the gangster drama that bagged Amitabh Bachchan a National Award for his portrayal of Vijay Dinanath Chauhan, were reportedly written by a spot boy—the only one in the unit who knew Tamil—and later corrected during dubbing.

Starting out with small roles in *Do Anjaane* (1976) and *Phool Khile Hai Gulshan Gulshan* (1978), Dada worked his way up to his first hit, *Mera Rakshak* (1978), in which he had a goat for a bodyguard. But it was as Gun Master G9, in the desi Bond thriller *Surakksha* (1979) that Mithun Chakraborty exploded in Bollywood. This was his first collaboration with singer-composer Bappi Lahiri and their *'Mausam hai gaane ka'* was a chart-topper. After that, it was imperative to rope in Bappi da for every Mithun film. Years later, when I prodded him on his once frequent collaborator, India's 'Golden Man' smiled fondly, 'We were a made-for-each-other jodi, the Royal Bengal Tigers who roared together and went on to give more than fifty hits.'

Surakksha and *Taraana*—both released in 1979—were followed by a series of box office duds, like *Prem Vivah* (1979), *Kismet* (1980), *Jeene Ki Arzoo* (1981) and *Laparwah* (1981) to name a few, and Dada was really low when he started shooting *Taqdeer Ka Badshah* (1982). To cheer him up, the film's director, Babbar Subhash, told him that he would make a film titled *Disco Dancer*, which would make him a superstar. 'The idea came to me one evening when Bappi ji and I were brainstorming on our film's music. His mother was in the next room doing puja, and as the fragrance of the agarbatti wafted in, I had an idea: Why not make a film about a street singer who becomes a disco dancer?' reminisced Subhash ji who believed the disco wave would sweep India too—just as it had in the West, thanks to John Travolta's *Saturday Night Fever* (1977)—and promptly registered the title *Disco Dancer*.

Dada loved the idea, seeing his own rags-to-riches story in Jimmy's story and spoke about the film all day. Publicist Jagdish Aurangabadkar who was on the set overheard him and leaked the news in the trade weekly *Screen*. Suddenly, Subhash ji had distributors queuing up for *Disco Dancer*—the only problem was the leading lady. After getting the thumbs down from Rekha, Zeenat Aman and Ranjeeta, he opted for a newcomer,

Kim. The casting coup was when Rajesh Khanna agreed to do his first guest appearance for free, grateful to the filmmaker who had stood by him when he was going through a bad phase. 'Kaka was supposed to feature in only one song, "*Goron ki na kalon ki*", but he ended up playing Jimmy's guru who returns in the climax to urge him to sing,' Subhash ji revealed.

However, to their misfortune, Biddu, who was on a high after '*Disco Deewane*' with the brother–sister duo of Nazia and Zoheb Haasan, released his first production, the much-hyped musical *Star*, on 22 October 1982. The film quickly ran out of steam despite Nazia's superhit '*Boom Boom*' and Zoheb's rendition of the title track. And suddenly, there was a cloud of doubt over *Disco Dancer*. If popular stars like Kumar Gaurav, Rati Agnihotri and Biddu couldn't work at the box office, how could one expect Mithun, a still struggling star, to pull in the crowds? Undeterred, Subhash ji released *Disco Dancer* two months later, on 10 December.

He watched the noon show with the audience at Bombay's Minerva theatre and was gratified to see that no one was going out for a cigarette or a loo break when the songs came on as was customary. By the end of the show, even the distributor looked happy and the filmmaker returned home to catch up on some much-needed sleep. 'I woke up at 6 p.m., learnt that no one had called and resigned myself to the fact that the film had flopped. Two hours later, the phone started ringing, and then it wouldn't stop. At midnight, Pahlaj Nihalani, a big producer at the time, dropped by. He wanted me to direct his next film. Soon, even top stars were sending out feelers and I knew my disco gamble had paid off,' Subhash ji recounted.

Disco Dancer was a craze, and not just in India. Even in Moscow, people were singing '*Jimmy Jimmy*' on the streets and in China it was adjudged the 'film of the decade'. In South

Africa, two stage performers thanked Subhash ji for giving them songs that were getting them plenty of money and appreciation. And when he started his next film, *Kasam Paida Karne Wale Ki* (1984), with Mithun and Smita Patil, a contingent of Israelis landed on the sets, greeting their hero with screams of, 'Jimmy... Jimmy'. Dada also came to be addressed as 'Pelvic Presley', 'Desi Michael Jackson' or simply 'Disco Dancer'. Decades later, when I asked Shoojit Sircar who was filming his Sardar Udham Singh biopic in St Petersburg with Vicky Kaushal, what kind of reception his team had received there, he exclaimed, 'It's wonderful! The Russians love Indians and our movies. You only have to sing "*Jimmy Jimmy, aaja aaja*" and you can get anything done here!'

With his career back on track, Dada was finally at peace, even in his personal life. In 1979, he had married model-turned-actress Helena Luke. The marriage lasted just four months. Dada then went on to marry another actress Yogita Bali, with whom he was paired in Shakti Samanta's *Khwab* (1980). In an interview in 1982, he confided that during his struggling days in Bombay, when he was often without work, to take his mind off his troubles, he would play football at Khar Gymkhana. Yogita ji who lived in the vicinity would pass by the football ground and gazing at the beautiful actress from a distance, Dada claimed he had a premonition that one day, this woman would be his wife. The marriage itself was an impetuous midnight decision. After they had signed the papers, the bride returned to her parents the next morning. Dada knew his conservative parents would never accept their daughter-in-law step out every morning for shoots, so he waited a few months for Yogita ji to wrap up all her film commitments before bringing her home. She never returned to the screen, happily settling down to a life of domesticity and giving him two beautiful sons, whom he named Mahaakshay, meaning 'immortal', and Ushme, meaning 'the first rays of the sun'. 'My grandfather was a scholar who would speak to us only in Sanskrit. So, I chose these unusual names for my sons,' he explained.

Then, Sridevi entered his life. Dada never acknowledged the relationship publicly, but they reportedly came close while filming Rakesh Roshan's *Jaag Utha Insan* (1984) and married in court sometime in 1985. They kept their secret for almost two years, but it took its toll with Dada admitting obliquely that he hated being dishonest to his close ones. Apparently, when Yogita ji guessed and confronted him, there were huge fights till he assured his wife that he would never leave her or their children. But in the process, it is said that he lost Sridevi who was not prepared to be the other woman in his life. She dropped out of three films featuring them and they never did another film together. All this is of course pure conjecture, stories thrown up by the rumour mills.

Yogita ji and Mithun had another son, whom they named Namashi, derived from Om Namah Shivay. The family was complete, but Dada had always wanted a daughter, and when he heard about a child who had been abandoned in a garbage bin by her birth parents, he adopted her and named her Dishani.

However, after eighteen years, fatigue was beginning to set in. It didn't help that since a surgery took him out of *maar dhaad dhamakas* (action films) and into family socials, none of his films had really hit the bull's eye at the box office. In July 1992, after he had signed half-a-dozen films, Dada announced that he would quit films after he had completed his present workload. No, he was not drunk. He had given up alcohol three years ago and turned vegetarian. He reasoned that after almost two decades, he had had his fill of stardom and was tired of going to the studio every day and doing the same old scenes. 'Maybe after five years I will become a sanyasi,' and I could see that as an eye-catching headline! Many of my colleagues were sceptical, insisting it was only a publicity gimmick. But I knew he had been serious. He had an apartment in Kolkata, close to my aunt's residence. Sometimes when I passed by, I saw saffron robes hanging from the clothesline. Enquiries revealed that Dada's sister was a sanyasin and whenever she visited, kirtan sessions were hosted in the apartment. Dada confirmed this, admitting that his sister and a cousin had renounced the world. 'We are disciples of Loknath Baba and one day, I might walk down the same path. Maa will take care of my family; they will survive,' he stated confidently.

To my relief he did not leave the industry. But he moved out of Mumbai, to Ooty, which had brought him luck. 'If even one shot is taken there, my film is a hit,' he told me, openly acknowledging that he was superstitious and also a well-meaning parent who believed that the picturesque hill station was a better place to bring up his children than a sea-facing bungalow on Madh Island.

The move did not pack him off into early retirement because by then he had hit upon a formula that was working for him. He would allot producers bulk dates, shoot the film in two months at one go, and ensure it released within six months. He kept his remuneration reasonable without compromising on his price. The budget was modest because he did not demand big names or lavish sets. The producer could sell the film for anything between ₹25 and ₹40 lakh in the major territories. This made his films 'safe' propositions and in case they flopped, Dada compensated by signing another film with the same producer, provided he was willing, and did not accept any money till the film was complete. That was how in 1991, when trade pundits were writing him off after a dozen flops, he still had another twelve films in his kitty. He couldn't sign any more because of the ceiling imposed by the producers' association. These films helped him pay off his loans, open three hotels under the Monarch Group and secure his children's future.

Mithun Chakraborty also made it to the *Limca Book of Records* as the only actor who had featured in 249 films in a national language as leading man, with 100-plus films made in the 1980s alone. There was a film releasing almost every other week. Eventually, quantity over quality proved his undoing. However, the occasional *Pyar Jhukta Nahin* (1985), along the lines of the Shashi Kapoor–Sharmila Tagore–Shatrughan Sinha romance drama *Aa Gale Lag Jaa* (1973), *Jallad* (1995), which bagged him the Filmfare Best Villain Award or *Elaan* (2005), another bad man role as dreaded terrorist Baba Sikander, redeemed his career graph and kept him in the running.

Vikram Bhatt, who directed his *Elaan*, pointed out that while Dada is undoubtedly a powerhouse of talent, he was always an underrated actor who did not get the acclaim and the credit he deserves—at least not enough. 'In a way he and I are very similar in the kind of films we make. They are "massy", so people say, "Oh, there's no talent required." But there is, and for me, Mithun Chakraborty will always be a great actor,' asserted the filmmaker who had glimpsed a childlike side to the star during the shoot in Ooty when Dada would cook for the entire unit and invite them to his hotel for dinner.

Like Rakhee, Dada's culinary skills are legendary within the film fraternity. Along with his cooking, he is also famous for his pranks. Padmini Kolhapure, his co-star in almost a dozen films after the surprise success of *Pyar Jhukta Nahin*, recalled how he would rag her endlessly, then, insist she couldn't laugh at his jokes. 'Sometimes he would tell me with a straight face not to rub my eyes early morning because it would bring bad luck. I didn't know if he was serious or joking,' she reminisced with a laugh.

I got a taste of his tongue-in-cheek humour during our interviews, when he would sometimes call me Didi in response to my Dada, and once even referred to himself as *Dadu* (grandfather), saying it was more apt given his advancing years! The ribbing fostered a familial bond and in 2006, when he came to Mumbai to introduce his first born Mimoh who had just signed his first film, *He—The Only One* (2010), Dada personally called to ask me to support my 'younger brother'. We agreed to a joint interview with father and son, but after a few questions, Dada left the floor to his twenty-one-year-old son who had golden locks, Yogita ji's face, referred to himself in third person and called his father Mithun, which amused me vastly.

Vikram recalled that when they were filming *Gunehgar* (1995) in Ooty, a sweet, roly-poly kid would follow Dada around. 'I later discovered that the little boy was his son. Mimoh never called him papa or daddy, it was always Mithun. And he never minded his son addressing him by his name. He never corrected him, and Mimoh never thought he was disrespecting his father by calling him Mithun. It was so sweet and the basis of the fabulous friendship they share,' he recounted.

He—The Only One was delayed, *The Murderer* remained unreleased and Mimoh finally made his debut with Raj N. Sippy's *Jimmy* (2008), which bit the dust. Vikram believes it was because he was projected as a dancing star, like his father. 'He is a hard-working boy, extremely polite and diligent, and a very good actor, but different from his father. Mimoh is not Mithun and comparisons between the two are unfortunate,' he reasoned.

Dada himself was pragmatic about *Jimmy's* failure, pointing out that it had also taken him a long time to be accepted by the industry. However, he was confident that Mimoh, whose name is a combination of his two idols—'King of Pop' Michael Jackson and the greatest boxer of all, Muhammad Ali—both of whom had fought their way to the top, would make it too. 'But he has to fight his own battles,' he asserted.

Three years later, his son got his first hit, Vikram's horror film *Haunted-3D* (2011), for which he reverted to his original name, Mahaakshay.

Meanwhile, Dada who had once worked around the clock, had almost disappeared from screen, sparking off rumours that he had been forced into retirement. The suggestion brought forth a roar, 'No one is going to kick me out, I will be the one to call it quits.' He, however, pointed out that after years of double and triple shifts, he was tired of routine stuff and had finally got picky choosy. There were select films that got him all charged up. One was *Swami Vivekanand* (1998), in which he played Ramkrishna Paramhansa, a performance that bagged him his third National Award for Best Supporting Actor, and the other, Kalpana Lajmi's *Chingari* (2006) as Bhuvan Panda, a priest by day who visited a prostitute he was obsessed with most nights.

The restlessness that had been apparent earlier, when he had spoken of renouncing the world, was gone. Dada admitted he had changed, from a God-fearing Brahmin, who had once chanted mantras at community pujas, to a man who believed that God was in him and kept him on the straight and narrow path, rather than in a temple, where if things didn't work out you could go to put the blame squarely on his shoulders. 'Do you understand what I am saying? Am I making sense?' he asked with a laugh at my bemused expression. I was too young then to grasp what he meant, but I understand today, that in his search for God, Dada had found himself. And this had empowered him into taking bigger risks professionally.

He jumped into television and became a household name with reality shows like *Dance India Dance, Dance Bangla Dance, Dhoom Dhamaka, Dadagiri Unlimited* and *Bigg Boss* (the Bengali edition). He made cash counters jingle in Bengal with blockbusters like *Juddho* (2005), *MLA Fatakeshto* (2006) and its sequel *Minister Fatakeshto* (2007) and wowed critics with films such as *Titli* (2002) and *Kaalpurush* (2005). Earlier, he had featured in a successful Indo-Bangladesh co-production, Shakti Samanta's *Anyay Abichar* (1985), now he experimented with regional cinema, experimenting with Bhojpuri (*Bhole Shankar*) and Odia (*Ae Jugara Krushna Sudama*), Telugu (*Gopala Gopala*), Tamil (*Yagavarayinum Naa Kaakka*), Telugu (*Malupu*) and Kannada (*The Villain*). Along the way, there were the regular masala movies like *Golmaal 3* (2010), *Housefull 2* (2012), *Boss* (2013) and *Genius* (2018) that he romped through and a *Guru* (2007) and a *Phir Kabhi* (2009) that he gave his heart to. Our interactions had dried up, but I was happy to see him, off and on, on screen. Then, he disappeared.

A bad back put him out of action for almost three years. It was an old injury he had suffered when doing an aerial stunt in South Africa for a Salman Khan movie, *Luck*, in 2008. He had landed on some hard rocks, lying unnoticed under the safety net, and the pain had returned, requiring a hospital stay and regular physiotherapy. 'He will resume work in January,' Mimoh assured towards the end of 2015. But instead of springing back, Dada resigned from the Rajya Sabha at the end of 2016, and made regular trips to Los Angeles, fuelling speculations that he was undergoing treatment for cancer. It was a rumour his sons vehemently refuted, but I was getting seriously worried. And then, in 2019, Vivek Agnihiotri's *The Tashkent Files* resurrected him in all his lost glory.

Just before the release of the film, I got a call from the publicist wanting to set up an interview with him. 'Tell me where and when and I will be there,' I promised. 'In a few days, I will let you know,' I was told. The call never came. It's been ages since I saw or spoke to Dada, so I did the next best thing. I reached out to Vivek who was in the midst of a hectic lecture tour, but agreed to a quick chat on the phone, during which he pointed out that with Dada, for the first time, he had connected with an actor on a professional, social, emotional and intellectual level.

'Though no one talks of it, Mithun da's awareness of the world—society and politics—is phenomenal,' he asserted. His film was a political thriller, trying to uncover the mysterious death of our second prime minister, Lal Bahadur Shastri, in Tashkent on 11 January 1966, just hours after signing a peace agreement with Pakistan to end the 1965 war. 'Was it really due to natural causes as propagated or was it "state-sponsored murder"? Given the complex subject, it was a difficult script to explain, so, when I got a call from Mithun da early one morning requesting a meeting, I immediately jumped to the conclusion that he wanted to opt out,' Vivek recalled.

However, when Vivek and his actress-wife Pallavi Joshi were seated opposite him, Dada confided that for the last couple of days he had been wondering about his character, political guru Shyam Sunder Tripathi, whose only mantra is to win, and wanted to know what he ate, how he spoke, even how he fell asleep. The last question in particular stumped Vivek because while other actors enquire about dialects, costumes, dialogue, no one had ever posed a query like this and he admitted he didn't know the answer. 'But given the kind of person he is, he would probably read a book or go through some papers before he nodded off,' he mused.

When they were shooting the scene where Shweta Basu Prasad's character, the journalist Raagini Phule, visits Tripathi at home and finds him asleep, Dada took a particular interest in the set decor, bringing books from home, and fan letters too, which he piled on a table beside a sofa, where, as the rest of the team finished lunch, he stretched out and dozed off. When he was woken up for the take, he mumbled, '*Haan haan* you say "Action", I am with you' and went back to sleep. That's when Vivek realized why he had asked that seemingly random question about how Tripathi slept—to set the scene, both on the set and in his mind. 'He was so convincing that one could believe that he was really sleeping,' he raved.

The filmmaker had been told that the actor didn't shoot for too long and gave only one shot a day, but on his set, Dada would reel off shot after perfect shot, which required him to memorize fifteen to twenty pages of monologues, without any complaint. In one important scene, where he addresses the committee, pointing to the different kinds of terrorists that exist, he was so brilliant he left the unit spellbound by his histrionics.

'Half an hour after it was canned, his wife Yogita called me on my cell phone since Mithun da doesn't carry one, to ask how the scene had gone off. I was surprised by her query till she revealed that for the last three days, he had been prepping up for this scene, afraid he might not be able to deliver. "Was he okay?" she asked nervously.' Vivek, who till then had believed from the way Dada behaved on the sets, that he was pretty casual about the film, was even more surprised to learn that he had been rehearsing diligently at home since the past three months, working to get every word and nuance right. 'When he is in the company of serious professionals, he is completely committed and excels in what he does. Actors like him have survived for half a century because they are constantly honing their skills. Like sadhus they are doing tapasya,' Vivek stated.

On the last day of the shoot, Vivek finished Dada's portions by 4 p.m., cut the cake in the customary wrap-up ritual, waved goodbye to him and returned to continue filming with the other actors. During the 6.30 p.m. tea break, he got a call from Dada's manager saying that the actor wanted to see him. Surprised that he was still around, the filmmaker went to his make-up room where Dada confided that the character was still haunting him. 'I have a question I've waited to ask but didn't want to disturb you while you were shooting. You took me for a reason, have I passed your test?' he asked humbly. Vivek couldn't believe a three-time National Award-winning actor was asking him this. 'I told him that I would cherish this experience all my life, and with tears in eyes, Mithun da replied that he would sit around a little longer to feel a part of the shoot because he didn't want to leave the film behind and go home. He finally left around 10.30 p.m.,' the filmmaker narrated.

The Tashkent Files went on to become a surprise hit, with an incredible 100-day run, and the filmmaker insisted he had Dada to thank for its success. Just before they kicked off promotions, Dada told Vivek that actors like Naseeruddin Shah, Mandira Bedi and he came from different political ideologies and their names had become attached to certain issues. 'No matter what we say, it will stir up a controversy and the focus will shift from Shastri ji. So, it is best that you speak for the film, since you know the subject best, with Pallavi and Shweta, but even they should not give interviews when you are not around,' he cautioned.

The studio was upset by his stand; even Vivek was perturbed for a day, but then he did as advised and quickly realized how wise Dada was because not once did the spotlight veer away from the film towards the BJP, the Congress or the Communists. After its release, it went on to strike a chord with the audience too, like Dada had predicted, and stayed in the theatre for 120 days. 'Every time we met after that, Mithun da would tell me with a twinkle in his eyes, 'See, *buzurgon ki baat sunne mein kitna fayda hai*, it pays to listen to your seniors.'

Vivek has now gone back to him with his next, equally contentious film, *The Kashmir Files*. And Dada was quick to give the nod.

Meanwhile, his youngest son, Namashi Chakraborty, who moved with his parents to Ooty when he was two and grew up watching his father's movies and idolizing Shah Rukh Khan and Govinda, has followed in his footsteps to become an actor with Rajkumar Santoshi's *Bad Boy*. Dada's daughter Dishani has featured in two short films and Mimoh too has a couple of films in hand. And Dada, like the proverbial Phoenix, has risen again. As he had once said, 'No one can kick Mithun out, till he is ready to quit.'

8

FAROOQUE SHAIKH: THE EXTRAORDINARY ACTOR

Zindagi jab bhi teri bazm mein lati hai humein,
yeh zameen chand se behtar nazar aati hai hamein

I was just a teenager when I saw *Garm Hava* (1974) for the first time. This was in the Doordarshan days when on Sunday evenings one was always at the movies. It didn't matter if the black-and-white screen bleached out the colour or if the 21-inch box scaled down the 70-mm grandeur of cinemascope—the magic never failed to cast its spell. The pain of Partition had never touched my life nor that of my family, yet the trials of the Mirza family, torn between its Indian roots and the pressure to relocate to the newly formed Pakistan, left an indelible imprint on my young mind. While Balraj Sahni's Salim Mirza was a class act, his younger son, Sikandar, also left a lasting impression, his eyes mirroring his growing disillusionment with the country of his birth, despite the fact that he chooses to stay behind and fight for his rights rather than follow family and friends across the border.

M.S. Sathyu, a big name in theatre but a first-time director in films, had discovered this final year law student on stage. Farooque Shaikh was on his way to following in the footsteps of his lawyer-father Mustafa Shaikh and had no intentions of becoming an actor. 'But it was an outstanding script and the film had something important to say, so when I was offered Sikandar Mirza's role, I accepted,' he explained years later.

It took eight months for the film to be censored following fears that it would trigger off communal unrest. Ironically, it bagged the Nargis Dutt Award for Best Feature Film on National Integration. The Farooque sahib I knew was the most secular man I have ever met and a true-blue patriot who didn't chant the I-love-India mantra, but would have never agreed to be a part of any film that was 'pro-Muslim' or 'anti-India' as was being alleged prior to its release. It eventually was India's official entry to the Oscars in the Best Film in a Foreign Language category.

Another incentive for Farooque sahib to veer away from his chosen path and get into acting was his idol, Balraj Sahni. They had worked together in Indian People's Theatre Association (IPTA) and during a two-month schedule in Agra, during which time his room was right next to that of Balraj ji, he bombarded the legendary actor with questions about cinema, a medium he was both curious and uncertain about.

The film was made on a shoe-string budget allotted by the Film Finance of India (FSI) and Sathyu sahib had to regularly screen reels for the FSI babus. Only if approved, was the next instalment released. Even Balraj ji received just ₹5,000 as his remuneration, but it was the highest amount paid to any member associated with the project. Still, *Garm Hava* was a film very close to his heart. Tragically, he did not live to see himself on screen, passing away a month before his sixtieth birthday, on 13 April 1973, and a day after he had completed the dubbing of the film.

His last dialogue was, *'Insaan kab tak akela jee sakta hai?'* which is heartbreaking, seen in the context of his younger daughter Shabnam's untimely demise. The scene with Salim Mirza running up the stairs after learning that his daughter Amina has committed suicide was drawn from real life. Sathyu sahib had accompanied Balraj ji home from Bhopal where he had been campaigning for the elections. He remembered seeing him fly up the stairs and burst into his daughter's room, looking at her lifeless form stone-faced, refusing to break down. They had recreated the scene on screen and that time too Balraj ji had not shed a tear. But the shock of his daughter's death had broken his heart.

Shama Zaidi who worked on the costumes as well as the story and screenplay with Kaifi Azmi sahib, recalled Farooque sahib asking Balraj ji the difference between acting in a play and in a film. 'It's very simple, really,' he was told, 'In films you just stand and don't move around much... You don't even open your mouth as much as you would in a play, so if anything goes wrong, it's easy to fix it in the dubbing, but when you are live on stage, there are no retakes, no chance to rectify your mistake.'

It was sound advice and, more than three decades later, another debutant, Aanaahad Singh Khatkar, during the making of the sports drama *Lahore* (2010), remembers being given some advice of his own by Farooque sahib who was a veteran by this time. 'You don't need diction classes or any kind of special training really, all you have to do is feel from within. Acting comes with experience,' he told Aanaahad who recalls him as a considerate co-star who never retreated into his vanity van between shots even if he was not in the scene. 'He would stand out of the frame and give appropriate expressions so I or another actor could react to him and not to an assistant director reading out the lines when close-ups were being taken.'

Lahore won Farooque sahib the National Award for Best Supporting Actor for a performance so natural it did not feel like he was acting. 'When he scratched his head, it seemed real and not a gesture that had been worked into the script. That came from being completely involved with the film's script. Every page brought forth a volley of questions that helped him get under the skin of his character,' Aanaahad explained, pointing to a scene in the film where Saurabh Shukla and Farooque sahib's characters are enjoying a game of squash. 'He had never played squash before, but on the screen, the court looks like familiar territory for him. His body language was amazing as was his command over the language.'

When we spoke about his debut film, Farooque sahib had chuckled over the fact that he had been paid just ₹750 for it, and even that took over two decades to reach him, after the nominal signing amount of ₹150. But money was never a criterion for him doing a film. He came from a family of zamindars in Gujarat, was a qualified lawyer and at one time had his own flourishing garment export business. Always impeccably turned out in his trademark Lucknavi kurtas, he looked like a gracious aristocrat himself, with an old-world courtesy that his vocabulary mirrored. The *tehzeeb* in his language made me squirm over my own *Bambaiya* Hindi, but fortunately, I can string words on paper, so I got his nod of approval.

During an eight-month stint as an editor of a trade weekly, I once had a copy of the magazine delivered to his home so he could read his interview. He called back to thank me and ask how he could subscribe to the magazine so he could read it every week even if he didn't feature in it. 'I like the way you write, not everyone can.' His words gave me the courage to request for a quick telephonic whenever the need arose. He never said 'no'.

In the course of one such interview, he revealed that for *Lorie* (1984) he wasn't even paid a rupee. Yet, his only grouse was that his director-friend Vijay Talwar had not given him enough time to grow a real beard. 'For half the film, I had to stick on an irritatingly itchy false beard because he insisted my character Bhupi [Bhupinder Singh] needed a beard to look suitably distraught as he helplessly stands by watching his wife obsess over a child who is not even their own,' he laughed.

Fortunately for Farooque sahib, not all his directors wanted him to sport a beard or even a moustache. In fact, clean-shaven, with his trusting eyes and a boy-next-door appeal, he looked tailor-made for a film like *Noorie* (1979). He had only worked in Satyajit Ray's period drama, *Shatranj Ke Khiladi* (1977), the little remembered *Gher Gher Matina Chula* (1977) and Muzaffar Ali's searing social commentary *Gaman* (1978) till then. *Noorie*, on paper, seemed like a good commercial Bollywood film with a decent budget and was a Yash Chopra production to boot. 'But it turned out to be an equally arduous shoot in Kashmir and none of us got any star treatment,' he joked later.

Noorie was filmed in the dead of winter in the Bhaderwah Valley with the unit camped out in a school shut for the holidays. Forget room service, the classrooms didn't even have attached bathrooms. Even transport to and fro from the location was erratic. 'Yet, no one threw a single starry tantrum,' Farooque sahib reminisced. It was the only film directed by character actor Manmohan Krishna, and from day one of the shoot, he was confident that the film would be a hit. No one believed him. Yet, *Noorie* was a superhit and made Poonam Dhillon who had played the titular role, an overnight star.

Even before *Noorie*, Farooque sahib was doing a weekly show on Doordarshan, which, to quote him, had made him 'moderately famous'. 'But as an actor I never aroused hysteria,' he was quick to add. He laughed over how awkward and gawky he looked in the film. 'I wanted to choke myself when I saw myself on screen.' Candid and self-deprecating, he was a refreshing change from the self-proclaimed geniuses who could do no wrong in their own eyes.

After *Noorie*, for over two years, Farooque sahib turned down almost fifty films because all the roles were 'boringly similar to that of Yusuf Fakir Mohammed in *Noorie*.' Finally, Sai Paranjape approached him for *Chashme Buddoor* (1981), a comedy revolving around three roomies and the neighbourhood cutie. He loved Sai's script, and the role of the shy, bookish Siddharth Parashar was right up his alley. Delighted with his reaction, Sai put him through to the film's producer Gul Anand and there they ran into a roadblock.

'I quoted my price and he offered a lesser amount. I reasoned that I did not do more than a couple of films a year so I would not compromise on my fee. He argued that his budget would not allow him to pay me that much. We parted ways over a handshake,' Farooque sahib flashbacked to that meeting with Gul Anand.

The film might well have slipped out of his fingers had it not been for his director's tenacity. When he told her that he would love to do her film but wouldn't play Siddharth unless he got his price, Sai spoke to her producer, Gul Anand, who eventually, albeit reluctantly, agreed to the figure the actor had initially quoted.

Chashme Buddoor re-released on 5 April 2013—the same day that David Dhawan's rebooted *Chashme Baddoor* also hit theatres. It was a first for Hindi cinema, both films arriving in the theatres on the same Friday. The Saturday before, our telephonic was set for 4 p.m. After several calls to him went unanswered, I began to panic as the Sunday deadline loomed. I called the editor and warned her that I might not be able to deliver the piece because Farooque sahib had inexplicably disappeared.

He called two hours later, profusely apologetic. He had been dubbing, and with the phone on mute, our appointment had skipped his mind. 'Is it too late for you?' he asked, more worried that I may have missed my deadline than him having lost out on an interview. 'It's never too late when it's you,' I assured him, wondering how he felt about the remake. Instead of the expected tirade about how cult classics should be left well alone, he told me that he was looking forward to seeing what Rishi Kapoor, whose *Rafoo Chakkar* (1975) he had loved, would make of Saeed Jaffri's Lallan Miyan.

Pakistani actor Ali Zafar, a huge Farooque Shaikh fan, who stepped into his shoes in David Dhawan's contemporary take, singled out his favourite scene from the original *Chashme Buddoor*. It was when Deepti Naval's salesgirl comes calling at the trio's bachelor pad in the hope that she will be able to sell them a packet of Chamko detergent. Ravi Baswani and Rakesh Bedi as Jai and Omi who had been unsuccessfully trying to woo Neha with a litany of lies, afraid that she would expose them to Siddharth, hop on to the balcony ledge, leaving him to open the door.

Since Siddharth was in the middle of shaving, Farooque sahib had to do the scene with shaving cream lathered all over his chin and cheeks. And because cinematographer Virendra Sahni was a master of retakes, he woke up the next morning with an itchy rash all over his face all thanks to having been smothered in shaving cream for too long! However, it was a small price to pay for a silver jubilee hit, which still draws an audience, almost four decades after its release.

In a career in journalism spanning three decades, I have met and spoken to many actors across generations, but there are few who are so quick to praise a co-actor. In Sai's *Katha* (1983), Farooque sahib played Bashudev, a human magpie who tricks everyone and steals everything, from money and rings to the hearts of daughters and wives and eventually, the thunder from his senior colleague Naseeruddin Shah. When I made the observation, he acknowledged that though his performance had fetched him rave reviews and compliments galore, he had his co-star to thank for it. 'It was because Naseer sahib was confident enough to underplay his character that the contrast between Rajaram Purshotam Joshi and Bashudev could be underlined, and I got so much praise,' he asserted.

Sai shared the script of *Katha* with Farooque sahib before anyone else and offered him the pick of roles. Since he had already played Mr Goody Two Shoes in *Chashme Buddoor*, Farooque sahib opted for the negative role much to her delight. The 'hero' image had never figured in his list of must-haves and after his untimely death, his much-loved writer-director recalled the playful one-upmanship between her two lead actors. Farooque sahib would tell her that if they were in a shot together, Naseer sahib's back should be to the camera, to which the latter would retort that his back was more expressive than Farooque sahib's face!

The year that *Chashme Buddoor* released, Farooque sahib was also seen in another film, from another era, remade by J.P. Dutta in 2006. In the original *Umrao Jaan* (1981), he played Nawab Sultan, a weak-willed aristocrat who doesn't have the courage to fight for the woman he loves and tamely submits to a match arranged by his mother. In real life, he was the polar opposite of the Nawab. He had met his wife Roopa at a sangeet mandal when studying at St Xavier's College in Bombay (present-day Mumbai). They belonged to different communities, but for nine years, Farooque sahib fought to convince everyone that he was the right match for her. Love finally triumphed, they got married and went on to parent two beautiful daughters, Shaista and Sanaa, whom he doted on.

Muzaffar Ali had earlier cast him as a migrant cab driver in *Gaman*. It was during the making of this film that he had told Farooque sahib that he was planning a film on Mirza Hadi Ruswa's Urdu novel, *Umrao Jaan Ada*. 'He knew the milieu well and was familiar with the language too. I was confident he would do a good job and when I read the script, I was even more convinced,' Farooque sahib pointed out.

Umrao Jaan was an absolute contrast to *Gaman*, a lavishly mounted spectacle that brought gasps of awe from the audience. Farooque sahib recounted how Dina Pathak, Rekha and he had shivered through an overnight train journey from Delhi to Lucknow in the dead of winter because the production guy had forgotten to arrange for bed rolls. 'We had been promised a good night's sleep, but forget about sleeping, we could barely sit without our teeth chattering. Dina ji had a shawl, but Rekha ji had only a dupatta to ward off the chill, yet not a word of complaint slipped past her lips,' he narrated, and as was typical of him, only focused on the discomfort of the ladies rather than his own.

On the return journey, everyone made sure that their bedding was on board before they boarded the train back to Delhi. But when they reached the capital, they discovered to their horror that this time the production guy had forgotten to arrange for cars to pick them up from the railway station. So, what did Farooque sahib do? He simply queued up for a cab, with Rekha ji, beside him. Fortunately for everyone, because he looked like a common man and his glamorous co-star had used her dupatta to mask her identity, they were not recognized.

Nawab Sultan may not have been every woman's dream

lover, but heartfelt lyrics from songs such as his *'Zindagi jab bhi teri bazm mein laati hai hamen, yeh zameen chand se behtar nazar aati hain hamein'* and Umrao's heartbreaking *'Justuju jisski thi usko to na paaya hamnein, iss bahane magar dekh li duniya hamein'* ensured that their brief on-screen romance crested the peaks of passion and plumbed the depths of despair. Perhaps because Farooque sahib was one of those rare erudite Hindi film actors who appreciated the wealth of words, not just *Umrao Jaan*, many of his other film songs are still unforgettable.

⁂

Once, when we were discussing *Saath Saath* (1982), which to me is memorable as much for its tale of relationships as its musical gems like *'Tumko dekha to yeh khayal aaya'*, *'Kyun zindagi ki raah mein majboor ho gaye'* and *'Yeh tera ghar yeh mera ghar'*, he pointed out that while Javed Akhtar may have written better songs individually but collectively the lyrics of this film are his best works. 'He will probably write a poem berating me for saying this,' he guffawed. Interestingly, this was Javed sahib's first stint as a songwriter, and while the film released much later, after listening to *Saath Saath* Yash Chopra gave him a break as a lyricist in *Silsila* (1981) and we got *'Neela asmaan so gaya'*.

Farooque sahib who worked with Rekha ji again in *Biwi Ho To Aisi* (1988) admitted that she challenged him as an actor and pushed him as a co-star because she was punctual to the dot, as he had learnt during 7 a.m. shoots in freezing Lucknow during *Umrao Jaan*. He also shared that she never read her lines but had them read out loud to her by the assistant director before every scene. To his amazement, during 'take' she got every word right.

Deepti Naval, with whom he reunited after twenty-eight

years in *Listen... Amaiya* (2013), also remembers the long conversations they would have on cinema, writing and life itself. Farooque sahib was delighted that their producer's bungalow in Delhi's Sundar Nagar where they shot much of the film, boasted of a wonderful collection of books and was close to the capital's famous eateries. This meant there was plenty of food for the mind and the body. His only grouse was that Miss Chamko continued to munch on her salads while he savoured his Mughlai meals. 'The *ghas phus* shows on her, while the solid food shows on me,' he rued, referring to the extra kilos he had put on.

Films like *Lahore* and *Listen... Amaiya* were few and far between, and because he was not interested in run-of-the-mill formula movies or the rat race, Farooque sahib slowly moved away from cinema and towards television. His performances as the poet-cum-freedom fighter Hasrat Mohani, Sarat Chandra Chattopadhyay's Srikant and the politician in *Ji Mantriji* were noteworthy but they weren't enough. 'I have become famous for turning down a lot of work,' he admitted with a wry smile when I complained that we missed seeing him on screen. 'But acting was always more a passion than a profession while filmmaking was all about storytelling. Stories that left you thinking long after the movie was over...stories that took you into a world beyond your own.'

Given how choosy he was, debutant director Sanjay Tripathy was surprised when he gave his nod to *Club 60* (2013). The story, penned by Sanjay himself, revolved around a middle-aged couple whose lives splinter after the death of their only son. Hoping to find meaning to their existence, the doctor duo shifts to Pune where their annoying talkative neighbour, Manu Bhai, introduces them to 'Club 60' for whose members life begins at sixty.

Farooque sahib who was sixty-plus himself, instantly empathized with the cynically depressed neurosurgeon, Dr Tariq Sheikh, he played, though he later admitted to Sanjay that he would have preferred to play Raghubir Yadav's garrulous Manu Bhai, pointing out that he could even speak Gujarati fluently. In response to Sanjay's protesting 'But sir, you could have told me this,' he laughed, pointing out, 'Well, you never offered me the role.' As was typical of him, once he accepted a role, Farooque sahib owned it, improvising on dialogue and turning *nalayak* to *namakool*, reasoning that since Dr Tariq was an educated Muslim, it was but natural that his vocabulary would have more Urdu than Hindi. He was an intellectual himself, well read and well spoken, with a balanced world view who could speak on any subject without getting argumentative or offensive.

Sanjay revealed that while on the set he appeared casual, cracking jokes and spreading laughs, but as soon as the camera started rolling, he instantly slipped into character and his performance underlined just how much of prep work he had done. 'He knew every word of the script and every nuance of his character. He was also always sensitive to his co-stars and was a friend of the unit, bringing them baskets of mangoes from his orchards and the best sweets Mumbai had to offer. He even hosted a dinner prepared by the best *khansamha* in Pune,' recounted Sanjay, adding that once Sarika ji and he had been drawn into a mithai-eating competition, which Farooque sahib won hands down.

Even after the shoot was over, he stayed in touch and would call once in a while to invite Sanjay home to sample some mithai he had ordered and send across biryani and sevaiyan over during Eid. On one occasion, he dragged the filmmaker off to Mohammed Ali Road and into a modest eatery by the name of Noor Mohammedi whose biryani and 'Sanju Baba Chicken' (named after actor Sanjay Dutt) he rated higher than any five-star meal! He sat on a bench in the dhaba with the other diners, despite being a familiar face as *Yeh Jawaani Hai Deewaani* (2013) in which he had played Ranbir Kapoor's father had just released, relishing the pungent dishes, which made his nose and eyes water.

Ghazal singer Talat Aziz who had collaborated with him on *Bayaan-e-Ghalib*—a unique fusion of theatre and music with Talat Aziz, Farooque Shaikh and Salim Arif on the legendary poet Mirza Ghalib, his ghazals and his letters—with Farooque sahib as Ghalib, bonded with him over food. 'When Javed [Akhtar] sahib, Shabana [Azmi] ji and Farooque sahib came to Hyderabad while on a tour, I got a tiffin of biryani, *mirchi ka salan* [stuffed chillies] and *baghaar-e-baigan* [stuffed brinjals] to the hotel and he was only too happy to dig in,' he reminisced fondly.

Sanjay added that Farooque sahib was very particular that the food should be fresh and be made from organic produce. 'Even his honey came from the jungles of Madhya Pradesh,' he informed, going on to reveal that while he was a *dil ka raja*, Farooque sahib didn't think twice about hopping into an autorickshaw if his chauffeur didn't turn up or his wife and daughters drove off with the car.

His *Lahore* co-star, Aanaahad, recalled Farooque sahib telling him that in Mumbai's terrible traffic, '*kaun gaadi ka bojh le ke ghoome* [who wants the burden of a car]'. One evening, when Shama Zaidi was trying desperately to flag down an autorickshaw on the road, he pulled up beside her in one and gave her a lift. When asked to pick her favourite Farooque Shaikh performance, Shama picked *Tumhari Amrita*.

This experimental play, directed by Feroz Abbas Khan and

written by Javed Siddiqui, was a story of unrequited love told through letters exchanged between Amrita Pritam and Zulfiqar Haider over thirty-five years, starting on her eighth birthday party. It was not like any regular performance. There was no theatrics, no lighting, just two people on stage reading these letters. 'My brief to them was to not memorize the words, but to react to them only if they were affected. For me, Javed Siddiqui was the star of this show. I wanted his words to reach Shabana and Farooque in the purest way and for them to give them back to the audience without any kind of corruption,' Feroz told me years later, adding they had an audience of eight at the first technical rehearsal, of which all eight nodded off.

Tumhari Amrita opened at Prithvi Theatre on 27 February 1992, on the first day of a three-day fest on Jennifer Kendal's birth anniversary. After the shock reaction at the rehearsal, Feroz came on stage before the curtains went up to prepare the audience for a play unlike any they had seen before. Still the reactions were muted and Feroz, already petrified, was convinced it was their biggest disaster. 'While Shabana and I were nervous and on edge, Farooque was always very calm, telling us everything would be fine. And later, when I spoke to people from the audience, I realized that though they may not have clapped as was usual, they were deeply affected. But till the last performance, despite Farooque's assurance, I continued to wonder every time if it would work that day,' Feroz confided.

He admitted that Shabana ji and the bohemian Amrita shared the same spirit and challenged each other. But Farooque sahib, while he was quick to grasp the character of Zulfi and understand his journey with extraordinary sensitivity, had more spine than him. 'Zulfi cracks at the end, Farooque never would,' asserted the director, who, watching them on stage, had pictured them in his mind as a couple—beautiful, cultured and happily married. 'When I told them this, they burst out laughing and when I grew to know them better, I realized it would have been a disaster of a marriage.'

However, they shared a friendship that went beyond the stage and the screen. Together, the trio took *Tumhari Amrita* not just across India, but also to the United States, even performing for the United Nations. They travelled with it to Europe and even went to Pakistan when the country was ravaged by an earthquake. Whether it was an earthquake or a chair in the university, the play supported several causes and various charitable organizations, making huge contributions socially.

The last performance was on 14 December 2013. As part of the Taj Literary Fest, they performed in front of the Taj Mahal, in front of 5,000-strong audience who watched it out in the open, in the biting cold, in speechless wonder. As the curtains came down, an overwhelmed Shabana ji told Farooque sahib that after twenty-one years, it was time for them to take the last curtain call and for Feroz to get himself new actors. He laughed her off saying they were good to go on for another twenty-one years and would perform it even when in a wheelchair. He then asked Feroz to send him some photographs of this particular show. 'I was surprised because he had never made such a request before,' the director confided.

Thirteen days later, Farooque Shaikh took his last curtain call—from the world.

I will never forget the day, 27 December 2013. I woke up to the news that while I had been sleeping, Farooque sahib had succumbed to a heart attack in a hospital in Dubai while on a family vacation. This was one obituary I had to write. I had to say goodbye.

I was in tears for most part of the day as friends and

colleagues spoke about the man and the actor. His *Club 60* co-star, Sarika, pointed out that it felt strange to refer to him as 'was' rather than 'is' while the film's director who got a hug from him after the first show and the promise of another film, revealed later that they had discussed some ideas, including a book whose rights Sanjay had bought. In the evening, when I was still in office, putting the finishing touches to his obituary, Shabana ji called. Ever since his wife Roopa had reached out to her with the news of Farooque sahib's death, she had been frantically busy. In the midst of making arrangements for his body to be flown home, she assured me that she would share memories of 'her Zulfi' when she had a moment. All day, there hadn't been time for tears, but while speaking about that last performance at the Taj, she finally broke down. 'Who will replace him in the play?' I asked, tears streaming down my own cheeks as I remembered the two of them together. 'No one can replace him. It's the final curtain call for me in *Tumhari Amrita*,' she replied between sobs.

Many years have passed since that fateful day. Sometimes I write a column on his birthday, but after that obituary, I haven't been able to pen another piece on his death anniversary. He was a man who had celebrated life through his show, *Jeena Iss Ka Naam Hai*. A compassionate human being, he not only connected with people, but stayed in touch. He was not tech savvy, but he was constantly texting with both hands on his Nokia phone, and there were wishes on Diwali, Eid and New Year. His *Lahore* co-star Aanaahad confided that he got regular texts from Farooque sahib, right up to his untimely death, asking, '*Barkhurdaar, kaise ho*? How are you doing? If you need any kind of help, do meet me,' while Talat Aziz sahib shared that he had got a last SMS from him, three days before he passed away, wishing him a Merry Christmas and a Happy

New Year. 'I could not bring myself to delete it,' he admitted.

I know the feeling. It took me a year to erase his number from my phone directory. But even today, I can still lull myself into believing that he's around and may just call one day to ask, 'So, what's this book you are doing?' and we can go on to talk more on his chapter. Why did God have to woo him away so soon? Maybe he promised him home-cooked biryani and a platter full of palatable stories, leaving us with only a handful of memories.

9

AAMIR KHAN: A MAN FOR ALL SEASONS

*Papa kehte hain bada naam karega,
beta humara aisa kaam karega*

I saw him for the first time on a life-size billboard, several of which had suddenly mushroomed on the skyline of the Maximum City. He had his back to the camera, and the catchline on the banner left me wondering, 'Who is this Aamir Khan?'

The next set of hoardings revealed his side profile, but he still remained faceless. Once again, I asked myself, 'Who the hell is this Aamir Khan?'

Even when the question was partially answered, 'Ask the girls next door,' the mystery of Aamir Khan remained unsolved because the girls next door didn't know him. It was only when the last in the series of billboards announced, 'See him in *Qayamat Se Qaymat Tak*,' that I realized he was another one of Bollywood's new faces.

With a little digging I discovered that Aamir Khan was actually a star kid—filmmaker Tahir Husain's son and the nephew of producer-director, Nasir Husain, whose *Teesri Manzil* (1966), *Yaadon Ki Baaraat* (1973) and

Hum Kisise Kum Naheen (1977) ranked among my favourite films. But just because he was the inheritor of a legacy and Nasir sahib was launching him, didn't mean that I had to like the desi Romeo or his debut film *Qayamat Se Qayamat Tak* (1988), which going by its title sounded like a Ramsay horror flick! In fact, I went to the theatre prepared to dislike both the film and its hero but came out humming, '*Papa kehte hain bada naam karega*'. In retrospect, the words were prophetic because never again did I or for that matter, anyone else ever ask, 'Who is Aamir Khan?'

Milind, of the composer duo Anand–Milind, who scored the film's music, remembers Aamir as a cute, fair boy, younger than both his brother and him. Nasir sahib's bungalow was under renovation at the time and he had shifted into a building that was a stone's throw away from the brothers' music room in Khar. There were plenty of story and music sessions there, with the producer and his son Mansoor who was debuting as a director with *Qayamat Se Qayamat Tak*. Aamir was present at every one of these sessions and one day, Milind casually suggested to Mansoor that he rope in his cousin to play Raj as he looked the part. Aamir had already appeared in Nasir sahib's *Yaadon Ki Baaraat* as a child of eight and then, eleven years later, in Ketan Mehta's coming-of-age drama *Holi* (1984) as a rebellious collegian. 'A fortnight after I made the suggestion, I learnt that Aamir had been cast opposite former Miss India Juhi Chawla,' Milind shared.

At the film's thirty years' reunion, Aamir recalled how they had shot the climax during the first schedule in Ooty. And like a true Romeo, he had hurtled down the cliff to cradle his dying Juliet in his arms after she is fatally shot. Everything went off perfectly till he called her 'Juhi' instead of 'Rashmi'. The mistake was rectified in the next take and the scene was completed to everyone's satisfaction. Everyone but Nasir sahib.

The story had been penned by the veteran filmmaker though he admitted that his daughter Nusrat and nephew Aamir had contributed a lot to the screenplay. Shooting was delayed because an ailing Nasir sahib had gone abroad for treatment. Even after he returned, the doctors advised another six months rest, which was when he handed over the reins to his reluctant son. Once he was in the saddle, Mansoor made some changes to the screenplay, which were reflected in the characters, their emotional graph and most importantly, the climax. Still in his early twenties, he argued that since the film began with betrayal, suicide, murder and the advent of doom, it had to end with another *qayamat*. His father didn't share his views because after the failure of the Rajesh Khanna and Asha Parekh musical romance *Baharon Ke Sapne* (1967), whose tragic ending had to be changed in the second week after a lukewarm response, Nasir sahib was convinced that unhappy love stories didn't work. But Mansoor believed that the audience didn't mind a good cry occasionally if it was justified. His father didn't agree and would call up every evening during the schedule in Ooty and insist that they also shoot a happily-ever-after ending. Mansoor eventually complied to appease his father. 'And till the time of release, the debate raged over which ending to go with,' Milind reminisced.

While several members of the team, including the distributors, wanted the film to end conventionally—Raj and Rashmi bringing the feud between their families to an end with the promise of marital bliss—Mansoor continued to push for a tragic conclusion. After hours of debate, he eventually prevailed upon everyone to go along with his vision. His music director duo was among the few who shared his conviction, but right till the evening of the premiere, Milind admitted that they were worried about the film's box office fate. For composer Chitragupt's sons, it was important that their entry into Bollywood does well, and both Anand and Milind, like the rest of the team, were a bundle of nerves till the interval when they heard guests curiously enquiring about the hero. 'By the time the film ended, there were hordes of people waiting outside to catch a glimpse of Aamir Khan and we went home relieved,' Milind smiled.

Qayamat Se Qayamat Tak, or *QSQT* as it came to be called, opened on 29 April 1988. It was a blockbuster and bagged the National Award for Best Popular Film Providing Wholesome Entertainment. It also picked up eight Filmfare statuettes when the awards commenced after a two-year break in 1990. I remember Aamir spent most of the evening running up to collect trophies for various members of his team who had not turned up. Eventually, he got one of his own too, but admitted later that he was disappointed the Best Actor Award went to Anil Kapoor for *Tezaab* (1988) and that the Best Debutant Award felt more like a consolation prize. 'If it had been for best newcomer over the last ten years it might have been more meaningful,' he stated.

Earlier in the evening, he had grooved to the peppy *'Papa kehte hain bada naam karega'* and made his own father proud. But Tahir sahib had never wanted Aamir to follow in his footsteps. Knowing the insecurities of show business, he had kept his four children away from film shoots and galas, but his son had inherited his passion for movies and there was no stopping him.

In the film, the song, *'Papa kehte hain bada naam karega',* appears twice, once early on when Dalip Tahil, who played Raj's father Dhanraj Singh, arrives at his son's college celebration after serving a jail term for murder. Sitting in the audience, he proudly watches Raj croon. A snatch of the same song plays in the end, after Raj and Rashmi die in each other's arms. Mansoor had sketched out the situation to Anand and Milind and one morning, mulling over it, the latter was sitting in the open veranda of their ground floor residence, strumming his guitar, when suddenly the tune came to him. He played it to his brother who loved it, after which they called veteran lyricist Majrooh Sultanpuri who came up with a brilliant mukhda, *'Papa kehte hain bada naam karega, beta hamara aisa kaam karega, magar yeh to, koi na jaane, ki meri manzil hai kahan.'* 'The thought was so universal that we instantly knew it would resonate with every parent and child. And to this day, we sing this song at every function on popular demand. It has also become Aamir's signature tune,' Milind recounted proudly.

That year, at the Filmfare Awards too, Aamir grooved to *'Papa kehte hain'* to a rousing reception. But the night before, during rehearsals, he had been on edge because he was not getting his facial expressions right. Only Aamir would spend a sleepless night worrying over something like this, despite knowing that the stage was far away from the audience. Even back then, Aamir was 'Mr Perfectionist', a tag he owns today. In fact, Milind disclosed that Aamir had learnt to strum the guitar for the song so he could appear convincing on screen.

Those days every successful Bollywood actor, from Amitabh Bachchan to Aamir Khan, went for concert tours across the United States, the United Kingdom and Canada. While performing on stage, Aamir would pick up a guitar and pretend to strum it when the song came on, while guitarist Raju Singh made music backstage. He got caught out once when the wire plugged to the electric guitar came loose and trailed behind him as he flitted around the stage even as the music continued to play! When hoots alerted him to this fact, Aamir who was still only in his early twenties, showed great presence of mind, taking the crowd into confidence and reasoning that even in the film, a singer gave playback for him while the musicians played their instruments. That was exactly what he had been doing on stage too. The confession brought his fans to their feet and they cheered even louder for him.

But after *QSQT,* Aamir was in danger of being dubbed a 'one film wonder' because the films that followed like *Love Love Love* (1989), *Awwal Number* (1990), *Tum Mere Ho* (1990), *Deewana Mujh Sa Nahin* (1990), *Jawani Zindabad* (1990) tumbled like nine pins. Lounging in his make-up room at Bombay's RK Studio while waiting for director Shekhar Kapur to set up a shot for the fantasy adventure *Time Machine*, Aamir was unfazed by the carping Cassandras. He admitted that he had taken some hasty decisions, but he was quick to add that he had started cutting down on his work. Given a chance, he told me, he would happily quit films for a year to sit by the side of his pregnant wife Reena. 'But there are commitments I have made that have to be honoured,' he reasoned, adding that he also wanted to buy a house of his own, for his wife and soon-to-arrive child. 'It takes me a year or two to earn the money I need, and when I do, I find that the price of real estate has gone up and the property I was looking to buy is out of my reach. And so, I have to start all over again,' he sighed. His words struck an empathetic chord because my husband and I having recently tied the knot, were also struggling to put a permanent roof over our heads. A few years later, both of us managed to buy our own apartments. And over the years, he did cut down his work, to a film or at best two, every year or every other year.

Scripts were carefully scrutinized, questions asked, the credentials of a director vetted and if necessary, changes incorporated before Aamir ran with it. In the process there were some casualties. Not many are aware that Lawrence D'Souza had first offered him the role of the polio-stricken poet in *Saajan* (1991). 'But how can a woman fall in love with a name? As soon as Pooja learns that Akash [played by Salman Khan] is not Sagar she promptly falls out of love with him. How's that possible?' he argued. The role was passed on to Sanjay Dutt after Aamir reportedly insisted on seeing the rushes of Lawrence's under-production film, *Nyay Anyay* (1990), irking producer Sudhakar Bokadia in the process. *Saajan* was one of the biggest grossers of the year, but Aamir was a marathon man, not a 100-metres sprinter. That's the reason why, thirty years later, he's still in the race while many of his contemporaries have long since dropped out.

Time Machine did not take off, despite him allotting a hundred and fifty days to the film. But with Indra Kumar's *Dil* (1990) and Mahesh Bhatt's *Dil Hai Ke Manta Nahin* (1991), Aamir returned to being the heartthrob of the nation. Back then I lived next door to the derelict Mukesh Mills where the *Dil* chartbuster '*Aaj na chodenge dum dama dum*' was being shot. Late one evening, I strolled across for a dekko and I was impressed to see Aamir matching Madhuri Dixit's *matkas* with *jhatkas* of his own. Indu ji, as Indra Kumar is fondly called, revealed later that he hadn't been able to shoot his favourite composition from the Anand-Milind album before the film's release because money had run out. But once the cash counters started jingling again, he decided to picturize a dance face-off between Aamir and Madhuri on the sets of his under-production film *Beta* (1992). The song was incorporated in the film as an 'added attraction' and brought the audience back for a second and third viewing. And *Dil* went on to become one of the biggest grossers of 1990.

Almost three decades later, when I met Madhuri during the promotions of *Total Dhamaal* (2019), another Indra Kumar film, she nostalgically recalled all the fun and frolic on the sets of *Dil* as she and her hero, along with the film's cinematographer Baba Azmi, romped around like carefree kids. One day, Aamir gravely asked to see her hand. Excited on thinking that he was a palmist, she trustingly held it out. Gently, he took her hand between his, intently peered down at the lines crisscrossing her palm and murmured, 'I can see that someone is going to make a fool of you.' Then, before the words could sink in, he spat into her proffered palm. Her eyes rounded in horror, Madhuri had looked down at the glob of saliva, too shocked initially to react because Aamir had seemed like such a well-behaved boy during the film's first schedule. Then, as the shock had worn off, she had picked up a stick and chased the prankster all around the studio, with a bewildered Indu ji hollering, *'Kya ho raha hai?'* [What is happening?]'

During his second film with Mansoor, the sports drama *Jo Jeeta Wohi Sikander* (1992), Ayesha Jhulka was urged by her leading man to try on a bangle he had bought. She had eagerly unwrapped the package and an insect had wriggled on to her hand, even as her scream had echoed around the studio. Yet, Ayesha has fond memories of the actor. 'Mansoor would praise me for my chaste Hindi, and one day, Aamir decided he and I would take a test to decide whose command over the language was better,' she flashbacked. Aamir goofed up on the spelling of *'khoobsurat'* but when Ayesha pointed out that 'beautiful' in Hindi was not spelt with a *chhoti oo-ki-matra*, he quipped that the lady he had been describing was only 'slightly beautiful' so he had refrained from using the *badi oo-ki-matra*. 'After that, whenever we met, we would joke over whether someone was *khubsoorat* or *khoobsurat*,' she laughed.

Having said this, Aamir's innate sense of mischief also caused a rift with his first co-star. Since he was a child, he had brought strays home and when filming Tahir sahib's *Tum Mere Ho*, in which he played a snake charmer, he had adopted a baby cobra. His family was far from charmed by his new pet and it was soon banished despite his pleas. Six years later, on the set of *Ishq* (1997), he had befriended another snake and had tried to convince his heroine, Juhi Chawla, to hold and pet it. The terrified actress took to her heels.

That year, they were shooting together on her birthday, 13 November, and after Juhi had cut the cake, Aamir had grabbed a chunk of it and smeared it all over her perfectly done up face. And like Madhuri, she had chased him around the studio with Indu ji egging her on. The fun and laughs, however, ended abruptly when one day, Aamir over-stepped his boundaries and made his leading lady cry. Juhi never did say what he had done, but she was so angry that she did not to turn up on the sets the next day. This angered Aamir who was a producer's son and knew just how much money her sudden absence had cost the producer. They did not speak for a long time. The following year, on her birthday again, Juhi had gone looking for Aamir. When told he was in a meeting with Amol Palekar in his vanity van, she had quietly returned to the *Ishq* set and cut the cake. However, it was not the same without her co-star, she admitted later. Still, it took a few more years for her to pick up the phone and attempt to bridge the gap. Aamir was quick to reciprocate, admitting that he had contemplated doing the same many times earlier, but refrained thinking she might rebuff him.

My own relationship with Aamir has had its own ups and downs, with long periods of silence in between. I met him for the first time at Satyam Dance Hall near Mumbai's Juhu beach where he was rehearsing for a concert tour. I requested him for an interview, expecting him to tell me that I should call his secretary and set up a date as was the common practice then. Instead, he whipped out an organizer, tapped a few keys and informed me that we could meet on a particular day between 4.15 and 4.35 p.m. before returning to his dance practice. 'Did you get the interview?' my editor asked when I returned to office still in a daze. I shook my head, saying, 'No, but we will, if we can wait three months.'

On the appointed day, Aamir was punctual to the dot, patiently answered every query I posed. In all the years that I have known him, he has never ducked a bouncer or been clean bowled by a googly. But once, before Amitabh Bachchan started the practice of videotaping his interviews so he would not be misquoted, misinterpreted or misrepresented, Aamir took me by surprise by putting a bulky tape recorder on the table between us. I was questioning him on his controversial exit from a film and catching my quizzical look, he pointed out that since I was recording his answers, it was only fair that he did the same.

Back then Aamir reminded me of Rodin's Thinker as he would ponder over every question for a long time, much to the exasperation of journalists. Once he even made me read out all that he had said so he could ponder some more and give me something that was 'just right'.

Then, one day, he stopped talking. Just like that.

This was at the turn of the century when upset with tabloids and magazines for aggressively probing into his personal life, Aamir hit back and stopped speaking to several English magazines, including the one I worked for. But even when we were on opposite sides of the fence, spotting me standing in the blazing sun one afternoon, waiting for his co-star to call me into her air-conditioned vanity van for an interview, he sent his man Friday across with a chair and the offer of chai. That's Aamir for you.

The two-year impasse did not affect either *Fanaa* (2006) or *Rang De Basanti* (2006), with both films going on to become huge hits. It was lifted a few months before he unveiled his first directorial, *Taare Zameen Par* (2007). I turned up at his office a little past 4 p.m. to find it already crowded with journalists, not just from dailies and film magazines, but also one from a financial paper who needed a crash course on his filmography. After a two-and-a-half-hour wait, we moved from Aamir's office to the waiting room of his Bandra residence, which was a five-minute drive up Pali Hill. By the time my turn came, I was hungry, weary and disgruntled because I wasn't home as usual with my young daughter. Perhaps that's why the questions came out a little too abrasive, even intrusive. I could see that he was getting upset, even angry, but to be fair, he answered every query, however provocative, keeping a tight leash on his own temper. But when we were done, he asked for a five-minute break before the next Q&A session to fructify himself.

The interview, I realize in retrospect, came out more harsh than hard-hitting, as his publicist pointed out. At the time the observation made me bristle. I went to see *Taare Zameen Par* seething. And as it had happened during *QSQT*, I came out loving Aamir Khan for changing the way we, as parents, perceive education, emphasizing that it's not just about rote learning, but creative development.

We did not interact for the next two years. Then, suddenly,

one day, I got a call, 'Will you interview Aamir for *3 Idiots* [2009]?' I declined. His publicist was aghast. 'Why not?' she prodded. I told her that I did not like talking to a star knowing the buzzer would go off any minute. Also, more than his upcoming film that was again on the education system and our quest for meaningless degrees, I wanted to chat with Aamir on his many commercials, which like his films showcased his versatility. 'Since all this will take a while and he is undoubtedly hard-pressed for time, I will take a rain check,' I reiterated. I hung up believing that I would never get another interview with Aamir Khan, but his publicist called back shortly to say I could take all the time I wanted, he was game.

I reached producer Vidhu Vinod Chopra's office somewhat sceptical, convinced that he would cut short our conversation once we were done with my questions on the film he was promoting. But true to his word, the highest paid and one of the most successful brand ambassadors of the country, spoke about some of his most memorable campaigns. Aamir admitted that he was the one who had come up with the brainwave of recreating his screen avatars from *Rangeela* (1995), *Ghulam* (1998), *Sarfarosh* (1999), *Lagaan* (2001) and *Dil Chahta Hai* (2001), complete with all their mannerisms and personality quirks, taking them along for a ride in his new spacious Tata Innova. When Prasoon Pandey, the creative director of the commercial selling the family car, had worried about finding the right costumes and accessories, Aamir had simply thrown open a few trunks. In them, Prasoon had discovered Bhuvan's dhoti, Siddhu's cap and chains and all the rest that had gone into making Akash, Ajay Singh Rathod and Munna unforgettable.

When the conversation turned to *3 Idiots*, which starts out with him as a college kid, Aamir revealed that when Vinod Chopra and director Raju Hirani had come to him with the role of Rancho, he had suggested that they take an actor who was twenty-two rather than one who was forty-four and expected to look twenty-two. But they had insisted on him because, in many ways, he was so much like the character who also did not like following rules. Perhaps that's why he has been able to break free of stereotypical roles and gamble his career on films such as these.

Soon after the interview appeared, I was taking a stroll around my building one evening when my cell phone buzzed. The voice at the other end introduced himself as Aamir Khan and invited me to a press conference the following day. I told the caller curtly that our newspaper did not cover press conferences. 'But this one will be different,' he promised. I wasn't convinced about either the interaction or the caller's identity. I believed it was a prankster friend who would call off and on pretending to be someone else and I told him as much. After he had rung off, I buzzed his publicist to warn her that someone masquerading as Aamir Khan was inviting journalists to non-existent press conferences. She laughed, 'It was actually Aamir, he took your number from me and said he would invite you himself.' Embarrassed, I dashed out in the middle of edition the next afternoon to check out Aamir's game plan. It infuriated me when he didn't turn up for the presser, his recorded voice informing the assembled media that he had taken off on a 'Discover India' tour as part of the film's unique promotional campaign and would be travelling through the country incognito. He dared everyone to spot and unmask him.

I was livid to be drawn away from my desk by a promotional gimmick. When I vented, I was promised an interview on his return. I didn't expect it to happen, but once again, Aamir kept his word, telling me over the course of an hour-long telephonic interview about his experiences on the road. One of the highpoints of his Bharat darshan had been lunch at cricketer Saurav Ganguly's home in Kolkata. Since he had dropped by on a Thursday, a vegetarian day for many Bengalis, the usual fish and mutton delicacies were not on the menu. But he had returned licking his fingers after his first authentic Bengali meal. When I asked for details, he called out to his second wife, Kiran Rao, who had spent the first eighteen years of her life in Kolkata, to help him with the names of the dishes. Together they slurped over *aloo posto* and *shukto, luchi* and *begun bhaja, mishti doi, sandesh* and *roshogullas*.

That day, I realized he was a foodie and despite having grown up on biryani and kebabs, didn't mind the occasional greens and grains. Still, it came as a shock when six years later, I reached his apartment around nine in the evening, to find him dining on a pile of vegetable sandwiches. Since at the time he was prepping for the wrestling drama *Dangal* (2016), and his weight had ballooned to 90 kilograms, I had expected him to be feasting like a king. But Aamir had chosen this time in his life to cut meat, fish, eggs, paneer and even his much-loved sweets from his diet. Nudged by Kiran, he had turned vegan just short of his fiftieth birthday after watching an hour-long video on YouTube. It had convinced him to make this lifestyle change in the interest of good health. Sipping tea laced with soy milk, he urged me to turn vegan too. I have to confess that I am still a carnivore.

One of the turning points of Aamir's career was *Raja Hindustani*. It was the highest grossing film of 1996 and the third highest earner of the decade after *Hum Aapke Hain Koun..!* (1994) and *Dilwale Dulhania Le Jayenge* (1995). *Raja Hindustani* bagged Aamir his first Filmfare Award for Best Actor. Dharmesh Darshan, the film's director, revealed that he had been warned that the actor ghost-directed his films.

'I asked him straight, how many directors would there be on the project.' His answer was simple, 'There will be only one director and that's you. A film is made from the vision of just one director.'

Dharmesh remembers Aamir as an intelligent actor with a lot of questions, one who actively and conscientiously participated in the filmmaking process, but was never difficult or interfering. When questioned on the subject, Aamir had himself asserted that on the set he makes his point known, but never imposes his will beyond a point.

Only once, during *Ghulam* (1998), reportedly watching Mahesh Bhatt nonchalantly read a novel instead of supervising the shot, he had walked up to the director and told him bluntly that he was not doing his job. It is said, he offered to make good the losses of the portions already shot and drop out of the film. But the Bhatts—Mahesh and his producer-brother Mukesh—had apparently suggested that they bring in Vikram Bhatt, who had been Mahesh's assistant on *Hum Hain Rahi Pyar Ke* (1993), as the director. Aamir had relented.

Vikram did not disappoint. *Ghulam* was a huge hit, and '*Aati kya Khandala*' immortalized Aamir as a playback singer. The song with an unusual conversational tone, had caught Aamir's fancy immediately, but he was surprised when Lalit Pandit, who was the composer along with his brother Jatin, having heard him casually sing on the sets, suggested he give his own playback. He only agreed when the composer duo promised that if he didn't like the recorded song, they would junk it, and no one would be wiser.

'Aamir practised daily for fifteen to twenty days and then wrapped up the recording in a couple of hours,' Lalit reminisced, all praise for Aamir's roadside Romeo act. His swag and the swagger were evident even twenty years later in the video of him performing '*Aati kya Khandala*' at Akash Ambani and Shloka Mehta's pre-wedding bash. But despite its phenomenal popularity, Aamir could not be convinced to croon again. He only returned to a recording studio after eighteen years to rap '*Dhakkad*' for his home production *Dangal*.

∽

Aamir's journey as a producer began with *Lagaan*, his first and perhaps his biggest gamble. At a time when producers were waiting in queue to make a film with him, he put his faith in Ashutosh Gowarikar, despite *Pehla Nasha* (1993) and *Baazi* (1995), which the actor-turned-filmmaker had directed earlier, not measuring up. The script was Ashutosh's and climaxed with a one-of-its-kind cricket match played in 1893 between the Brits and the villagers of Champaner. When no producer could be coaxed into backing the film, Aamir decided to produce *Lagaan* himself.

On 2 January 2000, Aamir and Ashutosh, along with a team of over 350 members, reached art director Nitin Desai's 'village' in Bhuj. The set had been built from scratch and stayed put for 5 months, 17 days and 10 hours. A team member remembers Aamir as the perfect producer, serving them tea and snacks when they assembled on the sets at five every evening. They would break for dinner at the stroke of midnight and continue till five the next morning. Before they straggled off to bed, Aamir would insist that everyone eat something, be it puris or toast, so they wouldn't be woken by hunger pangs.

The film was shot on a war footing and the outcome was an extremely engaging sports drama. *Lagaan* was the third Hindi film to be nominated for the Academy Awards in the Best Film in a Foreign Language Film category, after *Mother India* (1957) and *Salaam Bombay* (1988). Aamir had stopped attending award functions by then, believing that vested interests determined the choice of winners. However, he made an exception for the 2002 Oscars and for months, camped out in Los Angeles, trying to get the Academy's jury members to see his film. Thanks to his efforts, *Lagaan* made it to the top five.

I tumbled out of bed at the crack of dawn on the day of the Oscars, as excited as the rest of the country and convinced that Ashutosh and Aamir would bring home the coveted statuette. But *Lagaan* was nudged out by Bosnian director Danis Tanović's *No Man's Land* (2001) and the Oscar lost its shine for me that year. Fourteen years later, I relived that moment with Danis at a five-star in Mumbai, telling him how distraught every Indian had been when *Lagaan* had lost to his film. He quipped with a straight face, 'You are implying it was supposed to win. I liked the film too, but I'm glad I won.' Touché!

Satyajit Bhatkal, a young lawyer who had followed Aamir to Bhuj for a year to serve as a production assistant on *Lagaan*, has his own memories of the Oscars. He was standing on a chair, trying to capture the myriad expressions flitting across the faces of the fifty-odd unit members who had gathered around a television set at Aamir's office to watch the awards live. All of them broke down when *Lagaan* lost, after coming so close to making history. Their tears took Satya back to the last day of the film's shoot when he had sat atop a crane with his digital video camera, recording every emotion and reaction. There had been a lot of tears on that day too. Only Satya had remained far removed from the emotional scenes, almost forgotten by his *Lagaan* family till someone looked up and pointed, '*Satya upar akela hai* [Satya is sitting up there, alone].' All this went into his documentary *Chale Chalo: The Lunacy of Film Making*

(2003), which was also turned into a book, and traced the journey of Aamir's first production.

I watched *Lagaan* in the theatre in its silver jubilee week. It was my two-year-old daughter Ranjika's first film, and she was a ball of inexhaustible energy. I lost her during intermission when she quietly slipped out of the washroom. After frantically scouring the theatre, I returned to the darkened auditorium to ask my husband to help locate the brat only to find her playing her own cricket match in the aisles, her giggles along with the cheers on screen filling the hall.

A decade after *Lagaan*, I met Aamir and his nephew Imran Khan just prior to the release of *Delhi Belly* (2011), another Aamir Khan production. The black comedy was an 'adults only' film and so out of bounds for not just my daughter but also Aamir's own children, Junaid and Ira (his youngest son Azaad was born much later), who were then in their teens. In the course of our conversation, I learnt that Imran's tryst with Bollywood had begun in Film City on the set of Mansoor's *Jo Jeeta Wohi Sikander*. He was one of the child artistes in the film and was waiting to face the camera, in costume and full make-up, when his uncle, Aamir, spotted him. With a muttered 'Terrible!' he wiped Imran's garishly painted face and re-did the make-up himself. That image, for me, crystallizes Aamir Khan, the man, the actor and the filmmaker.

10

SHAH RUKH KHAN: COURTING THE BAADSHAH

Baazigar o baazigar, tu hai bada jaadugar

Years ago, when a young boy from Delhi was still hovering on the fringes of stardom, I had knocked on the door of his make-up room at RK Studio wondering if he would like to do a fun feature. Since I was working for a premier film magazine at the time and he was only a one-film actor, I had expected to be welcomed enthusiastically. But to my surprise, Shah Rukh Khan popped his head out the door to inform me that he was not interested. 'I'll wait to do a cover story with you instead,' he replied, flashing those now-famous dimples.

Back in the office, my colleagues shrugged off his refusal as 'arrogance', but I interpreted it as 'confidence'. I was proved right when this 'outsider' gambled his career on a role turned down by industry kids, Anil Kapoor and Salman Khan, as too big a risk, and got away with murder, literally. This time I went back for a cover story.

In a black tuxedo, his hair gelled back, Shah Rukh looked every inch the suave gambler and confided that one night in Mauritius, while filming Abbas-Mustan's *Baazigar* (1993), he had wandered into the island's casino and played the slot machines. With a beginner's luck, he had returned to his hotel suite flush with lucre. But after that he had never gone back, afraid that he might get hooked on gambling. How could a 'baazigar' think this way, I had countered, and SRK as he came to be known, had philosophized that life itself is the biggest gamble and in his case, his producers were risking their money and his directors staking their reputation on him. To Shah Rukh's credit, their bets paid off and the dark horse romped home with two big hits, *Baazigar* and *Darr* (1993). Only *Anjaam* (1994), ironically the first negative role he had signed, took the shine off the Devil's halo, but pleasantly shocked him by fetching him the Filmfare Award for Best Performance in a Negative Role.

The previous year, he had picked up the coveted statuette for *Baazigar*, and after shaking a leg with his wife Gauri at the after-party, the triumphant 'best actor' had driven down, with the film's composer, Anu Malik, and producers, Ganesh and Ratan Jain, to director duo Mustan Burmawalla and Abbas Burmawalla's Bhendi Bazaar residence since the men-in-white had given the function a miss. Abbas bhai and Mustan bhai recalled that it was close to four in the morning, when Shah Rukh came to give them a *jadoo ki jhappi* (hug). Since it was the month of Ramadan, many of their neighbours were already up for prayers and *suhoor* (the first meal during *roza* served before dawn). As word of his flying visit spread, almost 5,000 fans gathered below their building for a glimpse of their hero. 'Even after we moved out, that apartment continued to be a tourist attraction thanks to Shah Rukh's impromptu visit,' they stated.

In the early days, before publicists entered the picture and made me mentally tick off the allotted minutes, I would often visit Shah Rukh on the sets. Sometimes our interview spilled over a couple of days because we were constantly interrupted. Besides calls of 'shot ready hai?' there was always a steady stream of visitors wanting to meet him. From a producer wanting dates to a writer hoping for a story narration or a co-star just dropping by for a conversation, Shah Rukh never turned anyone away.

Once, when his make-up room at Chandivali Studio got too stuffy with never-ending guests and suffocating with clouds of cigarette smoke hanging over it, I stepped out. 'What happened?' he asked, returning from his shot, coming to an abrupt halt as he spotted me sitting on the stairs. 'Nothing,' I shrugged. 'Just too much noise and smoke inside.' Without any more questions, he sat down beside me to continue the interview, unmindful of the curious looks we were drawing.

Another late evening, when he was shooting for Ketan Mehta's *Maya Memsaab* (1993), yesteryear actor-filmmaker, Mehmood sahib rolled into Mumbai's Film City Studio in a wheelchair, plugged into an oxygen cylinder, which his wife Tracy was lugging. Shah Rukh rushed across, chiding, '*Bhaijaan,* why did you take the trouble of coming here? *Aap mujhe bula lete*' [You could have called me.] Mehmood sahib had come to request him to make a special appearance in his directorial *Dushman Duniya Ka* (1996), featuring Tracy and his son Manzoor Ali in the lead. Jeetendra had been signed as Manzoor's father, and Mehmood sahib wanted Shah Rukh to play Badru, his friend and matchmaker. 'But don't you think I'm a little too young to be playing Jeetu ji's friend?' Shah Rukh quipped tongue-in-cheek, even as he nodded his acceptance.

I learnt later that Mehmood sahib's farmhouse in Bangalore was located next door to Shah Rukh's maternal grandparents' home. During his visits there, he would romp around with the senior actor's kids. That's where he first met his idol, Amitabh Bachchan, when they were filming *Bombay to Goa* (1972). Neither of them knew then that years later they would share the frame in many films. For Shah Rukh, working with his 'hero' and discovering that like him, Big B also had to learn his lines and rehearse his scenes, seemed almost unbelievable. But that didn't make him a lesser hero to Shah Rukh. 'He's still *the* Mr Bachchan for me,' he had once told me with a faraway look in his eyes, 'I had dreams of being Babu, the *Satte Pe Satta* (1982) guy with the light eyes... I had dreams of lighting a dynamite with a beedi and coolly sauntering away even as it exploded a few feet from me, like Vijay in *Trishul* (1978)... I had dreams of locking the door, putting the key in my pocket and turning to the baddies to say quietly, "Only one of us is going to get out of here unhurt...", like another Vijay in *Deewar* (1975).'

As his memories ebbed and flowed, I flashbacked to the climax of *Deewar* that had a fatally wounded Vijay lying in the temple, his head cradled in his mother's (Nirupa Roy) lap, as he gasped his last breaths, '*Main thak gaya hoon maa, zindagi se ladte ladte thak gaya hoon... Ek baar mujhe sulade maa, sab theek ho jayega maa...*' (I am tired mother, tired of fighting in this life. One last time put me to sleep mother, everything will be right then).

Flashforward to *Baazigar* and we see a dying Shah Rukh lying with his head cradled in Rakhee's lap, saying brokenly, '*Ma mujhe apne bahon mein samet le, apne anchal mein chupa le maa, mein bachpan se tere pyar ke liye taras raha hoon maa, ab main jee bhar ke sona chahta hoon...*' (Oh mother, gather me in your arms, hide me in the folds of your sari, since childhood I have been yearning for your love, now I want to sleep, long and peacefully). Coincidence? Tribute? Neither. If Shah Rukh had his way, *Baazigar* might have had a very different ending, with him tottering menacingly towards Kajol's character, Priya, intent on pushing her off the roof, the way he had shoved her sister Seema (Shilpa Shetty) from the terrace just before the interval in a Jeffrey Archer-like twist in the tale. 'Panicked, Priya stabs Vicky in self-defence,' he recounted, pantomiming the quick jab with an imaginary dagger. 'He falls, and one of his contact lenses falls out. Then, slowly rising to his feet, Vicky lurches towards Priya again, one eye beady and brown, the other, green and gleaming menacingly.' As I visualized the scene play out, I shivered, caught up in the horror of the moment. 'Then?' I breathed, as he paused for dramatic effect. 'Then, in the scuffle that follows, Vicky, not Priya, would have gone over the edge... And "The End" would have flashed on the screen,' he concluded with a grin.

The distributors, however, refused to fall in with this audacious game plan, arguing that the film was already a commercial risk with a leading man playing a criminal. It needed a more conventional ending. 'If they had their way, *Baazigar* would have ended tamely, with the cops leading Vicky away in handcuffs, like it had happened in countless films before,' Shah Rukh sighed. Fortunately for him, his producer and directors stood their ground, insisting that after taking so many innocent lives, Vicky had to meet with a bloody end. And eventually, everyone agreed on a *Deewar-esque* ending.

Held close by 'his mother' Rakhee, Shah Rukh was reminded of his biological mother, Fatima Lateef, whom he had suddenly lost to multi-organ failure. 'One day she was laughing...talking...running... The next day, she was gone.' The pain of her death is still mirrored in his beautiful eyes.

I was in the audience when Rekha announced that Shah Rukh had bagged his first Filmfare Award for Best Male Debutant for *Deewana* (1992). In a black leather jacket and black jeans, the *baazigar* walked up to graciously accept the award, then, recalled emotionally that the first time he had won a medal in school—he was in third standard then—he had excitedly run home to show it to his mother. 'It was very sad, she wasn't there. The first time I am getting an award, a major award in the film industry, and she still isn't here,' he rued, and lifting the trophy to the skies added, 'This one is for you, mom.' Those achingly poignant words left many eyes in the audience brimming. However, in all these years, I have never seen Shah Rukh cry, despite his insistence that as a boy he was easily moved to tears. Death, and the realization that life is ephemeral, has perhaps dried up all those tears, cast a dark cloud over his life and left him with a lifetime of sadness. And it was this sadness in his eyes, along with a hint of madness, which convinced Sanjay Leela Bhansali that Shah Rukh was, indeed, his Devdas.

One late afternoon, sitting under a tree in Mumbai's Film City Studio, the actor had offered his own take on Sarat Chandra Chattopadhyay's tragic hero. 'Devdas would rather hurt himself than hurt others. But in doing so, he ends up hurting the people he loves,' Shah Rukh pointed out, the thought crystalized in one of his dialogues in the film, '*Babuji ne kaha, gaon chod do... Sab ne kaha, Paro chod do... Paro ne kaha, sharaab chod do... Aaj tumne keh diya, haveli chod do... Ek din aayega jab woh kahenge, duniya hi chhod do...*' [Father said, leave the village... Everyone said, leave Paro... Paro said, quit drinking... You said, leave the house... A day will come when He will say, leave the world] In the end, Devdas does give up the world for love, dying by the roadside, homeless and nameless. Would he die for love? 'No, but I can get very sad in love. That is something both Devdas and I share,' he admitted.

After Dilip Kumar, Rajesh Khanna and Amitabh Bachchan,

Shah Rukh Khan is the one Hindi film actor who has 'lived' through many death scenes. He says matter-of-factly, 'Death doesn't scare me, it is inevitable.' His only regret is that death takes away the nicest people, the ones you love the most. Apart from his mother, it snatched away his best friend when he was only fifteen. Mir Taj Muhammad Khan was a handsome man, over six feet tall, with light brown hair and grey eyes, a combination of Dev Anand, Gregory Peck and Clint Eastwood, going by Shah Rukh's rhapsodies. He was a qualified lawyer, but had never practised law; instead, he had become an activist and a nationalist whose illusions were shattered by post-Independence corruption and his life's dreams cut short by a sudden illness. Cancer took away his voice, but it could not take away the stories Mir sahib had told his son for years before he was silenced.

During Kamal Haasan's *Hey Ram* (2000), a fictional political drama set against the backdrop of the Partition of Bengal and Mahatma Gandhi's assassination, Shah Rukh recalled one such story when an Englishman on screen makes the first announcement after Gandhi ji is shot dead, saying, 'It was a Hindu who killed him.' One of the youngest freedom fighters, Mir sahib had explained to his son that though no one knew the identity of Nathuram Godse at the time, the announcement was made to prevent communal riots from breaking out following rumours that the assassin was a Christian or a Muslim.

Eighteen years later, Kamal Haasan revealed that Shah Rukh had bought the Hindi remake rights of *Hey Ram*. He was delighted, pointing out that he had been unable to pay the actor for his performance in his film because money had run out and he had tried to compensate with a wristwatch. It is another story that Shah Rukh went on to become the Indian face of an international watch brand. But despite the TAG Heuer watches,

Shah Rukh was invariably late for appointments.

Delays stretched to an hour, sometimes even a couple of hours, and after this happened once too often, members of my fraternity, including yours truly, started turning up late for appointments with him too. The last time we met, I was given a call time of 9 p.m. No one was expecting him to arrive before ten, and I was still in the local train, when I got a panicked call from his publicist. 'He's here, where are you?' she shouted across the wire. I told her that I would be there as quickly as was humanly possible, without jumping off a running train or doing a record 100-metre dash from the station. By the time I arrived, a fellow journalist had already been shown into his vanity van. An hour later, when I was seated across him in his swanky vanity, some friends of Bollywood's Baadshah dropped by to say 'goodnight'. While chatting with them, Shah Rukh recalled how a yesteryear superstar, notorious for his unpunctuality, had kept a director waiting for hours. When he had finally turned up, the filmmaker informed him that he would wrap up a shot with another actor first, before setting up the camera for him. 'I come late thinking you will be ready and you tell me you have yet to set up the shot,' he told the bemused director, and turning on his heel stalked out again. As I listened to that parable, I mentally told myself to never again take his unpunctuality for granted.

Journalists like me have overlooked his late comings over the years because once there, Shah Rukh is all there with quotable quotes in plenty, but it sometimes upset co-actors, even those who are among his best friends. Just before the release of their first production, *Phir Bhi Dil Hai Hindustani* (2000), I had spent days trying to coordinate a photoshoot with Shah Rukh and Juhi Chawla, his leading lady and co-producer. But as much as he loved the movie camera, Shah

Rukh then hated posing for magazine shoots and used every excuse, plausible and feeble, to wriggle out. Juhi, who knew him well, was always ready with a counter argument. When he pointed out that he was shooting, she suggested we do the session at the studio itself. When that proved inconvenient, she recommended his home. Eventually, he agreed to an early shoot at the photographer's studio in Goregaon. 'Be there at eleven, sharp,' Juhi warned, as her hairdresser had to leave by 1.30 p.m. He promised to be there on the dot, then, breezed in like a truant schoolboy when the hairdresser was on her way out. But one look at Juhi's stony face and he was out of his tee and cargoes and into Karan Johar's hi-fashion designer wear in record time. Still, it took a while for the ice to thaw, despite Shah Rukh's assurances that since they had turned production partners, such fights and disagreements over anything and everything were common. 'But at the end of the day we are still friends who are doing what we have always wanted to do,' he reasoned.

Juhi eventually succumbed to his dimpled charm and acknowledged that their company name, Dreamz Unlimited, including the 'z' in the Dreamz, had been Shah Rukh's brainwave. 'I guess he was inspired by Steven Spielberg's Dreamworks Production, but we had to register it as "Dreamz Limited" because you can't have an unlimited limited company,' she pointed out, ever practical. When I wondered aloud what made the film special, Shah Rukh quoted a line he had heard Shekhar Kapur say, 'It is not special to be special, but it's special to be ordinary.'

Phir Bhi Dil Hai Hindustani, despite its ambitious scale and profound message, didn't work. And after *Chalte Chalte* (2003), Dreamz Unlimited (or Dreamz Limited) folded up, and Shah Rukh went on launch his own banner, Red Chillies

Entertainment. However, Juhi and he did buy an Indian Premier League (IPL) franchise together and have been rooting for their cricket team, Kolkata Knight Riders, every year.

※

I may not be a friend, but I can safely say that mine is a name Mr Khan is familiar with despite the fact that there have been weeks, months, even years when I saw him only on screen and was convinced that he had forgotten me. But in 2012, when I was in Singapore, trying ineffectually to catch his eye during an impromptu media interaction, I requested a fellow scribe, who topped my five-feet-two-inch frame by several inches, to help out. He waved out and hollered, 'Shah Rukh, Roshmila and I would like a few words too.' Shah Rukh stopped in mid-sentence to ask, 'Roshmila? Where's she?' Then pushed his way through the crowd and reached out with a hug. I was plucked out of the *janta darbar* and escorted to his makeshift make-up room where between sips of tea and bites of a sandwich, the above-mentioned journo and I got our 'exclusive'. The special treatment, he pointed out, was because I was a name he could put a face to. 'Many of the younger lot are total strangers who seem to know me better than I know myself. It's hard explaining this other person they write about with so much of authority to my kids,' he quipped with his inimitable wit.

We chatted for close to an hour till the organizers gate-crashed and hauled him away, despite his protests that he hadn't finished his tea or his request that he be allowed to at least change out of the sweat-drenched tee. Once he was out of earshot, we got an earful for delaying him while 300 correspondents from around the world waited for him in another part of the hotel. 'But they are only strangers while he can put a face to my name,' I protested. No one was listening.

Of course, there's a price to pay too for being the 'familiar one'. Once, I got pulled up and hauled over hot coals because some reporter had written that a bicycle ride Shah Rukh had taken with his daughter, Suhana, down the Bandra promenade, was to promote an upcoming film. 'The next time I go biking with my kids, it will be on a street in London, away from the paparazzi. I don't have to use my kids to promote my films,' he raged, and I recalled seeing him strolling towards Hyde Park with Aryan and Suhana from the top of a Big Bus during a vacation in the Queen's City. When he finally ran out of steam, I pointed out that I had not written the offending article which, in fact, had appeared in another publication. He fixed me with a steely glare and snapped, 'Well, I don't know this other reporter, but I know you, so you have to listen to what I say.' I didn't dare argue. When you are courting a Baadshah, you take the bouquets with the brickbats, especially when he gives you an interview without having even seen the magazine you claim to work for because it is yet to hit the stands!

Yes, that happened for real. One monsoon afternoon in Mumbai, I changed two buses and cabbed the final leg, to clamber into his vanity van, wet and bedraggled, an hour late for our interview scheduled during 'lunch break'. He didn't bat an eyelash, simply asked for a cup of tea for me, then, got down to the business of answering my queries. Midway through, his wife Gauri who had been up all night with their seven-month-old son Aryan, called. He told her with a chuckle, 'Guess what I am doing, Gauri Maa? Giving an interview for a magazine that doesn't exist yet. It doesn't even have a name!' But that didn't stop him from speaking his heart out between shots for Karan Johar's debut directorial, *Kuch Kuch Hota Hai* (1998).

On the first day of the shoot at Mehboob Studio, he had

learnt that Gauri was pregnant. Their son was born during the making of the romance drama, which had him playing a father for the first time on screen to an eight-year-old girl. Holding the new-born Anjali in his arms, he was reminded of Aryan's entry into the world, though in the film the joy was clouded by a sense of doom that came from knowing that his wife, Tina, played by Rani Mukerji, was dying. Sitting by Tina's bedside, Shah Rukh recalled his mother's last days, when seething with impotent anger, he had deliberately set out to hurt her, telling her all the bad things he was going to bring upon himself, believing that if he could make her feel guilty, she wouldn't go away. Gauri once told me, in the course of a rare interview, that his life's biggest failure is that he couldn't prevent his mother from dying too early. 'A part of him went with her; he will never be a completely happy man again,' she had sighed.

Six months after our interview, *Kuch Kuch Hota Hai* opened on 16 October 1998, and went on to become one of Hindi cinema's biggest blockbusters. Our magazine had since been unveiled and the interview was slotted as a cover story. 'But a lot has changed since you met him last,' my editor pointed out, and suggested I might want to update my piece. Shah Rukh was shooting at Ramoji Rao Film City for Abbas-Mustan's *Baadshah* (1999) and asked him to book me on a flight to Hyderabad so I could meet him in person. Having just learnt that I was pregnant I was reluctant to travel even though it was just for a day. When I confided in his late manager, Anwar assured me that Shah Rukh would do the interview over the phone and I happily cancelled my ticket.

When he learnt this, the boss threw a fit. 'What makes you think Shah Rukh will speak to you over the phone? He is a superstar,' he hollered. I blinked, suddenly uneasy, and bravely promised him that he would. The man himself woke up way past noon after a night-long shoot and was ready for a chat. All he asked for was time for a morning cuppa. Then, he disappeared.

Three hours passed and a dozen calls went unanswered. My editor was livid, and I was in tears. Then, just when we were debating on an alternate story for the cover, Shah Rukh called, on the office landline, taking both the receptionist and the boss by surprise. Apologizing profusely, he explained that he had been caught up in an action scene. 'Let me get to my hotel room, then you can call me there,' he suggested. I hung up, and the boss groaned, 'Not again!' I smiled back reassuringly, this time confident of connecting with him.

We chatted for an hour—about *Kuch Kuch Hota Hai* and the highs of success; about playing brother to Aishwarya Rai in Mansoor Khan's *Josh* (2000); about Aryan's first birthday, which was just a few days away, among other things. By the time he hung up, I was the superstar. 'Was that really Shah Rukh Khan?' I was asked repeatedly over the next few days at the office. 'It was,' I would nod. 'And he gave you an interview on the phone?' Another nod. The 'Wow!' that followed played on a loop.

∞

For Shah Rukh, a film isn't just another day at the studio. Nor does it end after eighteen reels and two hours. Like life is a collection of memories, films too are a collage of moments. He carries the story forward in his mind and the characters become a part of his extended family. When I wondered what could have happened to Arjun and Ganga after they tied the knot in Subhash Ghai's *Pardes* (1997), pat came the answer, 'They would have a couple of kids, Arjun would get busy with his recordings and turn into a boring husband, and one day, tired of waiting for him to come home, Ganga might just walk out on him.' Ouch, I didn't care for this scenario!

I moved to the next—Rahul and Seema in Aziz Mirza's *Yes Boss* (1997), with the song *'Main koi aisa geet gaon, ke arzoo jatao agar tum kaho'* still echoing in my ears. 'I see Rahul Joshi at home, telling his young son that maybe if he hadn't married Seema, he might have had his own agency by now and his mom might have been a millionaire's wife,' he shot back.

I didn't want any more reel-life romances to be ripped apart, but couldn't stop myself from asking, somewhat apprehensively, 'Raj and Simran in *Dilwale Dulhania Le Jayenge* [DDLJ]?' To my relief, Shah Rukh saw them growing old together, still very much in love, still having a lot of fun. Phew! I sighed and gave myself up to the strains of *'Mehendi laga ke rakhna, doli saja ke rakhna'* wafting in from Yash Chopra's mustard fields.

In real life, Shah Rukh met his *dulhania*, Gauri Chibber, when they were still in school; she in the ninth standard and he in the twelfth. And even though he belonged to the 'other' community, had opted for an uncertain profession and in every way the wrong man for his Ms Right, there was no keeping him away from her. When her parents sternly warned Gauri to stay away from him, Shah Rukh popped up at her birthday party as Abhimanyu, his character from the TV serial *Fauji* (1988–1989). He was recognized, and all hell broke loose. When her possessive younger brother, Vikrant, shook a fist at him and hollered, 'I'll beat you to pulp,' Shah Rukh simply shrugged, 'Yeah, yeah, whatever you say.' When Gauri herself, torn between her love for her family and a man who was getting a little too possessive, broke up with him and went away to Bombay with some friends, like Rahul in *Darr*, he went after her. She recounted how after a week of partying and shopping, on the day that they were to return to Delhi, she had looked out of the window, and there he was, standing under the building.

Shah Rukh's version was more dramatic, even a trifle filmi. He narrated it to me, sitting on the steps at Chandivali Studio, with a glass of cutting chai in one hand and a cigarette in the other, that urged on by his mother, he had followed Gauri to Bombay with two friends. With money fast running out, the trio started sleeping on benches outside the Taj Mahal Hotel and spent the day searching for Shah Rukh's lady love. On the last day of their stay, with the last of his savings, they flagged down a cab for one last Gauri hunt. The cabbie took them as far as Aksa beach before their money ran out. Gorai Beach was close by and a despondent Shah Rukh decided he had to go there. 'Gorai... Gauri... Maybe...?' he murmured. She wasn't there, but while he was rushing to catch the ferry, shouts coming from a private beach, distracted him. One voice sounded familiar and he barged into a private party. 'And there I found her, standing in the water!' he mooned, years later. Maybe Gauri's version was the truth, but Shah Rukh, a natural-born raconteur, always made the mundane magical. On 25 October 1991, Raj took his *dulhania* home for real, with her family's blessings.

Meanwhile, *DDLJ* turned *Baazigar* and *Darr's* 'bad boy' into a 'lover boy', even though Aditya Chopra had to fool Shah Rukh into agreeing to a story narration by telling him that he was making an action film titled *Shashtra*. If he was uncharacteristically subdued in his first response to Adi's story, it was because it rang too close to home. 'Raj of *DDLJ* will always remain with me because he is me,' Shah Rukh later admitted, adding that Adi had wanted him to play himself, dressing the way he did, in jeans, shirt hanging out, hair ruffled. Then, with typical Shah Rukh humour, he had pointed out that since he couldn't let everyone see the real him, he had gone shopping in London and got shoes that matched his clothes—red, green, blue, brown and even mustard. I had refused to believe him till he had turned up in them for a photoshoot, and shot for us, dressed from neck to toe in a shade of greyish-green. Jeans, tee and shoes, all perfectly matched. Surprisingly, he looked pretty cool.

When I quizzed him on his favourite scene, he pointed to the one where Simran tells Raj that she is engaged and asks him if he will come to her wedding. While the conventional Hindi film hero would have smiled bravely and said he would, knowing his 'sacrifice' would endear him to the masses, Raj smiles and says, '*Nahin, main nahin aaoonga.* [No, I won't come.]'

Shah Rukh described it as an '*aankhon mein ansoon hoton mein muskaan*' (tears in your eyes and a smile playing on your lips) kind of a moment that he had seen Shashi Kapoor play out in countless films, as also Kamal Haasan in *Saagar* (1985). 'You only say "no" to someone you love. I would love to do the scene again just to feel that love,' he confessed.

On screen, Shah Rukh, despite his earlier antipathy to girl-meets-boy stories, has portrayed love in its many shades and moods. His trademark gesture of opening his arms wide, to embrace life, love and the world at large, makes you believe that the King Khan is always there for you… *Main hoon na!* But the fact is that he has changed, even if his phone number hasn't. Calls to him today invariably go unanswered, as do text messages. He still greets me with a *jhappi*, envelopes me in a cloud of nicotine, answers five questions in response to my one, but now interviews come with a time limit and Shah Rukh who once described himself as a 'childlike recluse', is happier in the company of his kids. Aryan wants to be a writer and a director and Suhana, an actor, while li'l AbRam is still a kid growing up in a world that has suddenly gone insane.

I can't imagine Shah Rukh without his kids. During *Asoka* (2001), while listening to him talk of the emperor as a rich, famous 'superstar' with the world at his feet, 'who is impulsive and selfish at times but they are the mistakes of a child who doesn't know better', we had four-year-old Aryan for company, running in circles around us. During *Devdas*, while he was decoding the tragic hero, I had watched Suhana walking around Film City, with her nanny following, picking up stones and fallen leaves, perfectly happy in her own company. Aryan was always a boisterous, playful child while Suhana was shy and studious. AbRam is a mix of the two—quick to befriend his father's friends, but at the same time just as happy to sit in his vanity van and watch TV alone or play with the cats and hens in the studio.

I met this 'cool kid' at Mehboob Studio while his father was promoting *Raees* (2017) and pretended that I was confused whether the fruit on the table in front of us was an orange or a lemon. The cherubic three-year-old was happy to educate me, pointing out knowledgably the differences in their colour and sizes. Since I was a few feet taller than him, I was in the league of his daddy, but I got an approving nod when I told him that one day soon, he would grow up to be bigger and taller than both of us and then, we would be the ones looking up to him. Shah Rukh who had been listening to our prattle with an amused smile, told his boy that I had a little baby at home. AbRam was instantly excited even after learning that my 'baby' was all of eighteen. Making me promise that I would bring her home someday, he ran off, mildly disappointed that I had to return to work and couldn't play football with him. 'AbRam has made me kinder and gentler,' Shah Rukh smiled, suddenly more approachable. Maybe he has, but for me Shah Rukh was always one of the kindest, most considerate actors around.

Once, after a photoshoot that went on till 8 p.m. at a photographer's suburban studio, he had invited me to drive down to Film City Studio with him where he would be shooting for the better part of the night. 'We can talk on the way and continue between shots,' he urged, taking the wheel as I hopped in beside him. Those were the pre-cell phone days, and by the time we reached the studio, the office with the only telephone in the vicinity had shut. So, I had no way of letting my husband know where I was. As I waited for Shah Rukh to finish the interview, I missed the last bus home... And then, the last train.

He returned from a shot to find me almost in tears. 'What's wrong?' he asked, looking concerned. I confided that I would now have to spend the night in the studio or worse, on the street. 'And when I get home, my husband will kill me!' I ended on a wail. He soothed me saying his car would drop me home. 'But how are you going to get home?' I sniffed. He shrugged nonchalantly, saying if the shoot ended before Kabir, his chauffeur, returned, he would hitch a ride with someone.

And so while he cadged a ride, I arrived in Vashi in a large, red, chauffeur-driven Pajero, well past midnight, surprising my anxious husband who was pacing the road outside, wondering what had become of me. That's Shah Rukh Khan, and that's what makes him a Baadshah for real!

11

SALMAN KHAN: PETER PAN WITH A SWAG

O...o...jaane jaana, dhoondhe tujhe deewana

My first interview as a just-anointed journalist was with Salim Khan, who, after blockbusters such as *Zanjeer* (1973), *Deewar* (1975), *Sholay* (1975) and *Trishul* (1978), had just split with his long-time scriptwriter-partner Javed Akhtar. I was sent to prod him on the break-up. Salim sahib was candid, maybe a bit too candid, because the interview was never published. This was the era when one tiptoed around celebrities, and tabloids had yet to bare their talons. Not the best of beginnings one would say, but despite the fact that his flood of words had been dammed before they flowed out on the pages of our magazine, the wordsmith remained fond of me. In fact, he insists, I owe my three-decade career to him. 'I brought you luck,' he reminds me with a chuckle every time we meet. The patriarch of Bollywood's Khan-daan has been like a father figure to me. And he was the one who introduced me to Salman Khan.

Despite my protests, Salim sahib graciously walked me to the door after we had wrapped up this first interview. I stepped out and turned back to thank him again and looked straight into a pair of large eyes curiously studying me from behind his broad shoulders. They stopped me in mid-sentence and in mid-stride. Salim sahib glanced back to see who had 'interrupted' me and smiled, 'This is my son Salman Khan. He is an actor.'

Salman was juggling two films at the time even though he had not really set out to be an actor. He had been assisting K. Shashilal Nair on *Falak* (1998), with plans of becoming a director himself, when Sooraj Barjatya offered him the lead role in his first film, *Maine Pyar Kiya* (1989). 'I urged him to say "yes" and Salman admitted that he had accepted the offer,' Farooque Shaikh, his co-star in *Biwi Ho To Aisi* (1988), told me years later. Salim sahib's eldest son had every intention of returning to direction after wrapping up these two films, but *Maine Pyar Kiya* gave him so much 'prem' that he remained an actor.

The career-defining, life-changing role of Prem came to him quite by accident. An actress with whom he had done a commercial, suggested Salman's name to Sooraj who wasn't sure if the son of a famous scriptwriter would even turn up for an audition. Salman himself was uncertain when he got a call from Rajshri Productions. The production house founded by Sooraj's grandfather Tarachand Barjatya was known for its family dramas—films such as *Dosti* (1964), *Uphaar* (1971), *Chitchor* (1976) and *Sawan Ko Aane Do* (1979)—and the actor wasn't sure if he wanted to play a *gaonwala* in a dhoti. But he did turn up for the audition, with no great expectations and no starry tantrums. The simple love story, *Maine Pyar Kiya*, was set in modern times and instantly struck a chord with Salman. Sooraj too liked his photographs, finding him young, fresh, with an endearing boy-next-door charm. But his screen-test wasn't impressive and the senior Barjatyas weren't convinced he was the right choice for Sooraj's all-important first directorial. They were even more sceptical when they learnt that Salman had already started shooting for another film, *Biwi Ho To Aisi*, which featured Rekha in the title role and him in the supporting role of her brattish brother-in-law.

Salman was aware that Sooraj was auditioning other new faces as well and left a list of names of his model friends with him. Much as he wanted to do the film, he felt some of these guys were more suited for the part, because they were not just better-looking but better actors as well. To Sooraj's surprise, he started sending them across for auditions, telling the director that he would be just as happy if he signed one of them. Decades later, Sooraj admitted that it was this large-hearted gesture of Salman that convinced him that this 'pure soul' was his Prem.

However, instead of being delighted, Salman was appalled when he was given the good news. He insisted Sooraj see the rushes of *Biwi Ho To Aisi* before deciding. He even confided to the director who had become a friend by then, that he thought he was terrible in the film. He didn't want Sooraj to see the film later and throw him out from *Maine Pyar Kiya* midway. The filmmaker, on his part, assured him that Salman was his Prem, but all through the making of the film, his hero was worried—more so when *Biwi Ho To Aisi* released before *Maine Pyar Kiya* and his lacklustre performance got him scathing reviews. What was worse, the film was a hit! 'Which means more and more people are watching my terrible performance,' he wailed. Sooraj only laughed and wondered why his eyes looked so large in the film.

Maine Pyar Kiya opened on 29 December 1989, two days after Salman's twenty-fourth birthday. It was one of the biggest grossers of the decade and is among the most successful films in Hindi cinema. The actor himself later admitted that had it not been for Sooraj, he might never have acted in another film.

Sooraj cast Salman as Prem in two more films after *Maine Pyar Kiya—Hum Aapke Hain Koun..!* (1994) and *Hum Saath Saath Hain* (1999)—before experimenting with other Prems. There was Abhishek Bachchan and Hrithik Roshan in *Main Prem Ki Diwani Hoon* (2003), Shahid Kapoor in *Vivah* (2006) and Sonu Sood in *Ek Vivah... Aisa Bhi* (2008). He returned to Salman sixteen years after *Hum Saath Saath Hain* with a double role in *Prem Ratan Dhan Payo* (2015), that of a royal, Vijay Singh, and his doppelganger, Prem Dilwale. Over a quarter of a century had passed, but while talking about his actor-friend, Sooraj admitted that every time Salman had zoomed into the set on his bike, he still saw his Prem in him.

Salman's leading lady in *Maine Pyar Kiya*, Bhagyashree, also has some fond memories of him. The eldest daughter of the Raja of Sangli, Vijay Singhrao Madhavrao, she had featured in next-door neighbour Amol Palekar's TV show, *Kachchi Dhoop* (1987), as a schoolgirl, but had no dreams of becoming an actress. All her dreams revolved around Himalaya Dassani, her classmate. The two were going steady, but under pressure from her parents, the couple had agreed to take a break and Himalaya had flown off to the United States. When her father refused to let her go abroad for higher studies, Bhagyashree reluctantly agreed to play the shy, sweetly smiling Suman, after turning Sooraj away at least half-a-dozen times.

The Barjatyas were family friends and hoping that the change in scenery would take her mind off Himalaya, her parents let her go to Ooty for the shoot totally unprepared for show business. While they were filming '*Kabutar jaa jaa jaa*', towards the end of the song, Sooraj instructed her to fly into Salman's arms when he returns home unexpectedly. Bhagyashree promptly burst into tears. It took three hours for her to admit to her flummoxed director and hero that she had never embraced a man before. What she didn't add was that she was petrified that after seeing the film, Himalaya's parents might call off the match. Both Sooraj and Salman offered to edit out the scene, but Bhagyashree eventually gave in. However, there were no real kisses or intimate scenes in this love story. Salman gave in easily because he doesn't think they are important to a film's success anyway.

In fact, Bhagyashree's leading man was the perfect gentleman all through the first schedule, asking for her permission before even reaching for her hand on camera. Then, inexplicably, his behaviour changed while they were shooting another song, 'Dil deewana bin sajna ke mane na'. Openly flirtatious, he was crooning the words in her ears, despite the presence of journalists on the set making her distinctly uncomfortable that day.

'I was missing Himalaya...my family...and suddenly, Salman was whispering to me that he knew who my *dil deewana* was,' she reminisced years later. After making her squirm awkwardly for a while, he finally admitted that he had learnt about Himalaya from a common friend and understood how unhappy she was. 'Why don't you invite him over?' he suggested 'No, no!' Bhagyashree exclaimed, her thoughts flying to her parents. 'He can come over pretending to be my friend,' he reassured her instantly. But she wouldn't succumb to the temptation.

However, once home, she returned to Himalaya and tried to convince her parents to agree to their match. After two refusals, Bhagyashree finally ran off to marry the love of her life in a temple in true filmi style. 'Himalaya's parents were there, along with a few friends. From my side there was only Sooraj ji and Salman. They were my family on my special day. Salman stayed till the end, long after all the guests had left, and even told Himalaya to take care of me or he would have him to answer to,' she smiled.

By the time the film released, she was pregnant. Yet Prem and Suman became the epitome of young love. In a Varanasi theatre, live pigeons were released every time '*Kabutar jaa jaa jaa*' played on screen, and in a Lucknow cinema, the management had to rewind the reel when '*Dil deewana*' came on. Salman's leading lady then went on a long sabbatical, returning to do a few films with her husband before retiring for good. Three decades later, Bhagyashree still remains the *Maine Pyar Kiya* girl. Salman went on to become a superstar with several more blockbusters to his name, but Prem remains his most popular screen avatar and a personal favourite.

He believes the character has his muse in Sooraj who is also a shy, soft-spoken, *sanskari* boy, growing up in an extended family of thirteen and holding fast to traditional values. I believe there's a little bit of Prem in Bollywood's brat too who hasn't moved out of his childhood home in all these years and is the quintessential family man. To his siblings—Arbaaz, Sohail, Alvira and Arpita—and their spouses, Salman is a fiercely protective brother who always looks out for their interests. To their kids, he is a doting uncle who teaches them to paint, bike and be themselves. At fifty-plus, he's still a mamma's boy and his father remains his hero whose approval still matters to him.

In Salim sahib's presence, Salman's swag and swagger disappears. He won't even light up a cigarette. Once when I was interviewing his dad, both of us sitting at the dining table at their Bandra residence, Salman suddenly strolled in, and pulling up a chair, gestured for his meal to be served. However, he had little interest in the food and was completely focused on our conversation. Those were the days when he didn't give interviews and that time too, he didn't utter a single word. But through his expressive eyes, and animated nods and head shakes, he made it clear what he endorsed and what he disagreed with. On that occasion too, his father introduced us with the very same words he had used the first time, 'This is my son Salman Khan. He is an actor.' By this time, Salman was more than just an actor; he was one of Bollywood's biggest superstars. But he had simply nodded as I smiled back.

∞

Salman had come along when his father had moved from Indore to Bombay with just ₹60 in his pockets and one film offer, *Baraat* (1960). A star cricketer, a trained pilot and a graduate, he could have chosen any career, but encouraged by his friends, Prince Salim—his chosen screen name—aimed for the stars. It took almost two dozen films for him to realize that he didn't have what it takes to be an actor. He then turned to scriptwriting.

Salman inherited Salim sahib's passion for writing. *Baaghi: A Rebel For Love* (1990), produced and directed by Nitin Manmohan, revolving around a colonel's son and a girl he rescues from a brothel, was his story idea. He had written it when he wanted to be director, and Javed Siddiqui polished it for the screen. He also went on to write *Chandra Mukhi* (1993), *Veer* (2010) and *Dabangg 3*. He has also written lyrics for songs like '*Selfish*' for *Race 3* (2018) and '*Main tera*' for *Notebook* (2019) as well as a few singles. However, after *Mane Pyar Kiya*, even his father acknowledged that Salman has great screen presence, great strength of will and the potential to be another Amitabh Bachchan. 'Once he decided to be an actor, he quit studies, spent a year building his body and taking acting lessons,' Salim sahib revealed.

Interestingly, even after the super success of *Maine Pyar Kiya*, Salman was out of work for six months before G.P. Sippy signed him for a revenge drama, *Patthar Ke Phool* (1991), scripted by his father. He played a cop, and the film is remembered for S.P. Balasubrahmanyam and Lata Mangeshkar's peppy duet *'Kabhi tu chalia lagta hai'* filmed on him and debutante Raveena Tandon. Raveena later admitted that the different get-ups they had donned for the song, from *Awara* (1951) and *Chhalia* (1960) to *Bobby* (1973) and *Julie* (1975), made it a fun shoot. 'But those days, Salman and I were not the best of friends and during our first film together, there were a lot of fireworks. Now, of course, we are older, wiser and friendlier,' she laughed while flashbacking to her first film.

Patthar Ke Phool was only an average grosser, but *Baaghi* (1990), *Sanam Bewafa* (1991) and *Saajan* (1991) were blockbusters. Salman had a winning streak of nine hits, followed by half-a-dozen flops like *Suryavanshi* (1992), *Chandra Mukhi* (1993) and *Chaand Kaa Tukdaa* (1994). During this time, trade pundits had started writing his obituary, distributors refused to touch his films and only C-grade producers queued up for his dates—the man himself remained as untouched by failures as he had been by stardom. He was confident he would resurrect himself like the proverbial Phoenix. This equilibrium, seen at different stages of his career and through many a personal crisis, is a trait he has inherited from his father.

Salman was too young to remember Salim sahib's early struggles in Bombay, but he saw him tumble from the pinnacle and hit a five-year low after his break-up with Javed sahib. But through it all, his father's attitude to life didn't change; nor did his lifestyle. Today, no matter what tempests he is battling, Salman lives life king-size, opening his home, heart and purse strings to those he has taken under his wing—be it actresses like Somy Ali, Katrina Kaif, Sonakshi Sinha, Daisy Shah, Jacqueline Fernandez, Iulia Vantur or young protégés like Sooraj Pancholi, Zaheer Iqbal, Ayush Sharma and so many more.

Jacqueline, who came from Sri Lanka and has found a

place for herself in India and Bollywood, openly acknowledges Salman and Sajid Nadiadwala as her mentors. They gave her *Kick* (2014), her biggest hit, when her career was floundering and expected nothing in return. Rather, they made her believe that she had done it all on her own.

Katrina confided that the most bizarre yet beautiful thing about their relationship was that even if they were not in touch for weeks, or even months, if something happened to upset her, Salman would show up, out of the blue. Despite not knowing anything about what had transpired, he would simply comfort her with his presence. It's a strange coincidence, but one she has grown to expect and accept.

Their friendship always makes me smile. During *Bharat* (2019), when I was interviewing Katrina, Salman strolled by, and quipped with a straight face, 'I have been waiting for you all my life and you are here.' She let the wisecrack pass without comment, going on to discuss promo shoots and Twitter chats with him.

There was a time when people expected them to marry. In fact, over the years, Salman's name has been linked with several women, from Sangeeta Bijlani and Somy Ali, to Aishwarya Rai, Katrina Kaif and Iulia Vantur. He is too much of a gentleman to bring up any names in conversation, but he did admit that marriage had been on his mind a few years ago. But, he had sighed, the person moved away, despite his anger and tears, his possessiveness and wisdom. And there was no point forcing anyone to stay when they didn't want to, he reasoned, as it would only make them unhappy and him, guilty. And so, at fifty-plus, he remains one of the country's most eligible bachelors who jokes that if marriage were to happen now, it would happen impetuously one night, and hit him with the realization the next morning.

Salman has often admitted in interviews that he wants a child of his own. Very early in his career, when people were calling him a brash and arrogant brat, he had wondered, 'If I am as bad as I am made out to be, why aren't little kids scared of me?' It is a fact that children open their hearts to him, and vice versa. During the promotions of *Ready* (2011), he kept the media waiting for over an hour for interviews while he sang and danced with a group of differently abled children. I sneaked into the auditorium and watched. He didn't break stride when one of the kids pulled at his shirt, hooted when another stripped off his own shirt to flex his non-existent muscles, and when one refused to leave, he cuddled her on his lap. There was not a flicker of irritation as the little one tugged on his hair and poked at his eyes while he was answering my questions. When she posed questions of her own, he answered them patiently. When the embarrassed mother was finally able to pry the child away—this is after he had set up a dance date with her for the coming week—he insisted on carrying her to the car himself and stood by waving till it had turned the corner.

On another occasion, when a heavily pregnant colleague visited Salman on the sets of his reality show *Bigg Boss*, he reprimanded her for running around in this condition, quickly stubbed out his cigarette and plied her with juices and all things healthy, along with dollops of advice.

Watching him around children, even unborn ones, I am convinced that he will make a great dad. But when I asked him why he didn't have any children of his own yet, he replied with a straight face that he would, if only he could find a way to keep the mother of the child away. When I suggested adoption or surrogacy, he roared with laughter, 'I'm fifty, but trust me I'm not too old for a man, not in India at least.' When I asked how he planned to become a father, he quipped tongue-in-cheek,

'Now, do I have to explain the process to you?' That kind of Puckish humour is typically Salman.

I have often been told I am soft on Salman. Maybe I am. Only he can make me dance to a '*Dhinka chika*' after a show of the nonsensical *Ready* (2011) or make me whistle from the balcony during *Tiger Zinda Hai* (2017) when he emerges from a room filled with poison gas, bare-bodied, and goes on to obliterate an entire army. Who cares if the critics call his adventures improbable and his fantasies impossible, Salman has never professed to be an 'arty' actor. He is an industry kid, a producer now, and for him, films bridge the divide between the classes and the masses. It doesn't matter if he doesn't win awards, what matters is that the theatres are full so those who invest in the film earn money from it. When *Tubelight* (2017) flickered and fused too soon, he returned money to the distributors with a heartfelt apology.

After three collaborations—*Sultan* (2016), *Tiger Zinda Hai* (2017) and *Bharat* (2019)—Ali Abbas Zafar, a biochemistry graduate, believes that the reason behind Salman's enduring appeal is his earnestness. His communication with his audience is simple and direct. No matter what character he plays, there's always a bit of Salman Khan in him and that is why he has remained a larger-than-life superhero even after three decades.

For me, Salman always makes great copy and I wait to meet him. However, his on-off equation with the press has made him an intimidating figure for many of my colleagues. I remember reaching Film City studio during *Tere Naam* (2003) for a promised one-on-one, only to find him prowling around like an angry tiger because of an article that had appeared in a daily that morning. The reporter who had written the piece was there too and that only made him angrier. It took hours to persuade him to a joint press conference. While many from my fraternity, including the one who had erred, kept a safe distance, I pulled my chair up right to his side so I could hear his murmur more clearly and get his attention too. When I asked him if he had liked *Devdas*, there was dead silence. After a long pause, just when everyone was expecting him to fly off the handle again, he replied that he hadn't because it didn't make him cry.

There was a time when Salman didn't like journalists because of their biased reportage and for years, didn't give interviews. But that didn't stop stories about him from appearing in magazines or being recounted in newsrooms. I heard about how he had chased a scribe who had written something derogatory about his then girlfriend around the studio, with every intention of beating him up. I also heard about how he had walked another up three flights of stairs at Mehboob Studio, then back down, up again and down, finally, telling the huffing-puffing reporter that he wasn't in the mood for an interview! I heard how he had kept a senior colleague standing in the blazing sun for a good part of the day, then, on learning that she was fasting and feeling faint, had rushed her into his make-up room, revived her with fruits, sweets and juices, and given her the interview of the year, only to tell her at the end to erase the tape as the conversation had been for her ears only.

I can add a few stories of my own to these. One evening, I raced into the studio, a few minutes after him, only to be told that tired of waiting, Salman had retreated into his vanity van to 'take a shower'. 'But didn't he just arrive from his home, which is just around the corner from the studio, five minutes ago?' I asked, baffled. His publicist nodded, unable to explain why he needed to suddenly take a shower at six in the evening. I had simply taken a chair and parked myself outside his vanity van. He stepped out, thirty minutes later, looking like a rock star. We did not mention the shower.

On another occasion, I arrived at a suburban five-star hotel only to be told that he was late. The publicist guided me towards the buffet table and insisted I have a bite while I waited. I was in the middle of lunch when the publicist reappeared, looking flustered, and asked if I would like to have the first go at Salman who suddenly wanted to do a few interviews before the press conference. I was ready.

I was ushered into a ballroom crowded with the entire marketing team of the brand he was promoting. Everyone was standing in attention, because well, Salman was on his feet too. I swallowed a chuckle. After we were introduced, he nodded curtly, and still standing by the table, rapped out, 'Start.' I flashed him a smile and asked sweetly, 'Can we sit down first?' There was a minute's silence when you could have heard a pin drop. Then, chuckling, he waved me to a chair, taking the one facing me. And everyone else sat down too, with sighs of relief. Phew!

Twenty minutes later, I got up to leave and reached for my cell phone that was on the table between us recording our conversation. It had pinged every time a text came through and even rung a couple of times. It pinged again as he was handing it over. 'Your phone rings more than mine, who's calling you so often?' Salman frowned. With a poker face I replied, 'Shah Rukh Khan. He has a press conference today at a hotel in the vicinity and is wondering why I am still here with you.' I swear I heard the congregation groan. Those were the days when 'Karan' and 'Arjun' were not even on talking terms. So, to bring up Shah Rukh's name in a conversation with Salman was suicidal. Everyone waited for him to pronounce, 'Off with her head.' The silence stretched... Then, he broke out into an appreciative guffaw. Salman, I discovered that day, is not an ogre, he only pretends to be one.

I got my interview, but he made the rest of the media wait for another hour or more before starting his press conference, and then kept it going for a good hour, hitting the other Khan's plans for a six. Their cold war continued for over a decade and ended with a *jadoo ki jhappi* at politician Baba Siddiqui's Iftar party. Since then, they have gone back to being friends. They root for each other's films on social media, make special appearances in each other's films and walk in and out of each other's homes, even if these visits mostly happen only after midnight. I learnt a long time ago that in Bollywood the sun rises in the West and sets in the East. That's why no one will take your call before noon and you get the best interviews after Cinderella has fled from the ball.

One Saturday, I went shopping. I still remember the date, 4 September 2011. It was pouring cats and dogs and, in the chaos, I lost my cell phone. I rushed home and bought another that same evening. The first call that came through on the new phone at around eleven at night was a request to interview Salman who was in a hospital in New Jersey, recuperating after surgery. It will be after midnight, I was warned. The interview happened closer to 2 a.m.

For close to seven years, Salman had battled Trigeminal Neuralgia, commonly known as the 'Suicide Disease' because the pain can drive a person to take his own life. There were times when he couldn't eat or drink, even live his life, because of five nerves that had wrapped around a vein leading to an aneurysm at the back of his head. The ailment was life threatening, and he had spent the days leading up to the surgery quietly at home with his parents. He then left for the US with brothers, Arbaaz and Sohail, and sister Alvira. Baby sister Arpita had been left behind with his parents to ensure that the annual

Ganesh Chaturthi and Eid celebrations continued just the way they always had been.

'How are you feeling?' was my first question. His answer was typically Salman even though the surgery had stretched to almost eight hours. 'I went into the operation theatre smiling and came out smiling,' he laughed, adding that seeing the media turnout at the airport on the day he flew out, he had asked his sister if he was going to return. It didn't surprise me that this man could be cracking jokes even before he had made a full recovery. Exactly three weeks later, he was in freezing Dublin, shooting for Kabir Khan's action thriller, *Ek Tha Tiger* (2012). The film was a blockbuster.

His illness isn't the only thing Salman has fought. Over the years, he has fought a number of legal battles too, which put him behind bars on a couple of occasions. When some of these cases were still in court, I was called for an interview but sternly warned not to bring them up. It was late at night and he was in the mood for a stroll in the parking lot of Mehboob Studio. In the course of our conversation, he was the one who alluded to the cases. Interview over, as the publicist hurried across, looking anxious, he turned to me and said almost accusingly, 'She asked me about the cases.' I almost tripped in disbelief, till I caught the glint of laughter in his eyes and realized I was being pranked.

Salman has grown up since our first encounter with him standing behind his father's back. His once-innocent eyes now have a worldly gleam. His fists bunch like that of a pugilist when he walks. Yet, for all his larger-than-life machismo, Salman for me remains a boy who, will never grow up, who if he wanted to invite a woman out, might still croon, *'Tan tana tan tan tan tara, chalti hai kya 9 se 12, khadi khadi kya soch rahi hai, chal ho jayee nau do gyarah...'*

Anu Malik, who composed this song for *Judwaa* (1997), recalled that when he was offered the film that came with the promise of a double dose of Salman Khan, he promised director David Dhawan he would come up with a song that would be on everyone's lips. He was thinking about it when he went on a concert tour to the US with Salman and Shah Rukh. Watching the former on stage and off it, the phrase '9 se 12' stuck in his head. In the 1990s, the last show at a theatre was this late night one and a favourite with couples who wanted to snuggle. Playing with the idea, Anu appended the phrase with the catchy '*Tan tana tan tan tan tara*' and one day, crooned it to David as he was lounging on a couch.

'In a flash David was up and told me abruptly that he had to leave. I silently berated myself for having overstepped my boundaries, convinced that the film had slipped out of my fingers. But on his way out, David complimented me on a great hook line, saying we had our song,' Anu reminisced, with a hat tip to Salman who has inspired many more funky tracks like '*Duniya mein aaye ho to love kar lo*', '*Ek garam chai ka pyaali ho, koi usko peelanewali ho*' and '*Oochi hai building lift teri band hai*', all songs only he could carry off. 'But I also gave him one of my most emotional and romantic numbers, penned by Gulzar sahib, "*Sau dard hain, sau rahatein, sab mila dil nashin, ek tu hi nahin*".' *Jaan-e-Mann* (2006) didn't work, but the song still tugs at the heartstrings,' asserted the composer.

Today, when I see Salman Khan, this is the song I hear because over the years, I have grown to understand that there are depths to this Peter Pan that the world may never see—a need to love and be loved in a way that completes him.

12

JOHN ABRAHAM: THE REAL ACTION HERO

Kisi ladki ko cheda, toh dhishoom

My first interview with John Abraham almost did not happen. Days into a new job, I went to meet him at a suburban nightclub, which in the light of the day, without the flashing strobes and ear-splitting music, was like a living room devoid of personality. John strode in a little after noon and spent a few minutes chatting with the assembled fourth estate, getting feedback on his upcoming release. After that, he retired to a far corner and we were beckoned in turns for our one-on-ones.

As I took my place opposite him, he greeted me affably, but as soon as I mentioned the name of my publication, his smile slipped and a tirade against yellow journalism followed. I had no idea what had set him off and told him as much. He frowned disbelievingly and groused that he had become a soft target for our daily gossip column. He was quick to add that almost everything that was written about him was fabricated. I understood his ire, but I wasn't prepared to accept his blame. 'I'm a new recruit, if you have problem with the paper, you could have struck us off your list. It's not fair to call me here and berate me in the presence of fellow journalists for something I had nothing to do with,' I shot back. For a moment or two there was strained silence between us, then, just as I was mentally preparing myself to be told to leave, his smile broke out again. He told me to ask what I wanted, and I walked away, still baffled as I tried to figure out the man, but with an interview in my bag.

When I got to know him better, I understood that John who grew up playing football, and now owns his own club, NorthEast United FC, is a sportsman to the core who always plays fair and square. He may dodge a tackle, but if you are straight with him, he can be brought around to empathize with your compulsion to raise prickly controversies, even ask intrusive questions or dig for an eye-catching headline. However, if you commit a nasty foul, you get the red card.

A few months later, my editor went to meet him to end the long-drawn cold war. I was busy with the edition at the office when the boss called, late in the afternoon, insisting that I rush across to Karan Johar's office, pronto. 'Why?' I asked, his SOS summon taking me by surprise. 'Because John is ready to give an interview, but he insists he will only do it with "that girl" whose name he can't recall,' he replied. I didn't wait to ask any more questions, just hopped into a waiting cab, telling the driver to press down on the accelerator, hard.

This time John greeted me like an old friend and we were soon laughing over whose dimples were deeper. We then went on to discuss his new film, *Dostana* (2008), in particular the now-famous scene where he emerges from the ocean wearing only a pair of sunshine yellow trunks. He revealed that Karan had prophesized, long before they started shooting, that he would make the girls swoon. John being John, had refused to take him seriously. But that day, sitting opposite me, he admitted, with a somewhat bashful grin, that Karan had been right.

Today, every actor—Salman Khan, Hrithik Roshan, Akshay Kumar, Tiger Shroff, Varun Dhawan and Aditya Roy Kapur—is going down the *Baywatch* route to show off their gym-acquired biceps and rippling abs. But back then, it took hours of introspection and discussion, and months of workouts, for a desi Adonis to throw off his shirt. John who always had an enviable physique, had simply shrugged, and asked when they were shooting the scene.

A decade later, flashbacking to that cinematic moment in Miami, he pointed out that while he has always been unapologetic about his body, he also hasn't flaunted it unless required. For the introduction scene in *Dostana*, he had gone to the beach with the film's Director of Photography, Ayananka Bose at 7 a.m. when there were no crowds milling around, quickly taken the shot of him walking out of the sea, and left in five minutes.

Dostana brought homosexuality out of the closet and into mainstream Hindi cinema. Abhishek Bachchan and John were voted the 'Jodi No. 1' of the year and his introduction scene, made him the nation's poster boy. Yet, today, a decade later, John will exclaim, 'Uff, how was I so brave as to pull down my trunks on camera. Fortunately, it was very aesthetically shot and did not look vulgar. I give Karan full credit for handling the subject with so much sensitivity and care.'

Standing tall at six-feet-one-and-a-half inches, it would be easy to dismiss John as just a gorgeous body and a pretty face. He himself admitted that in his early days as a model, that was the public's perception of him, and it would bug him endlessly. 'I made an effort to correct it. I would walk up to people and tell them in all seriousness, "Hey guys, listen, I'm educated.

Please understand, I know what's happening in the world too." But after a point I gave up, realizing that you are a prisoner of your own image. Since I was a model…a clothes hanger… I was being treated like one,' he sighed over the memory.

It was all the more frustrating because there is a sharp brain ticking in there. John is an economics graduate from Jai Hind College, with a Masters degree in management studies, from the Mumbai Education Trust. The son of a well-known architect, Abraham John, he was set on a career in advertising after an internship with Euro RSCG Advertising Pvt. Ltd. He joined Enterprise Nexus Communications Pvt. Ltd. as a media planner and his first account was The Times Group. And despite the backbreaking research, John was happy to analyse facts and figures to help the publishing house reach bigger targets and tap newer markets.

Then, modelling happened, quite by accident. 'One day, a model didn't turn up for a commercial and my boss, Hiren Pandit, told me to go and fill in for him. I finished my media plan, went there, wore the pair of jeans we were marketing and that was it!' he recounted, making light of a breakthrough many spend a lifetime chasing. Even today, John lives in a pair of jeans or cargoes, a casual tee and a pair of flip-flops or sneakers. And no matter what the occasion, he never looks out of place.

After that, he entered Maureen Wadia's Gladrags Manhunt and Mega Model contest with no expectations or aspirations. To his surprise, he was shortlisted for the international contest and flown to Manila where he missed winning the title by a whisker. However, he quickly gained popularity as the Cinthol Man, running through the jungles of Mauritius, chased by twenty top models. More ads followed, and John went on to work in New York, London, Singapore, Hong Kong and India.

And while he believes that had he been an inch shorter, he might have fared better on the ramp, he still ranks high amongst Indian supermodels and was the highest paid in his time.

For many, modelling was the launch pad to films. John featured in a few music videos of singers such as Hans Raj Hans, Babul Supriyo and Pankaj Udhas before Mahesh Bhatt spotted a star in the thirty-year-old model with shoulder-length hair and a sinewy body, who looked unlike any Bollywood actor of the time and could not even speak Hindi well. 'Bhatt sahib called me to his office one day and told me that he wanted me to do a film for his daughter. We shot for a day in Pooja Bhatt's office—only later did I realize that this could well have been my screen test,' John laughed years later, still grateful to his mentor for holding his hand at the start of his acting career and to his producer, Pooja, whom he describes as 'fantastic'.

Jism (2003) was a most unconventional debut with John playing a down-in the-dumps alcoholic lawyer who is fatally attracted to the beautiful wife of a millionaire. Their clandestine relationship eventually turns him into a killer. Many of his friends told him that he was crazy to start off with such a role, but John would not be swayed by their prophesies of doom. 'While making the film, Bhatt sahib told me something very interesting. He pointed out that if society accepts what is in their face, then *Jism*, revolving around an extra-marital affair, would be a success. If it doesn't, this film, he admitted, would fall flat on its face. Fortunately,' he exulted, '*Jism* worked and worked and worked.'

While the film's surprise success was encouraging, the public perception didn't change even after he entered Bollywood because *Jism* too had focused on his looks—body, sexuality and the whole package. While another actor may have struggled to break free of the stereotype, John having been a marketing guy, simply decided to position himself this way, earn his brownie points, then, when he had the power, do the kind of films he really wanted.

However, even during this year of 'fitting in', he was gambling with Anurag Basu's paranormal horror fantasy romantic thriller *Saaya* (2003) and Pooja Bhatt's *Paap* (2003), in which, as a cop investigating a crime, he falls in love with a Buddhist girl set on becoming a monk and their passion comes in the way of her vow of celibacy. Another out-of-the-box role was Vikram Bhatt's chilling *Aetbaar* (2004) where he played the role of a psychopath lover given to obsessive fixations and murderous rage.

The experiments with cinema continued. In 2007, he raised eyebrows as the narcissist chain-smoker K in Anurag Kashyap's neo-noir psychological thriller, *No Smoking*, whose slumbering soul searching leaves him with two less fingers. When I questioned him on what drew him to this film, I learnt that an avid reader of history, world politics and literature, Franz Kafka—one of the most influential writers of the twentieth century—ranks amongst John's favourite authors. '*No Smoking* was a very Kafkaesque-kind of film which is why despite knowing it wouldn't work, I did it. A good film does not necessarily have to be a successful film. Your conviction in what you do is important,' he pointed out.

Even Sanjay Gadhvi's action thriller *Dhoom* (2004), with which his career 'vroomed' off, was essentially a negative role. It's a different story that today, even after watching Hrithik Roshan and Aamir Khan in action in *Dhoom 2* and *Dhoom 3*, John remains the franchise's quintessential biker boy, still remembered for his on-screen wheelies and stoppies. He performed these daredevil stunts himself after his body double

Shashi met with an accident while filming the first action scene.

Sixteen years later, as one of Bollywood's last reigning action heroes, John continues to leap from unimaginable heights, break down doors and walls with effortless ease, pulverize bikes and cars, and is a one-man demolition army. However, now with a lot of money riding on him, he has become more cautious and started to pick and choose his action scenes with more care. He insists that he no longer takes unnecessary risks. This assertion, however, would only make his orthopaedic surgeon laugh. For him, John is a walking wounded who should be put on a retainer fee given how often he turns up with an old injury that has recurred during a shoot or worse, a new one.

By his own admission, John has torn the muscles of his biceps twice, has a hairline crack in both arms, has broken his left ankle and navicular bone, and for *Rocky Handsome* (2015) continued fighting despite a fractured rib cage. Before that, while shooting for *Force* (2011), he had torn a ligament and sustained around forty injuries on his back when while jumping from one moving goods train to another, he missed his step and fell on a pile of sharp stones. Yet, during press conferences for the film's promotion, he was a modern-day Hercules, picking up and hurling down bikes.

He upped the ante for *Force 2* by hauling up an E-class Mercedes Benz with people sitting inside and smashing it to the ground. Watching him in action, it was hard to believe that a busted knee during the film's shoot in Budapest, had almost put him in a wheelchair for life. I learnt about the accident while I was at work. John, I was told, had been chasing after the bad guy, broken down seven doors, before tripping on the handle of the last. Skidding down the corridor, he was headed straight for the wall and in a desperate last-minute move, had slammed his knee down to break the impact. Months later, when I met him—and after I had assured him that I wouldn't faint—he showed me videos of him being injected with a large needle that was plunged into his swollen knee in the local hospital where he was rushed to soon after the accident. 'It aspirated the clot and blood squirted everywhere. One of the older nurses fainted,' he confided, with his trademark crooked grin. And what did John do? He simply returned to the shoot, to slide down a rooftop, rupturing his knee further.

If that wasn't enough, for the next scene, he went zip-lining. He was hoisted up to 150 feet and was swinging between two high-rises when the film's villain Tahir Raj Bhasin cut the zip. 'I crashed through glass, bounced off the wall, rolled off the roof and fell twenty feet down,' he recounted.

He was back in hospital. This time, his swollen knee had to be cut open, the blood splashing on the face and glasses of the young doctor attending him. 'For six days, they continued to drain out fistfuls of clotted blood from the knee and on the seventh, I was told that the leg that had turned black, would have to be amputated.' It was, undoubtedly, his life's biggest scare.

Fortunately, before being wheeled into surgery while still in Europe, John called his doctor back in India who told him to strap up the leg and take the next flight back to Mumbai. It took three surgeries to keep him out of a wheelchair. When I spoke to him after the last, he was telling me ebulliently that his physiotherapist had promised he would be walking in ten days and flying within a fortnight.

I admit I was sceptical of him returning to action before six months, but John was back on the set in less than half the time. The first scene required him to break a door down with his leg. He did not blink. 'It was a one-shot, okay!' he exclaimed. 'How do you do it?' I marvelled. 'When you are living on the edge, you don't waste space,' he stated simply.

John's recurring ability to bounce back on the last count and deliver a knockout punch inspires respect and admiration in young actors such as Tiger Shroff. With films like *Heropanti* (2014), *War* (2019), the *Baaghi* franchise (2016, 2018, 2020), Tiger aspires to be like John one day. 'I did an ad with him once and I had the best time. We had our meals together, ate the same thing, and spent a lot of time chatting since our interests are alike. I would love to do an action film with John in which we have contrasting roles and yet we complement each other. I look up to him as a person and an actor,' gushed his younger colleague. When prodded on why he thinks John has ruled this action genre for close to twenty years, Tiger pointed out, 'He is among the very few actors who has not only sustained, but grown from strength to strength, and that is because he does such off-beat films.'

John has enjoyed rewriting the rules of commercial Hindi cinema. Not for him the mandatory five songs, six fight scenes and the girl at the end. Since *Jism*, he has been 'flirting with danger'. In the year of *Elaan*, *Kaal* and *Garam Masala*, John played Narayan, a dhoti-clad Gandhian in pre-Independence India, who falls in love with and wants to rehabilitate a widow, Kalyani, in Deepa Mehta's *Water* (2005). The film had kicked off in Varanasi five years before, with an entirely different cast of Shabana Azmi, Nandita Das and Akshay Kumar. But a day before they were to start shooting, there was a holdup over permits, and when the unit eventually turned up at the ghat, they were greeted by over 2,000 protestors angry at what they misconstrued to be the film's content and message.

When Deepa resumed shooting in Sri Lanka, John stepped in for Akshay. For him, *Water* was a relevant story that needed to be told. 'India was embarrassed and threatened by the film, but I wanted to be a part of it,' he asserted. The film premiered at the Toronto International Film Festival in the 'Opening Gala' section and was Canada's entry for the Oscars in the Best Foreign Language Film category. However, it did not fare well at the Indian box office. No regrets. 'My most successful choices before I became a producer were the films that failed, like *Water* (2005), *Kabul Express* (2006) and *No Smoking* (2007). I am known today for the films I did differently, that people had no faith in, and not for the regular commercial films,' he reasoned.

Eight years after *Water*, John returned to Sri Lanka as RAW agent Vikram Singh in *Madras Cafe* (2013), a political thriller he produced with Ronnie Lahiri. The film chartered the tumultuous years in Lankan politics, between the late 1980s and early 1990s, following India's intervention in the country's civil war, which lead to the assassination of former Prime Minister Rajiv Gandhi. The day, 21 May 1991, is etched in his memory. He woke up to sunlight streaming in through the windows. His mother had come into his bedroom as was her habit and pulled the curtains. In the bright light he could see that she was crying. When he asked her why, he learnt that Rajiv Gandhi, whom she had admired, had been assassinated. The suicide bombing in Sriperumbudur is clearly etched in my mind too because four days after it, I got married. There was no music and no lights since the country was still in mourning. Fortunately, curfew had been lifted so my husband managed to reach, but I remember Kolkata, usually the 'City of Joy', was still tense and grim.

The memory drove me towards *Madras Cafe*. I even got into a fracas with the publicist when she tried to stop me from entering a press screening in an ineffectual bid to control the enthusiastic crowds of journos who had come flocking.

I fought my way into the theatre, and *Madras Cafe* remains one of the most compelling films I have watched. It opened to mixed responses and was banned even in the United Kingdom despite being shot in London, as also the state of Tamil Nadu in India, for fear of protests from the Tamil diaspora. John was nonplussed. 'I had given my nod to the film back in 2006 when it was titled *Jaffna*, but Shoojit [Sircar] was unable to find anyone to back it. After three producers opted out, I offered to produce it myself knowing the film was way ahead of its time. One has to be brave to effect change and change comes only with conviction. I'm a guy who thinks for himself and am not influenced by five cronies who tell me this is good and that is not good. Tomorrow if two more films fail, I will still be the same person I am today. I revel in the fact that I don't have the pressure of being successful all the time because that would make me insecure. I'm not insecure because I am not afraid of failing.'

The words ring true because before *Madras Cafe*, John had produced *Vicky Donor* (2012), on the taboo topic of infertility, and turned it into a family film. I remember Shoojit telling me that when they were shooting in Delhi, curious bystanders often enquired after the film's title and then invariably asked, '*Yeh donor ka matlab kya hai*? [What's a donor?]' John gives full credit to his director for taking on such a serious topic and getting the message across in an entertaining way. On his part, he admitted that even when listening to the drafts, he knew he wanted to support the film because of its novel idea. 'The studio that distributed it was appalled that I was making a film like this but I decided I wanted to make this happen and did,' he revealed.

It was a brave decision, but John has never been afraid of courting danger, even when it came in the form of a death threat from one of the biggest terror organizations in the world. This happened during *Kabul Express* (2006) in which he played an investigative reporter in Afghanistan. The first two weeks of shooting passed without incident, then, director Kabir Khan, was summoned by the Indian ambassador and informed that the Taliban had sent out five men to kidnap and kill his two leading actors, John Abraham and Arshad Warsi, along with his executive producer Rajan Kapoor and him.

John and Arshad were promptly sent home and the rest of the team was packing up to leave when the Afghan security minister intervened, assuring the filmmakers of every possible security, should they agree to complete the shoot in his country. They were provided with a security cover of sixty commandoes, including rocket launchers, and travelled daily in a mile-long motorcade of SUVs with guns sticking out of every window. However, Kabir acknowledged that it was truly brave of both John and Arshad to return to Kabul to complete his first film, even after their producer, Aditya Chopra, had promised that he would recreate the war-ravaged country for them anywhere in the world.

If there's one thing John is not short of, it's courage. After returning from Kabul alive, he wanted to shoot his next film in strife-ridden Baghdad. He didn't get to go to Iraq eventually, but he did reunite with Kabir for *New York* (2009), a film on terrorism in the US post 9/11. A decade later, he took *RAW Rome Akbar Walter* (2019) into the Kashmir Valley, well knowing that he may not return alive.

With his grit and grace, John brings to mind Oscar Wilde's *Selfish Giant*—the only difference being that I can never imagine him walling his home from children! On a couple of occasions, when I dropped by at his office, housed in a rambling bungalow in a shady lane in suburban Mumbai, I ran into a pretty moppet who instantly asked his manager what I was doing there. When told I had come to interview John, his niece nodded, satisfied, and wandered off. The next time, she personally escorted me to a sunroom out in the garden where her uncle likes to meet people. When I pretended to struggle with the door, she pushed it open herself. She acknowledged my 'thank you' with a regal tilt of her head and walked away, leaving me to contemplate the jackfruit hanging from the tree above through the glass ceiling.

On another occasions, our conversation was interrupted by a volley of barks. 'That's Baliey, the newest member of my family,' John informed, even as the Beagle, displeased by the door separating us, barked louder. 'Let her in,' I pleaded, and a few minutes later, she dashed in, vetted me with several sniffs and licks, then, deciding that John was safe with me, plonked down between our feet. He shared that the rescued pup had come to him when she was three months old for just three days. 'But when it was time for her to leave, I couldn't let her go. And so, she stayed, in my home and my heart,' he revealed emotionally. One night, a few years later, when I called for a chat, John's voice was almost drowned out by canine commotion. 'Baliey?' I asked with a smile. 'Yeah, and she has a daughter too now, Sia,' he reported with paternal pride.

It's not often that John shares his 'family' with the world. While he is receptive to any career-related query, he can be really cagey about his personal life. I still remember that day in 2013—28 December—when I connected with him, post-midnight, at the airport, as he waited to board a flight to Los Angeles. By then, Priya Runchal and he had been going steady for three years, but I knew better than to probe. So, even though the holidays were upon us, I asked if the flying visit to the US was for a Hollywood adventure. 'No, I am going to ring in the New Year with Priya,' he replied, surprising me by bringing her name into the conversation himself.

But the real surprise arrived four days later, when on 3 January, a little after 4 a.m. IST, John and Priya Abraham wished the world a blessed 2014. 'How come you didn't know anything about the marriage?' my editor hollered. I merely repeated what had already been printed—that when I had asked John about any special plans, he had replied, 'None, I will resume work on 4 January.'

His dad, Abraham John, was not taken by surprise by the 'sudden' wedding, registered in a LA courthouse. He admitted to a colleague that it had been planned well in advance, but the news had remained a secret even from John's friend, Shoojit. When I caught him, he was just boarding a flight and after hearing the news, promised to call back in a couple of hours. Back on terra firma, Shoojit admitted that knowing how private the couple is, this was just how he would have expected them to make a lifelong commitment.

As promised, John returned to Mumbai on 4 January, and reported straight for his shoot. His bride, who had studied at UCLA—an NRI financial analyst and investment banker, who had worked at Goldman Sachs and the World Bank—stayed back in LA. She kept flying to Mumbai while she quietly finished a course at the London Business School. She topped it, then, returned to her husband's side to structure his business and handle his football team. He doesn't talk about his wife often, but when he does, his respect for Priya is as evident as his love. She is an equal partner in their marriage rather than just a pretty star wife on the red carpet. 'It's thanks to her that I can focus on acting and producing films,' he has often pointed out.

His next production venture, *Parmanu: The Story of Pokhran*, was a fictitious tale based on the nuclear bomb test explosions conducted by the Indian army at Pokhran in May 1998. John joined hands with Prerna Arora and Arjun N. Kapoor who had brought the script to him. The film rolled on 31 May 2017. It released a year later, on 25 May 2018, after a bitter legal battle.

A month earlier, on 1 April, John called me one Sunday and confirmed that the notice he had put out in a trade magazine was indeed true. He informed that he had wrapped up shooting by August, but cheques coming in late, then, bouncing, had delayed post-production and pushed the release thrice. Fed up, he had decided to terminate his contract with his erstwhile partners, alleging breach of contract. 'Will you go on record with this?' I asked and was surprised when he instantly agreed.

It was a harried evening for me the next day as I listened to both parties before filing my story. Prerna insisted that John, who had never line-produced a film before, was to blame for the delay, and at ₹35 crore, had over-charged them. John responded saying he would go broke but would never cheat anyone. He informed that he was yet to be paid ₹5 crore to which Prerna reacted saying they would pay him ₹3 crore on delivery of the film and hoped he would forgo ₹2 crore given the delay. 'If he wants to terminate the contract, he will have to pay back the ₹30 crore first,' was her final answer. John didn't, instead he filed three criminal complaints, she responded in kind, and the case eventually ended up in court. 'It's only because I am an honest guy, that I had the courage to go to court,' he pointed out later.

Many advised John to agree to an out-of-court settlement, but he was determined to fight it out. Those were tense weeks. A lesser man might have succumbed, but John stuck to his guns and eventually, got his money and the legal go-ahead to plan his release the way he thought best. After the judgement, many other fraud cases against Prerna Arora and Arjun N. Kapoor came to light. There was no gloating 'I-told-you-so' and no victory whoops from him. The pats on the back didn't impress nor did the other cases that eventually put Prerna behind bars. He told me with the worldly wisdom that comes from four decades of experience, 'It's a battle I fought alone, and I know that tomorrow, if I am in trouble again, I will have to fight alone again.'

The only good that came out of the nightmare was that he found a director-friend and a new production partner in Nikhil Advani. They grew close while working on *Satyamev Jayate* (2018) when John was battling for *Parmanu* and went on to collaborate on *Batla House* (2019), inspired by a real-life shootout, which happened on 19 September 2008, between a seven-member Delhi Police Special Cell team and suspected Indian Mujahideen terrorists allegedly involved in serial blasts. The film traced the legal battle of ACP Sanjeev Kumar Yadav who spearheaded the police team to prove that the Batla House encounter was not fake.

The film, fighting PILs, almost didn't keep its Independence Day date with the theatres. It was cleared by the court just hours before its release. I came out after watching it wondering where these two men had found the courage to bring this contentious case to the celluloid. Then I remembered something John had told me once, 'I'm a biker and driving on smooth roads can get boring.'

I can see him, a decade from now, still vrooming down life's fast lanes with the same care-a-damn disdain for formula, making his own choices, be it an *Attack* or a *Ray* or a *Gorkha*, and standing by them, no matter what the consequences. *Dhoom machale!*

13

IRRFAN KHAN

Rone do, jiya kare, rone do na ji bhar ke

Our first interaction was over his namesake. I was working for a film weekly at the time and, one day, he surprised me with a call on the office landline. 'We have never met, I saw your name in the paper and decided to reach out,' he offered by way of introduction, going on to inform me that a man by the name of Irfan Khan had been arrested in a drug bust. 'Obviously, it's not me, but since the news was reported, I have been bombarded with calls. Can you help me set the record straight?' he requested.

I knew him from the television soap *Banegi Apni Baat*, and though we had never met, I assured him that I would put out the news. But I was quick to add that the paper came out only once a week so there were still a couple of days to go before the next edition hits the stands. 'Can you wait?' I asked, uncertainly. He said he would and rang off. I kept my word. A few years later, in 2012, Irfan changed his name; he added an extra 'r' to Irfan. Then, for a while, he dropped the Khan. At one point, he even wanted to drop Irrfan and become nameless.

I remember asking him during Kabir Khan's *New York* (2009) if he had ever been singled out for any kind of embarrassment because his name is Khan. By then Mira Nair's *The Namesake* (2006) had arrived, and he was an international star. The query was random, perhaps triggered by the fact that the film delved on the prejudices perpetuated by the 9/11 attacks. I had expected Irrfan to laugh it off, but he surprised me by admitting that he had been stopped by immigration twice, in Los Angeles and in New York, in 2008 and 2009, respectively.

He recalled being asked for his passport, then, taken to a room at the airport and detained for hours, questioned along with several other 'illegals' while the officers did a verification check. No calls were permitted, to his legal counsel or even the chauffeur who was waiting outside. He was not even allowed to speak for himself. Perhaps it was yet another case of mistaken identity, but it left him feeling angry, humiliated and vulnerable. By then, he had dropped his surname from film credits, but had to retain it in his passport.

The next time it happened, Irrfan asked the officer straight why he had been issued a visa in the first place if they didn't want him to enter their country. This sparked off an angry altercation. When she heard about it, Mira sat him down and advised him to take such incidents in his stride and not risk getting blacklisted. Ironically, Irrfan went on to become India's most famous import to the West, who, after films like *A Mighty Heart* (2007), *Slumdog Millionaire* (2008), *The Amazing Spider-Man* (2012), *Life of Pi* (2012), *The Lunchbox* (2013), *Jurassic World* (2015) and *Inferno* (2016) was a household name even in the United States.

Meanwhile, he changed my name to 'Roshomilla'. The first time it happened, I corrected him automatically. But it happened again... and again. And I quickly realized that it was not an inadvertent slip but deliberate, with Irrfan rolling out the 'os' and unapologetically telling me that Roshomilla reminded him of Kolkata's *roshogollas*. I had grown up with this *mishti*-cized version of my name ringing in my ears, and after a while, it no longer sounded sweet. But Irrfan, in his irrepressible way, laughed off my disapproving frowns, and before I knew it, some of his friends, including *Maqbool* (2003) and *Haider* (2014) director Vishal Bhardwaj, were calling me Roshomilla. After a while I stopped arguing, consoling myself with the thought that a rose by any other name would smell just as sweet.

Our conversations flowed seamlessly, meandering into discussions we both knew were too philosophical to find their way into print, rippled with laughter and dappled with the golden glow of wisdom. 'Sufi' is a word I now hear often when people talk about Irrfan in the past tense. But I saw the mystic in him long before and cherished these interactions, which went on for a good hour or more, leaving me feeling evolved.

In later years, time grew short as both of us got caught up in our respective careers. I didn't see him for days, months, even years, and grew used to the occasional phone call, now rationed. Sometimes he would call me home and though I lived close by, I would come up with the excuse of being at the office by a certain time to duck out. He would grow impatient, then, reluctantly agree to a 'phoner', starting off by reprimanding me for being 'too busy'.

At other times, he would come on the line and frankly admit that he was not in the mood for a chat and was being coerced by his publicists. Had it been anyone else, I might have been affronted, even offended, but because it was Irrfan, I would sweet talk him into giving me five minutes. The interview would stretch for half an hour, and after ringing off, he would complain to his manager about this wily girl who knew how to trick him into staying on the line and saying more than he should.

When you are working with a monthly magazine or even a weekly newspaper, life is more relaxed and so are you. But once you get caught up in the hurry-scurry of a daily newspaper, life is all about deadlines. Just before *Hindi Medium* (2017), as I waited in his living room for Irrfan to emerge, I fretted and fumed as the minutes ponderously ticked by, before giving myself up to the serenity of my surroundings and the beauty of Rabindra Sangeet that ebbed and flowed around me. By the time he took the chair opposite me, my anger had melted. 'I had forgotten these songs, they took me back to my childhood,' I admitted, and with a mischievous twinkle, he quipped that he had that in mind, so he had dug them out that morning. 'Nothing like Tagore to calm a restless Bengali mind,' he guffawed.

There was a Bong in Irrfan too. His friend and *Life in a... Metro* (2007) director, Anurag Basu, who had conceived Irrfan's character in the film initially as a Bengali by the name of Debu, even done the first photo shoot with him dressed as a Bengali bridegroom in a *dhoti* and a *topor*, agreed. Even after Anurag changed his name to Monty, so he could chase after Konkana Sen Sharma's Shruti on a *dulhe ka ghoda*, Irrfan continued to exhibit some distinct Bengali mannerisms.

'Every year, his wife Sutapa comes to the Saraswati puja I organize in my housing society, and whenever he was in the country, Irrfan accompanied her. He loved the *khichdi bhog* (an offering to God) and the live music that played at the mandap all day. He was particularly drawn to the *bauls* (Bengali folk singers). He loved the music of the soil and would sometimes forward me a song, which had struck a chord with him or call to discuss it,' recounted Anurag, remembering his friend as a mystical minstrel, always in search of the meaning of life, which he sometimes found in a film, in a song or in a snatch of poetry.

One of his fondest memories is of flying kites with Irrfan while filming *Life in a... Metro*, despite them being on a strict deadline. 'His portions were rushed through in just eleven days, yet we managed to steal an afternoon. I asked him one day, "*Patang udayega?*" and he immediately agreed, arriving the next day with kites and *latai* in his car,' Anurag reminisced, admitting that while Konkana grew impatient and his cinematographer fretted over the fading light, they were like two little boys playing truant, yet managing to wrap up the day's scenes in the stipulated time.

Flying kites and playing gully cricket was a throwback to Irrfan's growing-up days in Rajasthan. A world he had left behind, much to his mother's disappointment, for the world of make-believe that had long fascinated him. He once recounted how he would queue up with the other kids in a narrow, dusty lane that ended at a small *janla* [window]. 'We climbed on each other's backs to reach the window, would push our hand through the narrow opening and wait expectantly with bated breath. If, when you pulled the hand out, there was a movie ticket clasped in the palm, it was an achievement. It took a lot of *dhakkas* and *mukkas*, bruises and scratches, to get into a darkened movie theatre those days,' he reminisced with the carefree laugh of a too tall, too skinny boy no one then had expected to light up the screen one day.

Success didn't come easy even though Irrfan had trained at the National School of Drama (NSD) and was a naturally gifted actor. '*Bahut dhakke aur mukke khane pade*. It took years of struggle, disappointment and perseverance, to break into Bollywood, then, Hollywood,' he recounted. He came via television, and Anurag who was part of that journey, admitted that those days, it was frustrating for Irrfan to be constantly running against time in the race to bank episodes. 'I remember discussing an episode of *Saturday Night Suspense* with him once and he had absolutely no memory of what we had shot. That's when I realized that he was sleepwalking through some of his roles, but he was such a brilliant actor, that no one ever caught on,' the filmmaker shared, acknowledging that though *Life in a... Metro* ranks high on his filmography, Irrfan's best work was with Tigmanshu Dhulia and Vishal Bhardwaj.

While Vishal's *Maqbool* turned him into a leading man, a star, it was in Tigmanshu's *Haasil* (2003) that Irrfan was noticed for the first time in Hindi films. As student leader Ranvijay Singh, he bagged the Filmfare Award for Best Performance in a Negative Role. The duo continued to impress in films like *Paan Singh Tomar* (2012) and *Saheb Biwi Aur Gangster Returns* (2013), the former bagging him another Filmfare trophy, along with the Best Actor National Award. When they couldn't collaborate because of date hassles, on films like *Saheb Biwi Aur Gangster* (2011) or *Bullet Raja* (2013), Irrfan admitted he missed Tishu a lot. 'I miss him when I'm watching one of his films... I miss him when I read an emotional story or a poem... I miss him when I am having a good time and he is not there with me,' he confided emotionally, revealing that he had accepted the *Saheb Biwi Aur Gangster* sequel without even reading the script because he had been longing to play a lover for a long time and Indarjeet gave him the opportunity.

There was a lot of Irrfan in Indarjeet. His parents came from Tonk, a *riyasat* in Rajasthan, full of dreamers reciting Urdu couplets. They didn't have much money, but they were happy because romanticism can be a great escape from the harsh realities of life. Growing up, Sahebzade Irfan Khan had flirted with the li'l *shehzadis* of his dreams too and grown to be a diehard romantic who yearned to play the poet-lyricist Sahir Ludhianvi on screen so he could recite the lines, '*Kabhi kabhi mere dil mein, khayal aata hai, ke jaise tujhko banaya gaya hai mere liye...*' Twice, opportunities to feature in the Amrita Pritam-Sahir love story came his way. Twice, they passed him by. But the book of Sahir's *nazms* never left his home. He continued to recite his verses, even if only in the shower, just to experience the pleasure and pain of Sahir's love.

There was a lot of love in Irrfan too that he wanted to share with the world, but not through trite 'I love yous' and coy smiles. His romantic idols were Dilip Kumar, Marlon Brando and Johnny Depp and he wanted his reel-life love stories to explore the complexities of human relationships. Perhaps that's what drew him to a film like Shoojit Sircar's *Piku* (2015) which, as the maker was quick to point out, was not a love story. It was a father-daughter story, with Irrfan driving the duo to Kolkata. Along the way, a relationship develops between Piku and Rana through unspoken glances and long silences—both knowing this time together is not forever. Even when one relationship ends, it doesn't lead to the consummation of another with the film ending with the two playing badminton, their future unmapped.

'Piku' stole a piece of Irrfan's heart, both the film and its lovely leading lady. Deepika Padukone, he admitted, is a glamorous heroine, but he saw flashes of an innocent and vulnerable girl when they were making the movie together, and it only added to her mystery and allure. Even after the film, he admitted with a laugh, that if she asked, he wouldn't mind picking her up from home and driving her to her shoots every day.

I once asked about his most romantic gesture. 'Carrying a girl's slippers in my hand as we walked together for miles, after one of them had snapped. I didn't think it was romantic, but she did,' he quipped. I could understand why because the Walter Raleigh-kind of chivalry is dead today. For him, time stood still when he went swimming with a (not the same one) lady at eleven in the night. 'We went into the deep waters, uncaring of how high the waves were, just letting them carry us far away,' he rhapsodized. Mesmerized as much by his voice as the tale, I asked breathlessly when he had trailed off, 'Then?' He shot back with that infectious grin, 'Then... nothing. You would have to censor it if I went further.'

He found love early, with his NSD classmate, Sutapa Sikdar. They tied the knot on 23 February 1995, in a quiet, informal wedding. Marriage, for him, was a legal formality, a certificate, yet, Irrfan was a more stable partner than so many seemingly-happily-married actor-colleagues. Once when I had asked him if he would remarry Sutapa, he had nodded, 'Why not?' then, had pointed out matter-of-factly that he wouldn't need to since they hadn't divorced.

His wife and kids kept him grounded. When success took him away from them to the US for the shoot of *The Namesake*, he admitted, on his return, that he had missed his family, but had enjoyed the long walks in the beautiful parks and streets not crowded with people and traffic like our Maximum City. Having grown up in a small town, spending most of his time outdoors, he grew claustrophobic within four walls, more so if the room was air-conditioned.

As soon as he could afford it, he moved away from the city's concrete jungle and into a bungalow in Madh Island. He loved sitting by the sea, watching the sun go down and the moon come out, watching the clouds sail across the sky, watching the monsoon showers. It took him back to his childhood days. But the 'escape' was short-lived.

He moved back to the city, into a larger apartment, with a view that while not so grey, was still depressing with all the ugly cables stretched out. 'Why did you leave your paradise?'

I asked, and he admitted that his boys were travelling a lot, needlessly, and couldn't have their friends come over or visit them. Even for him, the traffic bottlenecks had become a pain. 'Also, it's too much to ask a filmmaker to come all the way out for a narration or a discussion,' he reasoned, and I could see the regret in his eyes.

However, Irrfan could never stay down for long. Life, for him, was a roller coaster ride, its ups and downs pre-destined. A long time ago, he had learnt to surrender to his fate and enjoy the ride. He didn't like people who were serious and out to change the world. He took the lows in his stride…and the highs too.

When *Inferno* beckoned, he did not dump *Piku*. When he bagged a National Award, he didn't go partying, but quietly admitted that it felt good to have finally given the forgotten athlete, Paan Singh Tomar, his due recognition. When Ang Lee won the Oscar for Best Director for *Life Of Pi*, he was happy for him, but laughed that he was now being flooded with 'father' roles because Bollywood is always in a hurry to typecast you and didn't know how to slot him. When he was honoured with the Padma Shri, he reacted with a modest 'nice'. When he was a part of *Slumdog Millionaire's* winning team, he skipped the Golden Globes because 'my mother was waiting and I didn't want to disappoint her'. Even after the Oscars, instead of staying back in Los Angeles and cultivating contacts like co-star Anil Kapoor, he flew straight back home to *Paan Singh Tomar*.

I remember on the night he was to fly to LA, I was surprised to see a text from him simply sending me an unknown number without any explanation. It was while I was watching *Slumdog Millionaire* sweep the Oscars, including the Best Picture, that I realized why Irrfan had shared his overseas number with me. I sent him a congratulatory message. No answer. I wasn't really expecting one, so, I wasn't disappointed. Four hours later, he called to say that he had had enough parties for the night, he wanted to return home and hug his boys. 'I miss them,' he mumbled from his hotel room, admitting that the biggest high of the day had been having the kids from the movie jumping around director Danny Boyle, him and the rest of the team on stage during their winning moment. Also, that singer-composer A.R. Rahman and sound engineer Resul Pukutty had made history by winning three Oscars between them. The previous year, he had been in the running for the Oscar for Best Supporting Actor for *The Namesake*. He didn't make it to the top five. Momentarily, he was disappointed, but then the sun came out again. 'Live life with a smile,' he would urge, his own smile lighting up his craggy face. And then, because he was Irrfan, he would tell me that he thought about death too. There was no fear; only a sense of wonder at the magical, almost mystical, process of living and dying.

He was living the life of his dreams when suddenly, in early 2018, death swung by. He was diagnosed with a neuroendocrine tumour. 'Why now when his career is finally peaking? When he has the world at his feet?' was my first thought. The diagnosis was not encouraging and the subsequent reports from friends were depressing. He wasn't doing well, but he wasn't ready to quit either. Once the initial shock that he had cancer had worn off, Irrfan staggered to his feet, changed his lifestyle, learnt to live in the moment with Sutapa, Babil and Ayaan, and with morphine shots to relieve the pain, even completed a movie.

Just before the release of *Angrezi Medium* (2020), I was approached by the film's publicist for an interview. I almost jumped with joy. I hadn't seen Irrfan in over two years and I was ready to go to the end of the earth to meet him. But this time a meeting was not an option. 'A phoner then?' I entreated. That too was impossible because he was too weak. 'Send questions, he will reply with voice notes or dictate his answers to someone,' I was assured.

For three days, I wondered what to ask. I had never gone to Irrfan with questions before. On the third day, I was in office when the publicist called, saying everyone else had sent their questions and they were only waiting for mine. I assured her that she would get mine too in the next hour. Then I went back to my computer terminal and wrote him a letter.

I told him that my daughter who was in the third year, studying biotechnology, was keen to take admission in one of the universities in the United Kingdom that had accepted her. But my husband and I had convinced her to do her Masters in India before taking flight. Since his upcoming film was about higher education abroad, I sought his opinion on the subject. I wondered how different this dad was from the one in *Hindi Medium* (2017) or the one he was for real. I enquired about his co-stars and their equation. I questioned him on how he looked at life in the present, vis-à-vis his wife and sons.

I wasn't sure if he would remember Roshomilla after all this time. He did. On our last meeting, when Irrfan had learnt that I lived close by, he had invited himself over for a meal, saying, '*Kuchh machchi wacchi khilana*. [How about a meal of fish?]' I half-heartedly told him to drop by whenever free, knowing he wouldn't because I had never had any stars visiting me at home. But he persisted, asking for my address. I told him I lived in the '*mandir wali gali*' and he laughed, 'See Sutapa, she doesn't want us to come over. But I am going to go to the temple lane one day and shout for Roshomilla. Someone will guide me,' he warned, with that mischievous glint in his eye. I ended my letter telling him that when he was in Mumbai next—little knowing that he was already here—I would come by with that fish curry.

A week later, I got a call from the director of *Angrezi Medium* (2020), Homi Adajania, telling me that Irrfan had answered my letter. 'It's beautiful,' he assured me. I got the mail only towards the evening, and my heart swelled when Irrfan reiterated that he remembered Roshomilla, but chances were that he would call me *roshogolla* because that's what his wife had been feeding him. I didn't frown, I laughed, relieved that he hadn't changed. He went on to speak eloquently about his roller coaster ride and ended by saying that he wished to enjoy my fish curry someday, with me saying 'Bon Appetite.'

The letter arrived on 29 February. On 29 April, at around 11 a.m., I learnt through a WhatsApp text that he was gone.

It's hard to single out my favourite Irrfan Khan film because there are so many. But I remember going to watch a late-night show of *The Namesake* (2007). When we stepped out of the darkened auditorium, my husband was surprised to see my red-rimmed eyes, and even more taken aback when on our way home, I bawled into a balled-up tissue. 'What happened?' he asked, bemused. 'Irrfan... how could he die? He was the life of the film,' I mumbled between sobs. Used to my inexplicable mood swings, he called it a night.

Years passed, Ashoke Ganguli from *The Namesake*, with his mop of untamed curls—a throwback to Irrfan's NSD days—his sing-song voice and Bengali-accented English stayed in my heart. I often flashback to one particular scene. Holding his young son's hand protectively, Ashoke walks down a long, narrow path at the end of which is the vast expanse of the ocean and realizes he has forgotten his camera. He looks back at his wife, Ashima, who is standing by the car, holding their daughter. She waves back brightly, and he sighs. 'All this and now no picture... *haan... ki kori?* What to do?' He tells Gogol that he will now have to carry the picture in his head to which his son innocently asks how long he will have to remember the day. Ashoke laughs, 'Remember it always... Remember that you and I made this journey, that we went together to a place where there was nowhere left to go.'

It was one of his favourite cinematic moments too because the words were not contextual to the situation. They took him back to his boyhood, when he would accompany his father into the nearby jungle. There, since they never carried a camera, he would have to click a moment with his eyes and experience it later with his heart. Today, whenever I think of Irrfan, I hear Ashoke murmur, 'Remember that you and I made a journey, that we went together to a place from where there was nowhere left to go,' followed by a voiceover, 'Only when we go to a place from where there is nowhere left to go, do we really discover ourselves.'

I believe Irrfan found himself before his journey ended. As for me, a day after his untimely demise, struggling to express all that was churning within me, I wrote these words:

So far... And yet so near,
Conversations interrupted can continue now...
You know more about life today than I know about death,
Time is forever now...

You made me pause and ask where I was headed,
You would laugh when I said I knew all the answers now...
There are no more questions, just the need to talk,
To return to where we started
And know we will never be apart now.